SIMON

*For Ruth,
with love, like always!
Scott*

Scott Gibson

Scott Gibson

ISBN: 1481863509
ISBN-13: 9781481863506
Library of Congress Control Number: 2013900420
CreateSpace Independent Publishing Platform
North Charleston, South Carolina

This one's for my friends

Jim Hunt

and

Andy Anderson

I hope you aren't too disappointed...

With special thanks to Davis Bennett

To see the earth as it truly is, small
and blue and beautiful in that
eternal silence where it floats, is
to see riders on the earth together,
brothers on that bright loveliness
in the eternal cold—brothers who
know now they are truly brothers.

- Archibald MacLeish

Prologue

Neither the woman in the bed nor the boy in the chair had moved in several minutes. At this moment, he did not know if she was awake or even aware of her surroundings.

The thrumming sound from the machine pumping oxygen through the tubes inserted in her nose had a peculiar kind of cadence that had, after awhile, begun to sound like waves slapping a shoreline, he decided. If the tide was mechanically generated, that is.

He sat, straight-backed, in his seat, the palms of his hands resting on his legs just above the knees. He had brought a book, but it sat unopened on the floor under the chair.

He studied the inverted bag hanging from the metal rod at the head of the bed, an IV drip dispensing an occasional drop of something—morphine, he supposed, though he hadn't asked, and nobody had told him— that slid through the long plastic tubing and into the needle taped to the underside of her arm. *Did that hurt?* he wondered, the needle puncturing her paper-thin skin. Probably not. Probably whatever was in the bag took care of that discomfort, as well.

She hadn't wanted any sort of pain-killer if it was going to dull her senses, and so for awhile, they hadn't given her any. But the disease was aggressive and merciless and finally she had acquiesced, stoic even then, saying simply in a voice hardly more than a whisper through thin, straight lips:

"I guess you'd better, now."

That had been three days ago, and the difference in her since then had been marked. Whether it was the pain-killer itself or the resignation that had come with accepting it, she was changed.

1

On Monday, er face had been thin and taut, looking like the face of the woman he had known for years. By Wednesday, it was puffy and rounded, her cheeks pillowed out and her eyes sunken into her skull. He'd paused in the doorway of her room when he arrived after school, wondering for just a second if he'd wandered into the wrong place, or if the staff had transferred her to a new location. But no, he realized, swallowing hard and stepping forward. It was her, all right.

"Come on in," the voice from the bed had said. "It can't be as bad as all that."

It was one of her alert moments, and the eyes, though recessed, were still bright and dark. The voice weak, but gruff.

"Or is it?"

He'd settled his bag on the floor and stepped to the foot of the bed, considering. They had never lied to each other, and she would know if he started now. No matter how ill or mentally fuzzy things might have made her, she would know.

"Well," he said after a quick but thorough appraisal. "Your face looks fatter."

This had prompted a wheezy hack of a laugh.

That had been the day of their last extended conversation, or at any rate, any kind of exchange that could be called a real conversation. Since then, there were some days he visited when she was either asleep or didn't say a word. Other times, she would greet him and they would chat for a few minutes before he realized she didn't know who he was. The first time that happened, after he'd left her, he sat in his car in the parking lot, head slumped against the steering wheel, and cried. It was the only time—so far—he'd wept since all of this had begun.

Now and again, there were moments of coherence, precious interludes of five minutes or so, when they could talk the way they used to. Yet even then, he could sense the change, could tell that no matter what he might say or do, she was slipping away from him, gradually exchanging this life for whatever the next one would bring. She listened politely when he talked, but he could tell she was listening to something else besides him, and that other thing was becoming more and more important.

A nurse entered the room then. Katherine, this one was. He knew nearly all of them now. She smiled at him and crossed to the bed.

"How's she doing?"

He shrugged. "Don't know. She hasn't opened her eyes or said anything since I got here today."

Katherine nodded. She rested the back of her hand gently against the woman's cheek. Whether this served some medical function or was simply a gesture of affection, he did not know, but he liked that she always did it. She scrutinized the IV bag, held out the tubing and studied it, and then checked the needle and tape on the patient's arm.

At the foot of the bed, she held up the bag collecting urine, studying the level, and made a notation on her chart. Then she lifted the blankets and sheets and checked to make sure the catheter was securely in place. The boy averted his gaze, looking out of the window. When she was done, he said:

"It's hardly yellow, any more. The urine. It's almost clear."

She glanced at him. He was still looking out at the gray day.

"Yes. Doesn't really mean anything. It's not cloudy, and there isn't any blood. Those are good things."

As she left the room, she put her hand on his shoulder and squeezed it gently.

Katherine returned to the nurses' station and deposited the chart back in its assigned slot behind the desk. The other RN was seated at the counter, tapping at a keyboard. She did not look up from her work as she remarked, "He's in there, I suppose."

Katherine nodded.

"He shouldn't be. Especially now. When... When it's so close."

"Oh, what's the harm?"

"You *know* what's the harm. Liability. Insurance. Hospital rules. If he's in there when she... when it... Well, his parents could sue. Say he was traumatized, or something."

"I'll take responsibility." Katherine slid her hands into her pockets. "You can claim complete ignorance of the situation. I'll say you didn't know he was in there. They can sue me, fire me, whatever." She turned and looked back down the hallway over her shoulder.

"I think he's already as traumatized as he's going to get," she added.

Suddenly there was a soft, extended sigh from the woman in the bed. The boy leaned forward in his chair, wondering if she had just breathed her last. But instead, her eyes fluttered open. As if she already knew she'd find him waiting, she looked directly at him.

"It's you," she said. There was surprising strength behind the voice.

He had no idea how cognizant she was just now, whether she knew where she was or who she was addressing. And he knew it didn't matter.

"Yes," he told her. "It's me."

Chapter One

At seventeen and a half years old, Simon Perkins appeared capable of handling any of the eventualities life might throw his way.

This was due in part to the generally unruffled demeanor with which he greeted any news, good or bad. He was calm in a crisis and reserved in celebration, simply because it didn't occur to him to react otherwise.

Also, life *had* thrown him eventualities from an early age; time and experience had given him a certain understanding of the precarious nature of existence, and he'd made his peace with it.

These were the qualities others saw in him and identified as capability. Simon himself might have been surprised if he'd known that's what they were thinking, and most likely would have disagreed. But from all outward appearances, he didn't seem to spend a lot of time wondering what other people thought. This, of course, merely served to make people like him all the more.

Girls at school harbored crushes, secret or overt; no boys his age resented him, itself a significant accomplishment. Simon was a gifted student, a good athlete, and a reliable friend. He was widely liked, loved by many, and idolized, in particular, by his sister Madeleine and his brother Joshua.

This idolatry often took the form of demands, as it was doing now.

"Toask! Where's toask!"

"…And Judyann's uncle got this big trailer, and it's got a shower, and, and, a TV…"

"Uh-huh." Simon spooned peas onto plates, then slipped on a mitt and extracted a cookie sheet dotted with hissing, steaming tater tots from the oven.

"…and a place to sleep over the steering wheel! She says that when he takes them all to the lake, she'll get to sleep up there. Over the steering wheel!" Madeleine added once more for emphasis. Then, waiting a second or so, she complained, "You're not listening to me!"

"I am, I promise. She gets to sleep in the bed over the steering wheel." He was elbowing things out of the way to clear a space on the counter to set the cookie sheet. The oven mitt, he'd discovered, had a worn spot in it, and his fingers were beginning to burn.

"Not a bed, Simon! I didn't say it was a bed!"

"Well, what then? If it's a place to sleep over the steering wheel, what is it, if it's not a bed?"

Madeleine considered this as she watched her brother sweep a half-dozen tater tots onto each plate. Joshua used this interlude to renew his demands.

"Don't want that! Want toask!"

"You like tater tots, Bud. You love them!" Simon assured him.

"Maybe it's a bed," Madeline said dubiously. "A different kind of bed. Anyway, her uncle's going to take them to the lake."

"Uh-huh. Do you want peaches, or applesauce?"

"Peaches, I guess," she shrugged. She dipped her forefinger into her glass of milk and then stuck her finger in her mouth. "I wish we could go to the lake."

"I don't like peaches!" Joshua volunteered. "I don't like anything except toask for dinner!"

Simon glanced at the tall, slender girl in tight jeans leaning against the counter next to the refrigerator.

"You sure you don't want to join us? There's plenty."

Smiling, she shook her head, causing her long, soft hair to sweep back and forth. Simon grinned back at her, an exchange clearly designed to convey some secret message between the two of them.

This did not go unnoticed by his sister, who set her mouth in a firm, thin line, folded her arms in front of her and frowned.

"Will you take us to the pool tomorrow, Simon? Will you take us swimming?" she asked.

"I thought Kirk was going to take you." He ladled chilled peaches into three small bowls and carried them to the table.

"I want you to go, too. I want you to go swimming with us."

Using a folded dish towel this time, Simon pulled another pan from the oven.

"Sure," he said. "I'll go."

Occupied with setting fish sticks on the plates, he did not notice the girl by the refrigerator bristle. Her smiled faded, and she, like Madeleine had done a moment earlier, folded her arms over her chest.

Madeleine, on the other hand, was keenly aware of this small triumph, and decided she could be magnanimous in her victory.

"You do like tater tots," she reminded Joshua. "And fish sticks. And peaches. This is all stuff you like." She beamed at Simon as he set a plate in front of her.

"At least sit with us, Vanny," he urged the girl in the corner. "Don't stand clear over there."

Vanessa relinquished her position against the counter and moved to the empty chair between Joshua and where Simon would sit.

"Fish sticks and tater tots," she muttered. "Real healthy."

He gave a quick warning shake of his head. The kids—four year-old Joshua, in particular—needed only the very slightest encouragement to refuse anything served to them.

"Fish is good for you," Madeleine announced haughtily. She did not direct the remark to Vanessa, nor did she look at her. "It's brain food." She was currently inclined to like anything that her brother's friend did not.

Joshua found this extremely funny and broke into a series of hiccupped giggles. "It's brains! It's brains!" he exclaimed. Yet a moment later, when Simon, holding his own plate, plopped into the chair opposite him, his expression darkened and he folded his arms in front of him.

"Not going to eat this," he said, in a tone that left no room for equivocation. "I...only...want—"

With a businesslike click, two pieces of toast bounded into view from the toaster on the counter. Tilting his chair on its back legs, Simon reached over his shoulder, deftly snatching them and tossing them onto his brother's plate, nearly grazing Vanessa's nose in the process.

"There you go, Bud."

As the others contemplated this move in stunned silence, Simon picked up his fork, jabbed three tater tots, and poked them into his mouth. He quickly followed this with a heaping quantity of peas.

"...toask," Josh concluded lamely. He studied the golden slices as if he wasn't quite sure what to do with them. But after a few seconds of debate, he picked up one and began to gnaw on it.

Vanessa watched the three of them eat, unaware of the slightly pinched expression her face had acquired. In a matter of seconds, Joshua's mouth was ringed with crumbs. Madeleine had a white moustache, and in the process of returning her glass to the table, had managed to spill a quantity of milk across her fish sticks and peas. Simon's table manners were only marginally better. He ate as if he was participating in some sort of dining marathon.

"So," she ventured after another minute. "You're going to go swimming tomorrow."

In response she received a shrug of shoulders and a tilt of head that she took to mean Yes.

"I thought," she continued in a carefully measured tone, "That we were going to the senior picnic and then the concert at the fairgrounds." She was careful not to look at Madeleine who was watching them with bright, alert eyes over a fish stick she grasped in both hands.

"I can do both," Simon retorted carelessly. "If we're thirty minutes late to the picnic, who cares? It'll still be going on."

"Okay." She didn't really *mean* okay, of course. It meant they would need to discuss it later when they were alone.

"I'm gonna take your peas, Bud, if you don't want them." Simon reached across the table and began pulling Joshua's plate towards him.

"No!" his brother cried, dropping the fish stick he'd hoped no one had noticed he was now eating, in order to yank back his dish. "They're my peas, and I want them!"

"Just a few," Simon pleaded. "There's more there than you can eat."

"Huh-uh!" And to prove his point, Joshua used his hands to begin scooping peas into his mouth.

Simon stood, leaning across the table, trying to snatch a pea there, another there. In no time at all, there were peas and tater tots on the table, on the floor, and even a few in Joshua's mouth. Vanessa lunged for his glass of milk, rescuing it just seconds before it toppled over, though nobody seemed to notice or appreciate her quick reflexes. The laughing and the struggle for the food on Josh's plate continued to the accompaniment of Madeleine's shrieks of delight.

"If I was your mother," Vanessa informed Simon later, "I would never let you watch the kids." She had pulled the kitchen chairs away from the table and was sweeping up the fallen casualties from the dinner-wrestle. "Look at all this!" She thrust the dustpan upward for his inspection.

Simon, stacking plates in the dishwasher, grinned and barely gave her a sidelong glance.

With one foot, he nudged open the cupboard door under the sink.

"Trash goes in there."

"Honestly, Simon." She dumped the contents into the wastebasket, banging the dustpan against its side, mostly for emphasis. She returned the broom and dustpan to the pantry and then set about placing the chairs under the table. Task completed, she leaned against the counter watching while Simon spread plastic wrap over the leftover fish sticks and potatoes and placed them in the refrigerator.

"You've got food stains all over your shirt," she observed. "You'd better soak it before they set in. Take it off, and I'll do it for you."

He grinned. "You first."

"I'm serious," she said, though she was smiling, too.

Without ceremony, he peeled his t-shirt off over his head and tossed it at her. "I'm gonna go check on the monsters. Be right back."

He returned five minutes later, buttoning up a new shirt. Vanessa was standing at the small sink in the laundry room, rubbing a pre-soak on the spots of the other garment.

"What are they doing?"

"They're both on Josh's bed. He's asleep; Maddy's just about there. She's watching a DVD. I give her another five minutes."

"Then what?"

Simon stood behind her, and wrapped his arms around her waist. "I don't know. Got any ideas?"

She didn't turn, but smirking, elbowed him in the ribs. He laughed.

Forty minutes later, Simon crept into the kitchen from the garage in his boxers, his arms hugging his bare torso. He paused to rinse his hands under the tap, then climbed the stairs. As he passed Josh's bedroom, he peered around the nearly-closed door. Both kids were still asleep, two small forms under a quilt that rose and fell in time with a faint snore from one or the other. As quietly as he could manage, he padded down the hallway and back into his bedroom. Vanessa was pulling on her jeans.

"Where were you?" she asked.

"Getting rid of the evidence."

He laughed at the grimace she couldn't entire conceal. "You think I'm going to just leave one of those lying around where my mom can find it? Especially used?"

"That's disgusting."

"Tell me about it. I lifted up about half the junk in the garbage can and hid it partway down under some rancid coffee grounds. If you *really* want to talk about disgusting."

"Real romantic." She adjusted her collar and then flipped her hair away from her shoulders. "Help me make the bed."

"Are you kidding?" he demanded, pulling on his own jeans. "If you do it, it'll look too nice. That'll be a dead giveaway. Mom will know we've been doing something up here."

He sat on the edge of the bed to pull on his socks. Vanessa watched him for a second, then crawled across the tangled sheets and draped her arms over his shoulders. She pulled him back and then shifted so that she was lying alongside him. They gazed at the ceiling.

"Madeleine hates me," she said matter-of-factly after a moment.

Simon, stroking Vanessa's hair, nodded.

"Yeah."

Another second passed. "That wasn't what I wanted you to say," she spoke into his chest.

He considered this. "Well, Josh likes you. That's something."

"Oh, Joshua likes everybody."

Simon nodded, causing Vanessa's head to rock slightly. "That's true. But I like you. That makes two out of three. Four out of five, if you count Mom and Kirk. They think you're pretty nice."

Vanessa frowned at the ceiling. Simon had a knack for delivering answers that weren't entirely satisfactory, yet it was difficult to pinpoint precisely what was wrong with them. She decided to change the subject.

"Why do you have to go away this summer?"

"I always do." He sounded surprised. "You know that. I always work summers up in Stucker's Reach."

She ran her hand up and down his belly. "But it's our last summer before we go away to college, Simon. The last three months before we're going to be halfway across the country from each other. There are plenty of jobs around here. Better jobs, even, than bussing tables in some dumb restaurant in Stucker's Reach."

His hand had made its way up the small of her back, under her blouse and was tracing small circles between her shoulder blades. It caused a delicious shiver to run from the base of her neck down to her toes.

"My grandparents live there, Vanny. I stay with them. And it might be the last summer I get to do that."

For a mere second, Vanessa considered countering with, *Well, I guess you care more about your grandparents than you do about me.* But she thought better of it, having a strong hunch where that tactic would lead.

"And you really think you have to go swimming tomorrow?" she countered instead.

"Same thing," he retorted. "I'm gonna be away from the monsters all summer, and then I leave in the fall. I can go swimming with them and still make it to the picnic with you."

Without lifting her head, Vanessa allowed her hand to slide up Simon's chest, seeking its target. Her fingers circled one of his nipples and then captured it between thumb and forefinger and pinched.

"Ouch," he said calmly.

"*Still* think you need to go swimming tomorrow?" she asked, increasing the pressure.

She thought he was squirming in pain, but in fact, he was only moving enough to slide his own hand around to her breasts and under her bra to return the favor.

"Yes," he said. He twisted her nipple relentlessly. "The question is, how late are we going to be to the picnic?"

She was prepared to withstand the discomfort and to return it several times over, but the sound of a car pulling into the driveway below brought their contest of wills to an abrupt halt.

"Shit!" he hissed, sitting bolt upright and snatching up his shirt. "We need to get downstairs!"

Simon's mother and step-father stepped through the front door to find their son and Vanessa slumped on the living room couch gazing at the television. Simon's arm was thrown carelessly around his girlfriend's shoulders.

"Hey," he greeted them. "So how was dinner?"

"Delightful," Kirk Pointer retorted, tossing his car keys into the bowl on the entryway table. "Wilted salads, lukewarm chicken in gelatinous gravy, cherry cobbler with too many cherries and not enough cobbler. Long, dry speeches that I would testify under oath were exactly the same speeches given at last year's ceremony. In fact," he concluded thoughtfully, "I think they served the exact same meal last time, too."

"They gave Kirk a plaque for Distinguished Service to the District," Livia anounced, running her hand up and down the back of her husband's arm.

"Just like last year," Simon observed from the couch. "Maybe you guys got stuck in some kind of a time warp."

The humor was lost on his mother. "No, last year's was for teacher. This year, it was for being vice-principal," she clarified.

"Yeah, so watch it," Kirk threatened good-naturedly, bumping Simon's leg off the coffee table with a nudge of his knee. "You aren't graduated yet. I could still do you some real damage."

"Yeah? Only if you want me hanging around another year or so," his step-son returned.

"God Forbid." Kirk tugged at the knot of his tie, loosening it, and shrugging out of his jacket.

Livia, catching Vanessa's glance, smiled and rolled her eyes as she accepted the discarded garment.

"How are you, Vanny?"

"I'm good, Mrs. Pointer. Thanks."

"How were the kids?"

"Terrible, as always." Simon intercepted the question directed towards Vanessa.

"They take after their brother that way," she interjected, slipping out from under his arm and getting to her feet. She tugged at the hem of her blouse. "You should have seen how the table looked after dinner."

"I can well imagine. I take it they're asleep?"

Simon nodded. "On top of Josh's bed."

"Sounds good to me, too," Kirk said, yawning. "I'm headed up. Good to see you, Vanessa. 'Night, everybody."

"Night, Kirk."

"Good night, Mr. Pointer."

"I guess I'll go up, too." Livia leaned forward, standing on tiptoe to kiss her son on his forehead. "Thanks, Sweetie. Appreciate it."

"Sure, Mom."

Vanessa watched Livia's slightly plumpish frame ascend the steps and turned back to Simon.

"I like your mom. I like both your folks."

"Thanks." Simon sank back into the couch and patted the cushion alongside him invitingly. "I'm still going swimming tomorrow, by the way." Something in his tone and the way he smirked at her suggested he was hoping for more nipple-twisting.

Keeping her lips pursed, she shook her head. "I'm gonna take off. It's late, and they'll wonder what we're doing down here."

But she didn't move. Simon didn't pat the cushion a second time, but after a moment, she relented, and flopped onto the sofa next to him.

Kirk flushed the toilet and flicked out the bathroom light. He emerged from the bedroom as Livia was slipping a nightshirt over her naked form. He drew back the covers and settled in the bed, folding his arms over his head, watching her.

"Come here, you," he growled as she lifted her feet from the floor and slid them under the blanket. He rolled onto his side and nestled against her, nuzzling her neck.

"Not right now," she said, giggling under her breath. She swatted at him ineffectually.

"What are you whispering for?" he asked. "Nobody can hear us up here."

"I can't... I can't fool around with them downstairs. Simon."

"Are you kidding? We've done it hundreds of times when he was right down the hall. We made two more kids while he was barely twenty-five feet away!"

"Yeah, well..." she hesitated, fumbling for words. "He... He was asleep. Or at least alone. He wasn't directly below us, with a girlfriend."

Suddenly her entire body tensed. She turned her head so that she was nose-to-nose with her husband.

"How far do you suppose they've gone? Are they...you know... doing it?"

Kirk contemplated this for a second. His own amorous state faded slightly.

"Well... They're doing some things, I'm sure. They're seventeen, after all. Probably not... you know... *it*. Simon's not an idiot."

"If he's thinking with his brain, anyway." He didn't say this last part aloud. Though he suspected it was going through Livia's mind, as well.

As they lay in the darkness, each conjuring a variety of unsettling images, they heard the front door open and close. A moment later, a car engine flared to life and pulled away from the curb outside their window.

Footsteps ascended the stairs and they heard Simon's bedroom door close at the other end of the hall. As one, they both exhaled, muscles draining of tension they hadn't even realized they'd stored.

"He goes to his grandparents at the end of next week," Livia said softly, as if the mere words could invoke a magic incantation of sorts. "That should lessen the chances of anything, you know... happening."

Chapter Two

As they had told him they would, Robert MacKenzie's parents had come and taken him out of school at 10:00am. Now Robert sat with his folks in plush, upholstered chairs facing a dark oak desk and a man in a tailored suit on the opposite side.

He glanced curiously at either side of the room. It was just like lawyers' offices on television shows: Heavy, intimidating-looking volumes of books lined shelf after shelf. Another wall sported a variety of framed documents. Surely they couldn't all be diplomas. He knew that attorneys went to law school, but just how many did they have to attend, and how many awards were there to win?

The man on the other side of the desk let the pages of the document he was holding fall back into place. Clearing his throat, he set it on the desk, folded his arms and leaned forward, looking at each of The MacKenzies in turn.

"The house and most of the furnishings are to be donated to The Stucker's Reach Historical Preservation Society," he said. "I very much doubt that the property has much, if any, historical significance, but it will be up to the organization to decide whether to keep it or to sell it. A certain amount of money is to be used to establish a scholarship fund, and one or two other charitable organizations are to receive stipends.

"The rest," he concluded, lifting the top page of the document once again and scanning a few lines, "Certificates of deposit, stocks, savings, and the contents of three or four accounts, goes to Robert."

Robert shifted in his seat, acutely aware of the three sets of adults eyes fixed on him. For a moment, nobody spoke.

"Well," his mother said at last. A noncommittal word, yet it seemed to convey a host of emotions.

Nobody was mentioning figures, but Robert had a hunch that they were talking about a considerable amount of money. His fingers traced the scrollwork on the arm of his chair.

"What do you think about that?"

He raised his head to see that the attorney was looking directly at him.

"I… I don't know what I think."

Robert's father shook his head. "This is just amazing." He glanced at his wife. "I mean, did you have any idea?"

"Not in the least," she said. "I sometimes worried that he was spending too much time over there." She uttered a breathless laugh as if the reality was only now starting to sink in. "I wasn't sure what went on, or why she didn't just chase him off. Especially after I met her. Remember that?" she laughed again. "Later, though, I was…well, glad, I suppose, that Robert could be there to do things. To help out."

The lawyer shifted his gaze from Robert to Mr. MacKenzie.

"I would urge you to consult with a financial advisor, Jim. To decide how you want to proceed."

"That does bring up a point." Robert's father glanced at his wife and then leaned forward in his seat. "Robert received a nice scholarship this spring, but naturally, we've also applied for some financial aid. Will this inheritance jeopardize those, or is there some way to protect the money? Some place we can put it that will still allow Robert to get those other things?"

Dinner conversation that evening was lively and enthusiastic. From everyone except Robert.

"I can't believe it," his fifteen year-old sister Heather said, stabbing at the pile of string beans on her plate without ever actually lifting any of them to her mouth. "Why you, of all people?"

Robert, who had a different style, was idly pushing his own beans from one side of the dish to the other and then back again. Neither sibling was actually accomplishing much eating. He did not lift his gaze from the table, nor did he respond to his sister's question.

"It just goes to show," Mrs. MacKenzie said, "That if you treat people well, it will come back to you."

Robert did raise his face at this, giving his mother a sidelong glance and trying to read what he saw there. This was a concept that had never entered his mind, and he wasn't sure if it was one with which he wanted to be associated. At least, not in this instance.

"Yeah. Well, *I'd* treat bitchy old ladies well, if I knew they had money to give away," Heather muttered. She fixed her brother with a look of active dislike.

"That's not why we do things," her father admonished, though his tone didn't seem particularly sincere. He propped his elbows on the table, clasped his hands and rested his chin on them. "It is sort of amazing, though. You look at that house of hers; I mean, it's nice, and all, but nothing special. She lived there, what? A good thirty years or so, and it probably cost next-to-nothing when she bought it. So it naturally accrued in value. But she'd been a schoolteacher. Not a lot of money in that. Who would have expected?"

"She'd been married," Mrs. MacKenzie pointed out. "Maybe a lot of it came from her husband, and whatever he did."

He nodded. "Probably." His gaze shifted to his son. "We should probably set Robert up with an IRA or some other tax-deferred account. You turn eighteen in July, right? That's a little young to have an IRA, but if it saves you money now and starts building interest, it may be the way we want to go."

"I suppose Robert gets to keep it all," Heather sulked. There was no mistaking the sense of injustice in her injured tone. "Too bad it didn't happen sooner."

When her family stared at her with varying expressions of shock, she added hastily, "I just meant maybe he could have been popular in school, or something. Too late for that now."

"Oh, Heather." The usual gentle remonstration from her mother.

Robert took a bite of fish and then set down his fork.

"Tomorrow's Saturday," he said.

His family had become used to his non-sequiturs, and didn't generally spend much time pondering where they came from or what they meant. After an exchange of glances, they went on eating.

Robert was thinking that even though it had been quite a few months since she'd actually been there, he would like to go over to Eulamarie Scoggins' house in the morning.

Chapter Three

Simon stood in front of the empty storefront that had once housed Lilac Drugs and Novelties, studying the *For Sale or Lease* signs taped in each of the large picture windows. He leaned in closer, pressing his face to the glass and holding his hands to either side of his head to shield the sunlight while gazing within.

The interior was nearly empty. The rows of shelves had been removed. Towards the rear of the room the floor was elevated. This had been the pharmacy counter, he recalled, though the partition separating customers from the prescription medications and the person in charge of doling them out was gone. It looked odd, yet familiar, all at the same time.

The sounds of conversation and footsteps on the sidewalk behind him caused him to step away from the window and turn around. Three girls, his own age or perhaps slightly younger, were walking past. They gazed at him with a mixture of interest and shyness.

"Hi," one said, and the other two giggled ridiculously.

"Hi," he said back. They continued up the street. He watched them for a few seconds and then turned back to gaze at the squat, square empty building in front of him, its bricks so faded now he couldn't tell for sure if they'd once been red or perhaps yellow. He was trying to decide how this made him feel, this piece of his childhood now wrenched from him. Added to the mix was his impression of these girls.

They didn't look familiar, which meant either they were part of the early June influx of tourists, or they were kids whose families had moved to Stucker's Reach since he had left four years ago.

The drugstore held a variety of fond memories for him, but he wasn't sure if its unexpected absence this year was causing the odd feeling in the center of his chest, or if it was a symptom of something bigger, something that included the exchange he'd just had.

Every summer that he returned to Stucker's Reach, the town seemed just slightly less familiar than the time before. Businesses had changed or vanished; new buildings had sprung up; there were fewer faces he recognized and many he did not. Lately, he'd begun to feel as if he, not the strangers, was the intruder. Those girls, in fact, looked at him in a way that indicated that while they found him cute, they didn't think he belonged here.

Sighing, he stepped away from the dusty glass and continued down the sidewalk. There was still much that was the same, of course, including the enormous lake around which the town had been built. The museum, the park, the library. The Lodge, where he had bussed tables in the restaurant the past two summers. His grandparents, of course, and their comfortable house and the bedroom where he slept, the bedroom that had once been his dad's.

His pocket vibrated then, and he pulled out his cell phone. He grinned, staring down at the screen, then held it to his ear.

"Hey. What's up?"

"Nothing. Missing you. Wanted to hear your voice."

"Doesn't *sound* like nothing. Where are you?" Behind Vanessa's voice on the other end of the phone, there was the tumult of high-pitched yelps and shouts.

"At work, where do you think? Going out of my mind. Day camp totally sucks."

"For a minute, I would have sworn you were calling from my house," he laughed.

"No such luck. The little brats here are nowhere near as cool as Joshua and Madeleine."

Simon chose to overlook the fact that Vanessa had just paid his sister a compliment.

"Well, at least you're making money," he pointed out. "And it's good practice. I mean, if you're still planning to be a teacher."

"High school teacher," she clarified. "Not this. So... what're you doing?"

"Just walking through town. Looking at stuff."

"I thought you went up there to *work*."

"I start tomorrow."

"Lucky you. So, anyway, I have to go, since I'm watching about a hundred kids, but I was thinking about something."

"Yeah?" Simon stopped at the corner, waiting for cars to pass so that he could cross to the town square.

"Camp is closed the whole first week of July. Because of Independence Day Holiday. What would you think if I came up there? I know you probably couldn't take the whole week off, but we could still see each other. Hang out some."

"Well...sure. But how do you think you could manage it?"

"Not sure yet. Still working on it. I just wanted to know if you'd be okay with that. If you are..."

"Yeah. Totally."

"I gotta go," she concluded hastily. "We're not supposed to be on our phones when we're—"

And there the call ended. Simon dashed across the street, thrusting his cell phone back into his pocket. He was hoping Vanessa still had a job.

The town square was one of those things in Stucker's Reach that looked resolutely the same. A fascia-trimmed gazebo held court in the center of the lawn. Wooden sidewalks criss-crossed the grass, leading to the library, the Visitor's Bureau and a variety of lovingly-tended flowerbeds. He was waiting in line at the ice cream stand when he heard someone call his name. Turning, he found himself looking at tall, gangly Robert MacKenzie.

"Hey! Robert!"

"I thought it was you," the other boy said solemnly. He stepped forward, extending his hand. "I was coming out of the library, and I thought it was you."

Simon gripped Robert's hand in a clammy, slightly moist handshake. He simultaneously placed his other hand on Robert's shoulder and gave it a squeeze, then stepped back. They surveyed one another a few more seconds in silence.

Simon realized with an odd twinge that Robert reflected almost perfectly his feelings about the town. Here was his childhood schoolmate and sort-of-friend, looking the same, yet changed. His narrow face had filled in somewhat in the last few years, but the same freckles dotted the bridge of his nose and cheeks. His shoulders were broader, and he was taller than Simon now, by as much as three inches, yet neither of these things contrived to make him look even remotely more adult or intimidating. Even as a kid, Robert had possessed a strange ability to look both composed and unkempt at the same time. His brown hair, Simon noticed, still held the neat, even furrows of having had a wet comb dragged through it, yet he would bet it had been hours since that had happened. One side of his shirt collar was turned up. Dress shoes peeked out from under the cuffs of his jeans.

His hazel eyes gazed at Simon in pleasant expectation, a look Simon remembered all too well. Robert's standard, implacable expression was one of being at complete peace with himself, which, in the opinion of most of his contemporaries, was completely without justification.

"Well, yeah, it is me," Simon said finally. "Back here for the summer. How are you doing?"

"Are you getting ice cream?" Robert answered the question with a completely unrelated one of his own.

"Uh, yeah, I am," Simon said, turning back to the front of the line. "You?"

His companion shook his head. "But I'll stay with you while you eat yours."

Such a Robert-thing to say, Simon reflected, as he handed his money to the clerk. He hadn't planned on an audience while he had his ice cream bar.

They sat on a bench under the shade of the gazebo.

"I see your grandma and your grandpa around town sometimes," Robert informed him. "I guess you're staying with them."

"Yeah. I'm working at the Lodge again."

"It was too bad when you moved away." Robert sat gazing forward, hands gripping the front slat of the bench on either side of his legs. His intonation was so noncommittal that it was difficult to decide just who Robert was feeling sympathetic for—Simon or himself.

"Yeah. Well, when Kirk got that job offer in Denver, it was too good to turn down. So we had to go."

"You miss it here?"

"Yeah, sort of. Sometimes. Not as much as I used to." He took a bite of ice cream and reflected. "It's strange to think about it these days. My sister Maddy was two when we moved; my brother wasn't even born yet. This place was never home for them. Sometimes my mom and I will talk about our old house here, and stuff that we did, and I almost start to think that we're talking about some people that we knew once, not actually ourselves."

Robert nodded. "I would think about you sometimes, especially that first year when you were gone. Ninth grade. That was hard. After that, I sort of forgot." He shrugged dismissively. "What it was like, I mean. Having you around."

"Oh. Sure."

Robert darted a quick glance at Simon. "Was there anybody like me at your new school? That you were friends with? I bet not."

Simon couldn't help himself. He laughed.

"No. There was nobody like you, Robert. Not exactly, anyway." He looked at his companion. "You sure you don't want any ice cream? My treat."

Robert shook his head and then kicked at the grass under the bench with the toe of his shoe.

"No, thanks. I could afford it if I wanted some. I'm rich."

The last two words were offered almost sheepishly, as if he were confessing a dreadful secret about himself. Sagging forward, he turned his lowered face to squint up at Simon, smiling slightly.

Simon wasn't entirely sure what response was called for.

"Oh. Yeah?" he managed finally.

"I am. I didn't mean to be, Simon, I really didn't. But I am."

"Well... that's good, isn't it?"

"Yeah," Robert said. "It's good." His tone seemed nothing so much as obliging. He sat up straight, placing his hands on his knees. "So, you're working for the summer, and then going to college in the fall?"

"That's right. Are you working somewhere?"

"No. I'm supposed to go to an honor's camp, right after Fourth of July. It's sort of hard to get hired anyplace when you tell 'em you have to quit in the middle of summer."

Simon tossed his empty ice cream stick into the trash can alongside the bench. Robert seemed to take this as a sign that their conversation was over, and he stood.

"Well," he said. "Maybe I'll see you around before I go."

"Oh, sure." Simon got to his feet, swiping his hand on the leg of his pants. "I'm sure we'll run into each other lots. It's Stucker's Reach, after all."

He was turning to go when Robert added, "Maybe we could do something sometime. When you aren't working."

"Absolutely. We'll figure something out. See you."

He had taken maybe a dozen steps when Robert's voice drifted his way. "It's okay if you don't want to."

Simon turned back, planning to utter something. An assurance of some kind, he supposed. But he looked at Robert's retreating form, striding away in that nonchalant gait he abruptly remembered so well, and for a moment, his mind went blank. By the time he'd thought of something to say, Robert was far down the street and Simon was reluctant to call him back.

Chapter Four

"I noticed this afternoon that the drugstore is gone," Simon said. Because his arms were full, he used his hip to hold the screen door open for his grandmother. She slipped around him, bearing a platter of steaming bratwurst and sauerkraut, and carried it to the patio table.

"Oh, yes," she said almost absently, her focus on the meal at hand. She beckoned to Simon to follow, and he let the screen door bang closed and joined her. She relieved him of the bowls he was holding and placed one on either side of the sausage platter, then surveyed the arrangement with a critical eye.

"Melon wedges and potato salad," she listed. "And there's strawberry shortcake for dessert, but we'll bring that out later." Inventory complete, she turned to Simon, ready to resume the conversation.

"A shame, isn't it? Closed just after Memorial Day, so you barely missed it. Sit down, sit down," she urged. "That big new superstore on the edge of town has everything: Not just groceries, but a pharmacy, even a bank in it. Optometrist, too, can you believe it? Who do you suppose wants to get their eyes examined the same place they buy frozen peas and dog food? Wouldn't inspire a lot of confidence, I don't think." She settled in her own chair and unfolded a napkin in her lap.

Simon ladled a helping of melon onto his plate. "So the new place was siphoning off a lot of the drugstore's business?"

"Wasn't just that." His grandfather Axel interjected. He was in the process of spearing a braut and shaking it onto his plate. "J.J. Skeever's been making noises about retiring for awhile, now. I think this just made a good excuse."

"He tried selling it at first," Simon's grandmother added. "But nobody really wanted to take on that old place and all that dusty old inventory."

"Place won't stay empty long," her husband nodded confidently. "Somebody'll open a gallery or a souvenir shop there. Or another restaurant, wait and see. 'Nother touristy-type establishment. Can't have enough of those around here."

It was difficult to tell whether his grandfather was being facetious. He tended to deliver all of his statements—sincere or wry—in the same implacable tone. He hadn't even raised his face from his plate, so Simon couldn't judge by his expression, either.

"It gave me a weird feeling to see it. The empty space, I mean." Even as he said this, he realized that the weird feeling had returned. Only now it was because his grandparents appeared to be fairly indifferent to the change. Maybe it was because they lived here and therefore had had more time to adjust. Simon was feeling the loss more keenly. He scooped potato salad onto his plate, then added a sausage.

"I was going to suggest we grill the brats out here," Honey, his grandmother said. "In honor of your first dinner back with us." She propped her chin on her hand and watched the others eat for a moment. "But time just got away from me. And I don't think we've cleaned the grill since last autumn. So it would have taken too long. We'd be eating in the dark by then."

"This is fine, Grandma," Simon assured her. "I can clean it one of these days, and then we'll have a regular cookout."

She picked up her fork. "So, what else did you do today? Did you look up any of your old friends?"

He shook his head. "Not yet. I mostly just wanted to look around. See what's what. I'll catch up with whoever's left later on. I did see Robert MacKenzie downtown," he added after a hesitation. "We talked for a few minutes. Seems like the same old Robert."

Both his grandparents nodded.

"Yep. Robert," Axel said. His tone suggested that those two words explained all that needed to be said.

"He *is* a well-mannered boy, isn't he? Says hello to me in the market. Always seems to go along when his mother is shopping."

Simon grinned down at his plate. Both of his grandparents had a knack for saying more than they actually appeared to be saying. Honey's response had been just a little too bright, a little too artificial. Apparently she wasn't quite sure a boy Robert's age ought to be that dutiful about accompanying his mother to the grocery store. Every single time, anyway.

He remembered something else, then.

"Hey," he said, casually jabbing at his cantaloupe. "Do you guys remember Vanessa? The girl I've been dating since last fall? Well, um, she called me this afternoon. She gets the first week in July off, and wondered if it would be okay if she spent a few days up here. Around The Fourth."

Honey and Axel looked at one another. Axel's eyebrows did a twitch-thing, and then he went back to concentrating on his meal, leaving his wife to consider the question further. But apparently, some bit of vital information had been exchanged in that fleeting instant, for when Simon's grandmother, still chewing, said, "Well, I suppose that would be all right," his grandfather offered no objection.

Honey's brow creased, not in a frown, but in contemplation. She tapped the tines of her fork against her lip.

"We could set up a cot in the sun room," she said speculatively. "Vanessa could sleep on that. It's really quite comfortable, actually. Or if you'd rather, you could give her your bedroom, and you could stay on the cot. Three or four days, she'd be here, you think?"

"Uh…" Simon was at an utter loss. "I, I don't know. I'll find out, though. I'll call her later. I hadn't… Well, anyway, thanks."

This was an unexpected windfall. He hadn't been asking if it was okay if Vanessa stayed *here,* under this roof. He'd assumed that she was planning to make other arrangements for her visit—a motel, or perhaps a trailer park, since he figured what she'd meant was that she'd be coming with her family or with other friends, and he and she would see each other for just a few stray hours here and there. But *this*…this could be…

He shook off his reverie and cleared his throat. No point in conveying too much eagerness. He reached for another bratwurst and plunked it on his plate.

"These are really good, Grandma," he said. "Even if they weren't cooked on the grill."

"I'm glad you like them, Simon," his grandmother said.

Was it his imagination, or was she watching him rather closely just now?

* * *

Dark blue chased the fading amber sky over the foothills to the west.

Holding a bottle of beer in each hand, Livia Pointer stepped out onto the back porch. The heat of the afternoon and early evening had abated somewhat, though the air was still close and warm. Were it not for the alluring smell of freshly-mown grass, she would almost have preferred staying within the cooling embrace of air conditioning. But, no; that would be a shameful waste of summer.

"Kirk?" she called. "Where are you?"

"Here," came his response, though it wasn't particularly helpful, since he was nowhere in sight.

Rather than call again, Livia settled herself on one of the chaise lounges and set both bottles on the table between them. She would leave it up to her husband to find her—and the beer—when he was ready.

With a weary sigh, she leaned back in her chair. She rubbed the back of her moist neck, deciding at least momentarily that she was glad to have chopped off most of her hair a few weeks earlier. Kirk was constantly reassuring her that it hadn't made her ears look big; in moments like these, she was willing to believe him.

He appeared then, from around the side of the house, toting a ladder.

"Be right back," he promised, disappearing into the doorway that led into the garage. He reappeared seconds later empty-handed.

"What've you been doing?" Livia asked. "I could hear some banging and scratching noises while I was giving the kids their baths."

He threw himself onto the chair alongside hers and reached for a bottle.

"Sanding the eaves and the window sills. I'll start repainting the trim tomorrow night."

"In this heat?"

"I want to get it done before summer classes start next week. Anyway, it's not that bad once the sun goes down."

It was true he stood the heat much better than she did. "It's moments like these," she said, "I envy Simon, spending his summer up in the mountains."

"I see he mowed the grass before he left yesterday morning," Kirk gestured with his beer. They surveyed the back yard in silence for a moment. He sighed. "I suppose I'll have to take over that task from now on. Unless you think it's not too early to start letting Josh use a power mower."

Livia laughed.

"He and Maddie were just impossible all day. You know, it isn't that Simon's around that much of the day anyway, not with school and friends and especially since he got his driver's license; but I never quite realize what an influence he is on the other two until he's gone full time like this. It's like they've lost their anchor. They don't know what to do with themselves, so they divide their time equally between fighting, crying and driving me crazy."

Kirk nodded. "My self-esteem used to take a pounding. They were always twice as excited to see their brother walk in the door as me." He shrugged and took a gulp of beer. "Then, somewhere along the way, I just decided to go with the flow. We'll get our revenge, though. When Simon has kids, we can be the cool grandparents who spoil them rotten and then send 'em back home for him to deal with."

"But that's years off," she reminded him. "And he's off to college in the fall. What will we use for a diversion from now on?"

Rather than continuing the joke, Kirk grew quiet. Livia studied him curiously.

"Most parents hope college will make their kids buckle down and get serious, don't you suppose?" he said finally. "I kinda hope that it will make Simon cut loose a little. He needs that." Again he gestured towards the yard with his beer bottle. "He cut the grass before he left, for Pete's Sake."

She put her hand on his. "That's just his way."

"Was his dad like that? You know..." He fumbled for an appropriate word. "*Grounded?*"

Livia considered this for a long minute.

"Not especially," she concluded at last. "I certainly see traits of Larry in Simon, but most of what he is, he seems to have just picked up on his own. If I didn't think it would seem like I was trying to take credit where none is due, I'd say that maybe he just inherited the right mixture of things from both Larry and me to make him who he is: Better than either one of us."

"Not better," Kirk said, sliding his hand out from under hers in order to squeeze her fingers. "Just different. A newer model with all the latest accessories."

She laughed. "I used to worry that he got thrust into adulthood sooner than he should have. With his dad's death, and us getting married, and then having Madeleine and Joshy. But I don't think that anymore." With her other hand, she waved a gnat away from her face. "I think it was just always Simon's destiny to approach things the way he does."

They continued to hold hands across the table, sipping from their beers and watching night settle over the back yard.

* * *

"Too much iced tea," Axel lamented, returning from the bathroom and climbing back into bed alongside Honey. She didn't respond right away, and he turned his head to see if she was asleep. She was gazing at the ceiling, arms folded over her chest. He turned away then, closing his eyes while awaiting whatever thoughts she was processing and would almost certainly share.

"Do you think," she said at last, "That it's time for us to start thinking about selling this place?"

Axel shifted slightly, but said nothing, anticipating more information to follow. He was correct.

"It's more room than we really need, after all. Apart from Simon, we haven't had guests in a long while, and don't you suppose this is probably the last summer he'll be staying with us?"

"It's a thought," he responded without opening his eyes. "Where do you see us moving?"

"Oh, I don't know," was the careless reply. "A townhouse, maybe? Something with less responsibility?"

"Were you thinking of giving up the job? Retiring?" When she didn't answer right away, Axel offered some clarification. "I don't see that it makes a lot of sense to sell and then buy something else right here in town. That just seems like a lot of shifting for no good purpose. But if you meant further away, someplace warmer, or something like that... Well, then, it might be worth considering."

Still no answer was forthcoming, and he suspected she hadn't really taken her job in the city accounting office into consideration. It was a part-time administrative position, nothing particularly challenging, and they didn't need the income it provided, but it gave Honey a sense of purpose that he wasn't sure she was ready to abandon just yet.

"I didn't mean *right away*," she said at last. "But we should go while it's still our decision to make. You know: Before we have to be carted to a nursing home, or something."

"Oh. Well, sure."

"Just something to start thinking about."

"Mm."

Honey smoothed the blanket over her chest. "Stucker's Reach is changing, after all. It doesn't seem quite as much like home as it used to."

Another moment passed. Honey thought Axel had drifted off to sleep until he added:

"Just so you know, I don't plan on going to any nursing home."

* * *

Simon lay atop his bed, arms folded behind his head, toes wiggling as, in the darkness, the objects around him began to take on shape and focus.

This had been his father's bedroom, the room in which his dad and his dad's younger brother—Simon's Uncle Gordon—had grown up. Few remants of their childhood remained now: Just a couple of trophies atop the bureau, an indentation on the back of the closet where an errant basketball had smashed the dry wall, and a faint scent that Simon had come to associate with his father. It was a mixture of cedar and soap, and would have been here, no matter whose room this was, yet for as long as he might live, the smell would instantly conjure up the image of his dad.

He'd held the room in a kind of reverence as a child. In the last few years, when he'd begun spending the summers here, that feeling had settled into comfortable familiarity. Last night and tonight, however, his first two nights back, it seemed different again. He shifted on his pillow, his gaze traveling from one wall to the next, in search of something that might explain this.

But there was nothing. In fact, as much as the world—and the people in it—might change outside this room, nothing within these four walls was altered.

Simon thought about something else then; it wasn't the first time he'd contemplated it, but it had been awhile now.

What if, by some cosmic happenstance, his dad were to be restored to life? Not just moments after his death, back when Simon was five. But right now, with everything in the world having proceeded along the same course; his mom married to Kirk, Simon now seventeen and graduated from high school. And with a six year-old half-sister and a four year-old half-brother. And all of them living a hundred miles away from here.

His dad would be happy for them, he was sure. Simon had long since abandoned any sense of disloyalty that came from the simple fact that he and his mother had continued to live their lives. There was much about his father's memory that had receded into a kind of half-remembered haze, but he understood with absolute conviction that his dad had not been the kind of man to harbor resentment. But a new and jarring thought had come to him just now.

If, indeed Larry Perkins were plopped back down on this planet, alive and kicking, would there be a place for him? What would still be left? His family was no longer his. The town he'd grown up in and had found work in had changed. Only by degrees, if you looked at it from one day to the next, but in adding up the years, it had changed a great deal. Even Simon, seeing the alterations from one summer to the next, probably didn't understand how completely different Stucker's Reach—and the world—would seem to someone who last saw it thirteen years ago.

And that new thought abruptly sent a jolt through Simon's chest. For a few seconds, he fought to draw in an ample breath, his heart was beating so hard. *Thirteen years.* Twelve and a half, actually, but the fact remained: Simon had now lived much more of his life since his dad's death than he had before it.

In the darkness, he lifted his feet to the floor and sat up. Standing, he crept as softly as he could across the paneled, creaking floor into the hallway and across into the bathroom where he carefully pushed the door almost closed and turned on the light. He studied the face that looked back at him from the mirror over the sink.

Simon had been told ever since he could remember how much he resembled his dad, but he couldn't see it. The light brown hair and darker eyes he'd inherited from his mother; everything else just seemed his. He was nothing so much as pleasantly nondescript.

If tomorrow they were to pass on the street, would his father recognize him anymore?

He looked at his reflection a moment longer, searching without success for some feature he might trace to an old photo or some veiled memory. Finally, he clicked off the light and returned to his room and his bed.

It was only natural, of course, that as Simon lived more days, new experiences would force older ones into the background. Previous summers, lying in this bed, he'd been a virgin. With the removal of that, life had taken on different experiences and priorities that rendered much of what had come before as vague and dreamlike.

This room was just a room, he realized. It was shaded by memories and trophies and smells, but increasingly less a part of the person he was now, and even less the person he was on his way to becoming.

This made him just a little bit sad, but not overwhelmingly so. And as sleep gradually overtook him, he had a fleeting image of his dad, standing in front of an empty storefront, bewildered, and wondering where the drugstore had gone.

Chapter Five

Heather MacKenzie was a bully.

She wasn't a bad person, really, and she would outgrow this unpleasant trait in time. She'd had a sickly childhood, full of allergies and maladies, and her parents had compensated by catering to her whims and inadvertently fostering an ongoing sense of privilege. By twelve, she'd outgrown all the illnesses, but not the entitlement. She held court over her small circle of friends with a shrewd combination of cajoling, threats, and guilt-trips. By fifteen, she'd so mastered these techniques, she was scarcely aware she was using them.

Her brother Robert, chauffeuring Heather and her friend Mindy to their afternoon jobs at the miniature golf course, either chose to ignore their back seat conversation or was preoccupied with his own thoughts. In any instance, this was all to the best. They occasionally looked at his reflection in the rear view mirror or at the back of his head, then leaned close to one another and exchanged muffled comments behind a cupped hand, followed by explosive laughs. They might have been talking about anything under the sun and their glances at him merely coincidence. But the derisiveness with which Heather treated him upon their arrival was precisely delivered.

"You need to pick us up at five forty-five, and don't be late. We're going to the movies tonight." She slammed the door and strode away without a look back.

"You are such a *bitch*," Mindy giggled, with a glance over her shoulder in Robert's direction.

"Oh, please!" Heather retorted loudly. "It's not like he has a *job*, or anything to do. At least not until he goes to geek camp next month. So he might as well take us places."

It seemed unlikely that Robert, still sitting fifteen feet away with the windows rolled down, didn't hear this, but if so, he gave no indication. He waited another minute or so until traffic was clear, then pulled his car away from the curb, circled, and exited the parking area.

Robert stood inside the pleasantly cool foyer of The Stucker's Reach Savings and Loan less than a quarter-hour later, hands dangling at his sides. Though it was several more minutes before anyone seemed to take any real notice of him, he remained unruffled, perfectly at ease in his spot on the carpet, gazing with interest around the lobby.

"Can I help you?" a woman asked finally.

"Yes, please. I want to talk to somebody about opening a checking account."

"Oh." If he noticed the startled expression that flickered across her face for just an instant, he gave no indication. "Well, certainly. Just follow me, won't you?"

He did, trailing after her to a desk in a walnut-paneled alcove. The air, he thought, glancing around him, seemed not just still, but heavier back here.

"Have a seat," and I'll get the paperwork," the woman instructed. She moved around to the far side of the desk and plucked a folder from a rack on a side table. She settled herself in her chair, but did not open the folder. Instead, she rested her arms across it and smiled at Robert.

"A checking account, huh?"

"I'm going to college in the fall. Actually, I leave in a couple of weeks, because I'm going to an honor's camp first. So I need to set up a checking account with a debit card first. I have money in the bank here already. It's in a money market fund and also some in a savings account. I would like to transfer some of it from one of those." As he was speaking, Robert had reached into his pocket for his wallet, withdrawn his driver's license, and slid it across the desk, past the nameplate: *Ruth Sparks.*

Both the young man's expression and tone were unflappable. Ms. Sparks scrutinized him while trying to give the appearance of not scrutinizing too closely, and then picked up the license.

"You have a birthday coming up," she observed. "A big one, I see." This provoked no reaction from him. He simply continued to study her with an even, mild expression, not quite smiling. The juxtaposition of self-composure and adolescence was oddly intimidating, and she quickly handed him back his license and opened the folder.

"All right; this packet contains the application and information. Since you already have accounts with us, it will make this simpler. But, since you aren't yet eighteen..."

"My dad is supposed to be meeting me here," the young man said. He shifted in his chair, looking over both shoulders. "He said he'd swing by at the end of his lunch hour."

"Oh. Well, tell you what..." She plucked a pen from the cup near her elbow and handed it to him. "Why don't you start filling out the top form then, and he'll probably be along before we're finished. In the meantime..." She turned to the computer and tapped a few keys. "I'll pull up your information. Let's see, that was capital M, small A and C, right?"

"Uh-huh." He was already absorbed with filling out the application. Head lowered, he did not see Ruth's frown as she looked at the columns that had just flickered into place on her screen. After some hesitation, she started to ask to see the driver's license again, but then she noticed she could read upside down the information he'd entered already on the form.

Robert E. MacKenzie. And yes: The birth date and Social Security number matched.

"How... How much were you thinking you wanted to transfer into a checking account?" she asked.

Robert looked up then, an unfocused look on his face as he pondered this.

"I don't know. Fifteen hundred, I think my dad said. Enough to cover an emergency, but not enough to go crazy with."

She nodded, her gaze drifting to the computer screen, scrutinizing a second time the amounts posted to these accounts.

"That seems sensible," she said. "Where are you planning to go to college?"

"California Polytechnical," he reported. This time he did not look up. "I'm going to study Architectural Engineering and Design."

"That's very impressive. I bet you were very good at math and science, then."

"Uh-huh." Abruptly, he set down his pen and pushed the completed form back towards her. "Maybe," he said, "I should transfer two thousand. The catalog says some of the courses require loading extra applications on your computer." The look he gave her was a searching one. "Do you think?"

She turned the paperwork so it was facing her once more. With very little time and effort, Robert had managed to smudge quite a bit of ink across the page and crumple its corners.

"I wouldn't really know," she told him, unconsciously running her hand over the creases. "It's been awhile since I've been at college, and I certainly never studied anything as complicated as the classes you'll be taking. At any rate, though, once you've set up everything electronically online, you would be able to move money from any account to any other account. So it doesn't matter how much you want to start out with. You can always add more."

Brow furrowed, Robert watched her intently as she spoke. He appeared to be carefully evaluating each word as it left her lips, examining it with some sort of mental slide rule, or whatever objects a would-be architectural engineer might employ. Even when she stopped talking, he continued to scrutinize her so closely that she felt she had somehow failed him by not providing more data. And now they were left looking at one another in silence. What was keeping this young man's father? She cast covert glances at the clock on the far wall while tossing off innocuous questions in an effort to keep them both occupied as they waited. Good Lord, what kind of a lunch hour did this boy's dad take, anyhow?

"Do you want to call him?" she inquired finally. Like all of the other questions lobbied at him, Robert MacKenzie responded to this one with indifferent brevity.

"That's okay. I can wait." Clearly he felt that she could, as well.

"Well, look," she said finally, summoning a regretful sigh and gathering up the papers, "I have a meeting starting in a few minutes. Why don't you sit over there in the reception area until your father gets here? There are magazines and things to look at. I'm going to go ahead and flag these pages that need his signature." She gestured to another desk across the way. "If I'm still unavailable when he gets here, just go talk to Monica. She can pull the forms from my desk, and finish processing everything."

"All right," Robert said agreeably. He watched as Ruth affixed colored arrows to his application and slipped it back into the folder. She dropped this into a hanging file and closed the drawer. As she stood, he rose from his own chair and followed her back out into the lobby. There, he accepted her extended hand and shook it solemnly.

"And thanks so much, Robert, for continuing to bank with us here," she said by way of parting. "I wish you all the best at college."

He nodded, then settled himself in a chair alongside an end table burgeoning with magazines. He selected one and was already leafing through the pages as Ruth left him. She resisted the impulse to wipe away the lingering effects of his clammy handshake until she'd turned the corner and was out of sight.

Robert waited several more minutes, seemingly absorbed in his reading, but in fact mostly just lifting his face now and then to give the nearly empty room several cursory inspections. Just one teller appeared to be on duty, and Monica, the woman at the other desk, was on her telephone. After she'd concluded her call, she gathered up some papers from her desk, smiled at Robert, and went into a small room behind the counter. Robert lowered his magazine.

A woman entered the bank with a baby in a stroller. She moved to the teller's window and began a lively conversation with the clerk, who, enchanted by the small child, leaned across the counter to beam down at her.

"Well, hey, there! Look at you! Look at you, sweetheart! Oh, isn't she precious? How old is she?"

No other customers were waiting for service, and the teller was able to engage in a lengthy conversation with the young mother. Monica was in the back room for another few moments, and when she returned, she, too, dallied to admire the baby. So absorbed, was she, in fact, that she hadn't noticed at first that Robert was now sitting in the chair next to her desk, a folder lying across his lap.

"I'm so sorry," she told him, crossing the lobby. "I didn't realize you had moved over here."

"That's all right." He placed the paperwork on her desk. "The other woman said you would be able to help me finish this if she wasn't back yet."

"Oh. Yes, certainly. What are we doing for you today? Oh, establishing a checking account, I see," she said, answering her own question as she opened his folder.

"My dad couldn't wait," Robert said. "He had to get back to work. But he said we could call him, if you had any questions, or if you needed anything else." He pointed to the signatures next to the colored flags.

Monica looked at Robert, then lifted the forms, studying each page in turn.

"No, it looks like everything is here," she said slowly. She set the application on her desk, frowning. "So... Your dad... He was just here...?"

Robert extracted a card from his shirt pocket and placed it alongside the folder.

"Here's his business card. That's his direct number, right there. He should be back in his office by now, if you want to call."

"No," she concluded after a moment's consideration. "No, this should be fine." For another few seconds, she appeared to be wrestling with some inner conflict, but then straightened in her chair and offered Robert a broad smile.

"All right, then," she said briskly, reaching into a drawer. "I need to take your fingerprint, and then we'll get you a pad of temporary checks. The regular ones and your debit card will be sent to you in the mail in a week or so. Will that be okay?"

"That will be okay," he said agreeably, taking back the business card and returning it to his pocket.

Chapter Six

Simon had been filled with a jittery anticipation all day.

He'd awakened earlier than usual and then been unable to go back to sleep. After twenty minutes of burrowing determinedly into his pillow, forcing his eyes to remain closed and trying to will away conscious thought, he'd sighed, tossed aside his blankets, and risen to greet the dawn.

By eight o'clock, he'd taken a fifty minute-long jog along the lakeshore, showered, washed his car, and fixed pancakes for his bewildered grandparents.

Honey, accustomed to little more than some tea and half a grapefruit in the morning, thanked Simon profusely and tottered off to work feeling unpleasantly bloated.

Axel sat on the porch with a mid-morning cup of coffee and the newspaper. Simon, having washed the dishes and cleaned the kitchen, kept him company. After fifteen minutes, Axel lowered his newspaper and studied his grandson over the rims of his glasses.

"Good Lord, Boy, will you calm down, or find someplace else to burn off that excess energy? You've driven me so far past distraction, I can't even see it in the rear-view mirror any longer."

Simon, who had been drumming the palms of his hands on his kneecaps in a staccato beat, looked startled. He stopped drumming, but his legs continued to twitch from side to side.

"Oh. Sorry."

Axel continued to peer at him without comment until the twitching also ceased. Then he folded his paper and set it to one side. He took a sip of coffee and gazed out across the yard.

"So tell me a little about her."

Simon shook his head.

"I'd rather you just meet her," he said. "That way, you can form your own opinion."

His grandfather nodded. "You're taking tonight off, then?"

"Yeah. And Thursday and Sunday. I'm going to bring her here for dinner Thursday night. Grandma said we should have a cookout, the four of us. And since Sunday's her last day here…" He allowed the sentence to trail off.

"I hope you can find enough to keep her entertained a whole week in pokey old Stucker's Reach."

Simon looked startled, as if this was an eventuality that hadn't even occurred to him until now.

"Oh. Well, sure. I mean…" He paused, considering. Axel cleared his throat, though it was really just a means of disguising a smile he felt coming on, a prudent move, because now Simon was looking at him.

"That shouldn't be a problem, should it? There's… Well, there's boating, and water-skiing, and maybe fishing, and, well, there'll be the fireworks on The Fourth, and the cookout here on Thursday…"

His grandson still appeared so stricken that Axel couldn't help but feel a little guilty for having introduced the topic. He reached across the small table to slap him on the shoulder.

"And there's you," he pointed out. "I doubt she cares very much about anything besides that."

Simon didn't appear to be convinced. He was still listing events.

"And the place she and her folks are staying," he added. "I guess her parents are friends with these people; they have one of those big houses on the far shore, with its own beach, and stuff."

"Uh-huh." Axel didn't volunteer that he'd been rather relieved to learn that they wouldn't be hosting the girlfriend all week, after all. He just wasn't up to the demands of that sort of peppy socialization. "Forget I said anything, Simon. What you're going to find is that the whole seven days zip by so quickly, you'll wonder where they went. Vanessa isn't going to be bored."

Whether that did the trick, he could not be certain, but Simon leaned back in his chair and was quiet. The drumming of fingers on knees returned, but Axel decided to let it slide for now.

"Hard to believe another June has practically slid away out from under us," he observed. Privately, he found himself wondering just how many more Junes he would be treated to. He was staring down the barrel of seventy-five, and practically every month anymore, it seemed that one of his compatriots succumbed to some age-related malady, or other: Ted Berskin, Eulamarie Scoggins, Warren Tomlinson...

"Hey, Doo-Dah," Simon said, interrupting his reverie. "Remember how we used to go out hunting for old aluminum cans? Do you still do that sometimes?"

In spite of himself, Axel unleashed a small bark of a laugh. He wasn't sure if it was the question itself or the reappearance an old nickname his grandson had once bestowed upon him. Either way, it had the effect of chasing away any approaching sense of melancholy.

"Nope," he said. "Not for awhile. They have these civic groups who've adopted stretches of the highway, and they keep the ditches pretty cleaned up anymore."

"Oh." Simon considered this for a few seconds, then brightened. "Well... We could still take a walk, couldn't we?"

Vanessa and her family, Axel knew, weren't expected to arrive until late afternoon. And while, as far as he was concerned, June had rocketed past in the blink of an eye, for Simon, the next few hours threatened to drag interminably.

"Sure," the older man said, tossing his newspaper onto the table along-side his unfinished cup of coffee and hoisting himself out of his seat. "We could do that."

"So, anyway... hi!" Vanessa greeted Simon with a self-conscious little giggle as he emerged from his car.

"Yeah, hi," Simon returned, his hands flopping like awkward, useless flippers at his side.

This moment of reunion was dismayingly anticlimactic.

The call telling him that, finally, she and her family were in town, had come at quarter 'til seven. He'd jumped in his car and driven quickly along the road that looped the lake. He had no difficulty finding the house, since he'd previously made a scouting trip after Vanessa had texted him the address. It was a spectacular, log-hewn two-story home settled on a rise with an expansive lawn that rolled gently down to a strip of sandy shore fronting the water. The driveway rose and curved well beyond an entry gate, and Simon, once inside the compound, felt abruptly intimidated and out of place. He'd parked some distance away from the house, as that seemed somehow more respectful. A sizable group of people were clustered on a second-story deck, and it was from this that Vanessa had disentangled herself and come rushing down the grass to meet him.

Yet, as if she, too, suddenly felt intimidated, she'd slowed her headlong dash to a sedate walk perhaps thirty feet away, closing the remaining gap in a casual stroll. They stood three feet apart, acutely aware now that they were under the bemused scrutiny of everyone up on the deck. Simon had an uncomfortable feeling that some of the laughs floating through the air were at his expense.

"I… I wasn't sure where I should park my car," he began.

"Oh." Vanessa cast a hasty glance over her shoulder at the people up at the house. "Here is probably fine. It's… It's so awesome to see you!" And finally, she launched herself at him, wrapping her arms around him.

Now the laughs from the house swelled, joined by a few *Oohs* and cheers, but for the moment, Simon didn't care. His flippers felt like hands again, and he threw them around her waist. They hugged, but did not kiss, not in front of the audience.

"I have…missed you…so…freaking…much!" she declared, and, her head obscuring the view from the deck, she managed a secretive kiss on his neck.

"Me, too," he said. They stepped apart, holding hands and gazing at each other another moment.

"Come on!" she said at last, tugging at him as she turned and started back up the hill. "Come meet everybody!" Instantly, Simon's nervousness was back, but he allowed himself to be pulled across the yard and up the set of steps to the deck and the throng of people awaiting them there.

Honey was on the phone when she saw headlights appear in the driveway. She glanced at the kitchen clock, wondering if she'd lost track of time and been talking far longer than she'd realized.

"Looks like Simon's back," she said. "It's not even ten."

"That's okay, Mom," her son Gordon said. "I need to hang up anyway. I've got some stuff to do."

"Gordie!" she admonished. "Are you still in the office? At this time of night?"

"Well, I wouldn't have been, if I weren't still talking to my dear old ma," he retorted. "There's just one or two things to wrap up, and then I'm headed out."

"I should hope so. You should have said something." Her tone, Gordon recognized, was a distracted one. She was, in fact, watching Simon, who had just come through the front door and was giving her a half-wave on his way down the hall to his bedroom.

"It's all right," Gordon assured her. "We're done here. Go get the scoop from Si; I know you're dying to, and you can only spread your mothering skills so thin."

"Oh, hush," she said, before setting down the receiver. Honey stood by the table in silent debate, wondering if she would seem too eager by venturing as far as Simon's doorway to ask about his evening. Before she could move, however, he saved her the trouble by reappearing.

"Where's Grandpa?" he asked, moving past her into the kitchen. "In bed already?" He pulled a soft drink from the refrigerator and leaned against the counter, peeling back the aluminum tab and taking a gulp.

She nodded. "He was reading. Probably asleep now." By way of demonstrating availability and receptiveness, she took her own drink and settled herself in one of the kitchen chairs right in front of him.

"Has she changed much in four weeks?" she inquired.

Simon laughed and straddled the chair on the opposite side of the table. "No, but it was strange. Not her—*she* wasn't strange; but it wasn't how I'd pictured it, our first time back together. We didn't have any time alone tonight, just the two of us. I guess I should have expected that. ... But I didn't. It felt like there was this sheet of glass between us the whole time. We could see and talk to each other, but we almost weren't in the same room."

With his forefinger, Simon traced idle patterns across the tabletop.

"It'll be fine, I know," he continued. "It's just… Well, our first night in town is over, and it felt like it never really happened, you know?"

"It was all the other people," Honey acknowledged. She took a stab at describing the situation. "Vanessa's parents, and the people they're staying with: They all know you're her boyfriend and how she feels about you. All of sudden, you were both under a microscope. You hadn't counted on that."

Eyebrows raised, Simon exhaled a long breath.

"You should see that house where they're staying, Grandma. These people must have some serious money. They were grilling these big Porterhouse steaks, and they asked me how I wanted mine cooked, and when I said I didn't need one, they insisted. So we're eating this big fancy meal, and the adults are drinking this wine that's like, two hundred dollars a bottle. Later, everybody was planning to get into a big Jacuzzi they have in their back yard, on a bluff overlooking the lake. They offered to loan me a bathing suit so I could get in, too, but I decided I'd just come home."

Honey considered this for a second.

"You could have called," she said. "I would have brought your own bathing trunks over, if you'd wanted."

Simon shook his head. "No, it wasn't that," he said slowly.

He struggled to describe his feelings in a way that didn't seem selfish or petulant. It wasn't that he had wanted Vanessa all to himself; but he did want *her* to want to be with just him, not having quite so much fun in the company of all those people. There had been a moment or two of silent concern as he'd watched her over dinner tonight, laughing and relaxed and, well, comfortable in this fancy place.

Their hosts had a fifteen year-old daughter who was clearly enamored of Vanessa, and she had proposed all kinds of exciting-sounding activities they could do together. They had a stable of jet skis, she said, and a speed-boat, and friends with a bigger boat, and an island. It was around this point that Simon had excused himself and said good night, because he didn't want to hear what else these people or their friends might come up with to distract his girlfriend for the next five days.

Vanessa, already in her bathing suit, had offered to walk him to his car, but he'd told her No, that was all right, she should go ahead and get into the Jacuzzi. And that's what she had done, without further persuasion, telling him she'd see him tomorrow, then. Simon had taken his leave, vaguely dismayed that it had been so easy for them to part company.

As if sensing his thoughts, his grandmother reached across the table and patted his hand.

"She's come all this way to see you, Sweetheart, not a fancy house or a hot tub. Just wait. Tomorrow will be a whole different story."

"Yeah, I guess."

He looked so solemn. Honey bit her lip, half in sympathy, and half to hold back a smile. She drew back her hand and settled it in her lap. It was enough that he was willing to share his feelings; she could not expect that he would be open to predictions, no matter how well-intentioned. Better to go a different route.

"Tell me about Vanessa," she said. "How did the two of you meet? And when did you know she was the one?"

He shrugged and continued to prod the table with his finger, but she could tell he was nonetheless pleased to have an excuse to talk about her.

"It's no big deal." Then, after a respectable hesitation, he launched into an account of their early courtship. Honey smiled and nodded attentively and tried not to let her thoughts wander too much.

Yet again, Simon slept fitfully. Excitement and anticipation had kept him from dozing soundly the previous night. And now, his brain filled with fresh images of Vanessa, courtesy of the conversation with his grandmother, he rolled from side to side in the darkness, trying hard not to analyze the evening and therefore analyzing it every time he let down his guard.

Towards morning, spent, he fell at last into a deep sleep that carried him far past his usual waking time. As sunlight filled the room, he gradually became aware of the world taking shape around him. With his eyes still closed, his other senses lured him back from oblivion: The sound of a neighbor's lawn mower, accompanied by the scent of freshly cut grass. The soft pillow cushioning the back of his neck. The murmur of his grandparents' conversational tones out in the kitchen.

It was another sound—a familiar, yet out of place one—that prompted Simon to lift himself on his elbows, blinking and listening closely.

Yes. There it was again.

He threw back the covers and clambered out of bed. Tugging up the waistband of his sweatpants, he padded barefooted down the hall to the kitchen, where he stopped in the doorway, blinking several more times as he took in the scene before him.

His grandfather, baseball cap parked atop his head, sat at the table, one arm thrown over the back of his chair. His grandmother leaned against the counter, wiping her hands on a dishtowel. And, seated opposite his grandfather, finger threaded through the handle of a coffee mug, was Vanessa. As one, they shifted their gaze to Simon, who, for the moment, could think of nothing to say.

"Hi," Vanessa greeted him.

"Beginning to think we needed to send a search party in for you," Axel commented.

Honey merely smiled. She folded the towel and set it behind her. Vanessa set down her mug, pushed back her chair, rose and crossed to Simon, throwing her arms around his bare shoulders, kissing him lightly on the cheek.

Simon was astounded, delighted, and self-conscious.

"What are you doing here?" he asked when they stepped away from one another. "How did you find the house, I mean?"

She laughed. "It wasn't hard. This is Stucker's Reach, after all."

"No, I mean… That isn't what I…" Flustered, he shook his head and stopped. It wasn't that he doubted her ability to navigate the town; it just hadn't entered his mind she would ever show up here on her own. But this was wonderful. All of last evening's feelings of doubt and frustrations were swept away. He grabbed her again, and in full view of his grandparents, pressed his lips to hers in a long, hard kiss. Releasing her, he instructed, "Don't go anywhere! I'm gonna go get dressed!"

"Brush your teeth!" she called after him, as he dashed back to his bedroom. "You've got awful morning breath!"

Simon showered and dressed as quickly as he could manage. The image of Vanessa parked at the kitchen table, having coffee and chatting up his grandparents suggested a sort of casualness he wasn't sure he liked all that much. If anybody had a host of potentially embarrassing stories—and photos—of him to share, it would be the two people entertaining his girlfriend just now. Though, he reflected philosophically as he spat toothpaste into the sink, it was probably too late to worry about that now.

"Where'd everybody go?" he demanded upon his return to the kitchen. Vanessa was now the sole occupant of the room. She handed him a cup of coffee and settled herself at the table again.

"Your grandmother's weeding in the back yard. I don't know where your grandfather went. He patted me on the head on his way out, though." She giggled. "I like them. I like them both a lot. They don't seem…you know…*old.*"

Simon took a sip from his cup before he remembered he didn't actually like coffee.

"So," he said. "I thought maybe you'd be jet skiing or something today."

She grinned and finished her own cup in a single gulp. "Who gives a crap about any of that?" she retorted. "I just want to spend the day with you. You can show me all the places you hung out while you were growing up."

By mid-afternoon, Simon had conducted a tour of all the sites he could think to share: The house he'd lived in prior to moving to Denver. The school he'd attended. The Lodge, where he was currently busing tables in the evening. Now he and Vanessa were having lunch in The Snack Shack, a popular lakeshore restaurant whose dilapidated architecture served to reinforce the name.

"So, what do you do?" she queried, dipping her breaded fish fillet into tartar sauce. "I mean, with your free time. Do you still have friends here?"

"Yeah," he said vaguely. He was struck suddenly by the realization that he'd been in town an entire month already. What *had* he done, and who had he done it with? Surely there must have been something besides working five or six shifts a week, and hanging around with his grandparents. "Nothing much so far," he concluded lamely. "A couple of hikes. One party."

The party had been an impromptu after-work-one-night kind of thing, involving co-workers, only one or two of whom were former classmates or friends. Most of Simon's fellow wait-staff and restaurant employees were college students or older, and generally when they relaxed, it was at one of the local bars, precluding the under-twenty-one crowd from joining in. But there had been one gathering at somebody's house, with a keg, and Simon had gotten pleasantly buzzed and had a pretty good time. It hadn't really led to further socializing, however.

A gradual kind of ennui seemed to have taken hold over the past four years. With each summer, Simon discovered that he and his childhood friends had drifted still further apart, the natural outgrowth of different experiences and pursuits. What interested the kids of Stucker's Reach didn't necessarily interest kids formerly from Stucker's Reach. He and his old buddies were friendly when their paths crossed, but they seemed to exhaust all avenues of conversation in increasingly shorter amounts of time, and no longer actively sought one another's company. This was disappointing, but not bitterly so. Simon was content with his time here, all the same.

He wondered if his answer would cause Vanessa to point out once again how much more fun it would have been if he'd stayed in Denver, with her, this summer. But it did not. She sipped her Coke, wadded up her napkin, and said:

"You have to be at work at five, right? Let's do something until then. I don't care what."

They left the restaurant and ventured down to the beach. The lake, fed by streams carrying the winter run-off, was chilly most any time of year, yet hundreds of determined people bobbed in the dark blue water in the roped-off swimming section. Further out, boats skimmed past, some towing water skiers.

"I would love to try that," Vanessa declared, pointing to an individual the size of an ant, suspended beneath a bright orange parasail that floated high overhead. "Have you ever?" When Simon shook his head, she added, "Could we, do you think? Maybe not today, but sometime this week before I go back?"

"Probably," he said cautiously. "I think it's pretty expensive, and we'd need to make a reservation, especially since it's a holiday week." He pointed to a canopied section of floating dock some distance away. "That's where you rent water craft and bumper boats. They can probably tell us where to go for the parasailing, too."

Vanessa looped her arm around Simon's waist as they strolled across the boardwalk to the rental counter. His was draped across her shoulder, one thumb stroking the back of her neck. They had to dodge countless groups of people, some moving purposefully, some drifting aimlessly, lost in their surroundings and the moment. Simon felt a kinship with the latter. He would happily have walked the entire shoreline like this, content to have no destination in mind. How had he not realized until just now how much he missed her?

"A hundred twenty-five bucks for thirty minutes," the clerk informed them at the rental desk. He hunched across the counter, studying them indifferently as he chewed his gum. "That includes some instruction first, and you have to sign a release." He scrutinized them under sandy colored eyebrows. "Or, if you're under eighteen, you have to get a parent's or a guardian's signature."

"Okay, thanks," Simon said, turning away. He was waiting until they were out of earshot of the clerk to say that either one of those things made it impossible for him. But before he could say anything, they found themselves standing nose-to-nose with Robert MacKenzie.

"Hi, Simon," he said. His eyes drifted to Vanessa, scrutinizing her unabashedly, and then shifting his gaze to Simon once more. "What're you guys doing? Going paddle-boating?"

"No," Simon told him. "We were—"

Robert was addressing Vanessa now. "—The paddleboats are pretty fun. But stay away from the blue ones," he informed her. He frowned. "Well, most of the blue ones are fine. But there are two of them that don't work very well. One keeps wanting to go in circles. The other's just really slow. Better to just get a green or a red one."

"We're not doing the paddleboats, Robert," Simon assured him. They remained where they were, the three of them, chiefly because it hadn't occurred to Robert to step out of their way.

"Oh." He received this information solemnly. "What *are* you doing, then?"

Simon felt an irritation rising in his chest, a not-unfamiliar sensation that frequently occurred in conversations with Robert, at least in years past. "Look—" he began.

"—We were asking about the parasailing," Vanessa said, seizing the conversation. She dropped her arm from around Simon's waist and extended her palm. "I'm Vanessa, by the way. We thought it looked like fun."

Robert accepted her outstretched hand and shook it. "Parasailing," he repeated. He appeared to be digesting this bit of information, but his next question was, "Are you Simon's girlfriend?"

"Yes," she said, her smile growing wider. "From back home. From Denver, I mean. It's nice to meet you. I was just asking Simon about some of his friends from when he lived here."

"Yes," Robert acknowledged. "Simon and I were friends when we were in middle school."

Both of them looked abruptly at Simon as if seeking validation of this fact.

"Uh...yeah," he said, feeling oddly ambushed. "That's right."

"The parasailing is pretty expensive, I bet," Robert said.

"It is," Vanessa told him. "A hundred and twenty-five dollars for thirty minutes." He looked at her again.

"It's pretty expensive," he repeated, as if it was important to drive home that point. "And it's dangerous enough that they make you sign a paper saying you won't sue them if you get hurt. And your family can't sue them if you die."

"Yeah, we *know.*" The barely-concealed annoyance in Simon's tone caused Vanessa to give him a sidelong glance. Robert, on the other hand, seemed oblivious.

"Are you going to do it?"

"Probably not."

"Oh."

At last, Robert stood to one side, allowing them to pass. He followed on their heels as they crossed from under the canopy into the sunlight once more.

"You're up from Denver?" he asked.

Vanessa nodded.

"I didn't know Simon had a girlfriend. He didn't tell me that."

Near the water's edge, they stopped. Vanessa turned, squinting in the bright light.

"He didn't?" she inquired, addressing Robert but looking at Simon. She was still smiling, but there was an odd sort of expectant look on her face.

"No. But the last time we talked was at the beginning of June. Maybe you weren't his girlfriend then."

Simon felt a curious sort of helplessness. A part of him wanted to tell Robert to shut up now, and to go away. Another part of him wanted to say to Vanessa, *"You can understand why I didn't, can't you? You can see what a… what a different sort of person Robert is, right?"*

But, strictly speaking, Robert hadn't done anything wrong. And to say anything right now, to yell at Robert, or to try and explain that their one single conversation since Simon had been back in town had been mercifully brief, too brief to mention anything as important as Vanessa, well… he would just come off sounding defensive. And guilty.

A bold move was called for.

He took a half-step behind her and slipped both his arms tightly around her waist, kissed her on the temple and then pressed his cheek against hers.

"Vanny's been my girlfriend for a year now," he declared. "She's up for the week."

Robert seemed unimpressed. "Anyway," he said, and for just a second, it appeared that he was going to let that single word constitute an entire statement. "It was nice to meet you. I hope you enjoy your vacation. Parasailing, or whatever."

He lifted his chin, squinting overhead, and reflexively, the others did the same. There was only the clear blue sky and the sun, however, beaming back at them.

"Thank you," Vanessa said when they were done looking up. She shaded her face with one hand to bring her eyes back into focus. "It was nice to meet you, too."

He drifted away then, rather like an unmoored boat, floating on a receding wave.

"So, anyway," Simon said, as they resumed their own stroll in the opposite direction. "What are you going to do tonight?"

Her shoulders rose and fell in a shrug.

"There's a concert in the park, or something. Krissy was telling me about it, so I guess that's what we're doing."

Krissy, Simon remembered, was the fifteen year-old daughter at the house where Vanessa and her family were staying.

"Oh, yeah," he said. "Symphony Under the Stars. Happens a few times each summer. People bring picnics and sit on blankets while they listen. Is that what you're going to do?"

"I guess." Vanessa tried to mentally sort through all the chatter Krissy had levied at her last night and this morning. "She's got some friends who are going, and she invited me, too." She faced Simon. "I think it lasts until ten, or so. Why don't you head over after you get off work, and meet up with us?" She squeezed his hand. "Maybe we could do something."

"Sure," he nodded. Giving it some added thought, he said, "Probably be closer to ten-thirty before I can get there. Do you guys have to be home by a certain time? Or does she, anyway?"

"I don't know. Don't worry about it. I'll think of something," she assured him.

They left it at that, and spent the rest of the too-brief afternoon sitting side-by-side on one of the docks, dipping their bare toes into the chilly lake.

Chapter Seven

When the sun dipped behind the mountains, the air turned abruptly cool, and Vanessa, who hadn't thought to bring a jacket to the concert, found herself grateful for the body heat of the people surrounding her on all sides.

There were more people gathered on the lawn of the town square this evening than she imagined living in the entire town, certainly more than she had seen up until now.

The crowd consisted of all sorts, comfortably sharing grass-space. She would not have suspected orchestral music to be such a draw, or to appeal to such a variety of types—families, couples, old, young… Perhaps the social aspect, rather than the music itself, was more the appeal. Certainly that was the case for Krissy and her friends, who barely remained seated more than five minutes at a stretch before wandering off somewhere when they spotted somebody else they knew. And that was just as well, since when they did sit, they chattered nonstop, ignoring glares and shushings from those within earshot.

Vanessa, who didn't know anybody, was happy to remain cross-legged on the ground in a cocoon of warmth. And the entertainment, she decided, was pleasant enough. There was something spellbinding about music floating over a sea of unmoving heads in the crisp air. She'd been to rock concerts, where the crowds stood and shouted and sang along. Those were rousing, adrenalin-pumping experiences, as different from this as one could possibly imagine. Nobody sang along here, nobody raised their arms above their heads. But the quiet, shared affability—except for when people were frowning at Krissy's group—created a sense of community. Lifting her gaze, she regarded the outline of the spruce and pine trees looming over the park and, beyond them, shadowy mountain ridges fading into the night.

From here, she couldn't see the lake or hear the waves slapping relentlessly against the shore, but the air was heavy with its murky scent.

Until now, city-born-and-raised Vanessa had never contemplated life in a small town. It had, she decided, certain attractions. Nothing compelling enough to make her want to move to one, of course, but she could see why some people did. More importantly, it gave her fresh perspective on Simon and how life here must have shaped him.

The concert ended shortly after ten. She struggled to her feet, brushing grass and leaves from the seat of her shorts. She looked around, trying to find Krissy or any of her friends in the hordes of people folding blankets, packing up baskets and moving off to their cars, but without success. The girls were no doubt off socializing somewhere.

Hands tucked into her pockets, Vanessa made her way through the crowd, stepping carefully across flowerbeds to get to the wooden sidewalk. There, she paused for a minute, leaning against a tree trunk, away from the exodus of the crowd. In front of the bandstand, musicians were packing up various instruments while other workers collected and stacked the performers' folding chairs. A lone figure hovered over the gazebo railing, inspecting the process. It was, Vanessa realized belatedly, the boy she'd met on the shore this afternoon. He appeared to be carrying on a conversation with one of the musicians.

She removed her hands from her pockets and folded them across her chest, idly watching. Even from this distance, it appeared that the discussion was fairly one-sided. The woman setting her viola into its case was making no eye contact with Robert. She nodded now and again and seemed to be giving terse responses to whatever comments or questions he was directing her way. Her body language alone suggested she was trying not to engage him any more than necessary. Vanessa wondered if Robert was simply unaware, or choosing to ignore these signs.

As she continued to watch, faintly amused, Vanessa gradually became aware of another feeling rising within her, one which left her slightly conflicted. She was trying to identify it when somebody tapped her shoulder.

"Here you are," Krissy said. "So, we're going over to the drive-in. You think you and Simon want to join us when he gets here?"

"I don't know."

"Well, he knows where it is. Just tell him *the drive-in*. And Mom's picking us up there at eleven."

"Okay. Thanks."

Krissy followed Vanessa's gaze to the gazebo. A curious hissing noise escaped her lips.

"That's my friend Heather's brother" she said dismissively. "The one leaning over the railing, practically standing on his head in the flowers. Even she thinks he's a weirdo. He's like, super smart, but probably going to be a serial killer or something, someday. Anyhow," she concluded, "Maybe we'll see you over there."

During this enlightening assessment, Vanessa had not taken her eyes from Robert. As the other girl talked, Vanessa realized her own impression of the boy was pretty much in line with what Krissy was saying.

The conflicting feeling that had been rising within her was one of embarrassment, mortification for Robert, clueless that his presence wasn't welcomed by the woman with the viola; she just wanted him to go away and leave her alone. First, it had been entertaining to watch, but now it was painful.

Vanessa recalled her own meeting with him earlier this afternoon, and she wondered what he had been doing between now and then. Probably going from one such interaction to the next, all day, creating awkwardness every time. How did he not recognize the effect he had on people? Or was it possible that he did, but he was so hungry for socialization that he didn't care?

Now the musician with the viola was escaping, carrying her instrument case hastily across the grass, not looking back. Robert was watching her go, and as the woman brushed passed Vanessa, he transferred his gaze to her.

Oh, shoot.

Their eyes locked, Vanessa's and Robert's. What could she do, but lift her hand in a half-hearted greeting. He nodded back.

And then, to her surprise, he turned away and strolled in the opposite direction.

For a split-second, she wondered if he somehow knew what she had been thinking.

Business in The Lodge's dining room had been slow, probably because so many people were attending the concert, instead. But a loud and enthusiastic party of ten had arrived around 8:30 and lingered, ordering more wine and chatting. Simon, working the later shift, was required to hang around until the restaurant was empty.

At ten-twenty-five, he clocked out, shoved his meager share of the tips into his pocket and dashed out of the building to his car. Vanessa wasn't answering her cell, and he hoped it wasn't because she was mad that he was so late.

Ten minutes later, he drove past the nearly deserted town square, glancing out the open window for some sign of her, but without success. Though the concert was over, cars still occupied every parking slot along Main Street, as many concert-goers had retreated to the bars and pubs. Simon was forced to double-back several blocks and leave his car on a side street. He jogged back to the park.

He waved at a couple of buddies who'd shouted, "Hey, Perkins!" from across the square, but didn't stop or cross to meet them. Instead, he mounted the steps to the gazebo and paused, turning slowly in every direction.

Music drifted from the open doors of a couple of the bars, disparate styles meeting and clashing in the night air. A great many people were wandering up and down the sidewalks in front of the storefronts even this late in the evening. But nobody seemed to be waiting for him in the park.

Simon descended the steps on the opposite side of the gazebo and hopped over the hedge of columbine bushes that fronted the museum. He was passing the courthouse when he heard:

"Looking for someone?"

There was Vanessa, sitting at the top of the granite steps leading into the building's second floor entrance, leaning back on her arms, legs stretched down the stairs in front of her. She grinned at him.

"Hey," he said, surprised, not just to find her here, but that, waiting with her was Robert MacKenzie. Simon climbed the steps and settled himself on Vanessa's other side. "What are you doing up here?"

"Robert said this would be a good vantage point. We watched you come down the street and then go up and stand in the gazebo, looking around. I wondered how long it would be before you'd find us."

Simon couldn't think of anything to say to this. Even the apology he'd prepared for being so late remained undelivered.

"Krissy's mom is supposed to pick us up at the drive-in in ten minutes," Vanessa informed him. She had pulled her cell phone from the pocket of her shorts and was pressing in a number. Both boys watched as she held it to her ear.

"Hey, Krissy, it's me," she said. "Simon just got here. ...Yeah, I know," she added with a hint of exasperation in her tone, though she threw Simon an amused glance. "So, anyway, would you tell your mom that he's going to bring me home later? Let my folks know I'll be in by midnight. ...Yeah. Bye." She shoved her phone back into her pocket and then nudged Simon with her shoulder. "Okay. We've got an hour and ten minutes. Maybe a little bit more, if I want to stretch it. So, what are we going to do?"

He found he was still at a loss for words, perhaps because both Vanessa and Robert were looking at him expectantly. All the activities he'd had in mind were designed for two, not three. But as he considered this, she turned to the other boy and squeezed his arm.

"Well, good night, Robert," she said, and then stood. Turning, she held out her arm to Simon, and when he took her hand, she pulled him to his feet. They descended the steps to the sidewalk, turned back to toss a final wave at the other boy, then headed up the street.

It was a glorious night, Simon reflected. As they walked away from the hub of downtown, the sound of music and laughter faded, overtaken by the whirr of cricket-chirps rising from the tall grasses near the water's edge. Overhead, the aspen trees bobbed gently on a barely noticeable breeze. Vanessa, shivering a bit, huddled against his side.

"Cold?"

"Yeah."

"City girl," he taunted, but pulled her even closer and rubbed her outer arm vigorously. "We'll be at the car in another minute," he promised.

Outside of town, he drove them down a rutted lane lined on either side with tall, yellowish buffalo grass. The road ended in a small clearing on a bluff. There, he turned out the headlights and shut off the engine. For a few moments, they watched the whitecaps rising out of the lake, captured briefly in the moonlight before vanishing once more, reclaimed by the dark water.

Then Simon and Vanessa crawled into the back seat and, with some awkward thrashing and manueuvering, managed finally to consummate their reunion.

Afterward, they lay panting into each other's ear, Simon holding himself up on his elbows, trying not to rest his full weight atop her. Vanessa laughed suddenly.

"The windows," she said. Simon, his face and neck beaded with sweat, lifted his head to look, and laughed, also. They were surrounded by fogged-up glass.

"Air," Vanessa pleaded. "I need air!"

They hadn't bothered to get entirely naked, and this was now proving to be problematic. Simon's shorts and underwear were tangled around his ankles and he was having no success in tugging them up once more. After a moment of useless struggle, he scooted backwards and fumbled for the door handle behind him. Allowing it to swing open, he staggered out into the open air, nearly falling into the bushes.

They raised and re-fastened their clothing in silence. Passion spent, now they both felt slightly foolish.

"Not real romantic, I suppose," Simon muttered. He wiped his damp forehead with the back of one hand.

Vanessa had gotten out through the door on the other side of the car and was running her fingers through the tangled strands of her hair.

"Well, at least I'm not cold anymore," she offered.

Dressed, they both climbed back into the front seat. Simon started the engine and backed down the single-lane road out to the highway.

"Eleven-forty," he commented, glancing at the digital clock in the dashboard.

She sighed. "Yeah. I probably better get home."

Simon nodded. After a pause, he shifted into forward and pulled out onto the blacktop that curved around the shoreline and would take them to the houses on the far side of the lake. Vanessa rested her hand on the seat behind his head, stroking the back of his neck.

"So, tomorrow night's the barbecue at your grandparents' house, right?"

"Yeah. And I have tomorrow off from work, remember. I thought we could take a hike, or go out on the lake, or swim at The Lodge, if you wanted. I have pool privileges."

"Oh."

For just a second, Vanessa's fingers stopped moving. Even the tone in her one-word response put Simon on his guard.

"What?"

"Well, my mom and Krissy's mom and Krissy and I have appointments at a spa tomorrow. It's pretty much an all-day thing. It's something they set up even before we got here. I just found out about it this evening. But, you know what? I can get out of it. I'll say I have other plans, with you."

"No, don't do that."

"You sure? I don't mind."

He shook his head. "How often do you get to do something like spending a day at a spa? We'll just get together tomorrow evening. What time do you think you'll be done?"

"Six, I think is what they said. But… Are you really sure it's okay?"

Simon had driven through the gate and up the driveway to the expansive carport that fronted the house of Vanessa's hosts. He put the car in park and turned, squeezing her shoulder and leaning in to press his lips against hers.

"It's okay," he reassured her after the kiss.

But, was it? he wondered as he drove away. He *wanted* it to be okay, but the conversation prickled, just a little.

Had Vanessa forgotten that he'd taken tomorrow off, especially for her? Simon didn't want her to pass up the opportunity, but he would have liked a stronger indication that she felt bad about not spending the day with him. Instead, she mostly just seemed relieved that she wouldn't have to alter her plans.

Also, in his eagerness to manage a little intimacy with her, he'd forgotten to ask just what she and Robert MacKenzie had been talking about when he'd happened upon them on the courthouse steps earlier this evening.

Vanessa herself was thinking about Robert as she padded across the floor of the darkened bedroom and eased herself between the sheets, trying not to disturb Krissy, slumbering just a few inches away.

It was herself she'd seen earlier when she'd listened to Krissy's sneering appraisal of the strange boy. How often through the years had she made those same kinds of haughty, uninformed judgments about people? She'd never given it a second thought until hearing the pointless venom in the younger girl's comments.

Standing in a place where she had no stake in the local social standings had enabled her to see things through a different lens, and for a moment, Vanessa found herself wishing she could somehow reach through time and take back all the nasty little barbs she'd levied in school hallways and in giggling clusters at parties.

But she couldn't.

What she could do, while she'd been waiting in the town square for Simon, was easy enough.

"Hey! Robert! Robert, it's me!"

Robert MacKenzie paused. His shoulders arched in a defensive sort of way, and he turned slowly, as if anticipating something vaguely unpleasant might be about to occur.

Out of breath, Vanessa stopped a few feet away. She had run a fair distance to catch up to him.

"I saw you across the park," she said. "I guess you were at the concert, too?"

He nodded. "I saw you, too. But not Simon."

"He's at work. He should be here in a little while."

They faced each other, Vanessa smiling, Robert still looking guarded.

"I just wanted to say hi again," she added finally. "You're the first one of Simon's friends I've met since I got here."

"Are you here for the whole summer, like he is?"

"No, just for the week. Then I have to go back to my job. I'm a counselor at a day camp. In Denver."

Robert processed this information thoughtfully.

"I'll bet it's noisy," was his verdict.

Vanessa laughed.

"Nobody has ever said that before. When I tell them what I do, I mean."

"Well… Isn't it?"

"Absolutely! Very." Then, noticing his still-tense posture, she added, "I don't mean to hold you up. If you were headed somewhere."

"Not really." He shifted his feet, relaxing just slightly, then frowned, as though trying to recall if he might have had some destination in mind before this interruption. "Just waiting for the movie to let out. I'm picking up my sister and some of her friends."

"Oh. Well, I guess we could wait together. Couldn't we? Me for Simon, and you for your sister."

From there, they had gravitated to the courthouse steps, talking about...

...What had they talked about?

Drowsiness was clouding her thoughts, now, making it difficult to recall specifics. Robert was not an easy person to converse with, though; Vanessa could remember that much. It required... so much... effort...

Chapter Eight

Gordon was surprised to find his nephew standing in the delicatessen section of the grocery store, staring fixedly into one of the refrigerated cases.

"Simon?" And when the boy turned to look at him, he added, "Whatcha doing?"

Simon gestured to the case. "There are a *lot* of different potato salads," he said. "I never knew."

His uncle joined him, and together they studied the rows of packaged containers.

"I take this to mean," Gordon said at last, "That you are planning to buy some potato salad."

"For tonight. For the cookout."

"Ah." They both looked a few seconds longer, and then Gordon added, "You know, I don't suppose it really matters; they probably all taste pretty much the same."

Simon nodded. He leaned forward, apparently ready to make a selection.

"Starts at six," he said. "I sure wish you could come. I mean, you've barely met Vanessa. I was hoping she'd get to know you better this week."

"Me, too. But we're headed out of town this afternoon. I'm just picking up a few things for the car trip. Next time. Or, if I get down your way at the end of the summer before you head off for college, maybe we can spend some time together then." Gordon glanced around. "Is she here with you right now?"

Simon shook his head as he placed the container of potato salad in his basket. "She's doing something with her mom and some friends today."

Simon's tone was light, but something in it made Gordon study his nephew's profile closely.

"You took today off from work, didn't you?" he asked.

"Yeah; it's no big deal. It gives me a chance to get stuff together for tonight. Do you think I should get macaroni salad, too?"

"Depends. Do you like macaroni salad? Does she?"

"I guess. And, I don't know."

"Then don't. Get something you know you like. I vote for lemon meringue pie, but that's if I was coming. And, Simon?" He waited until his nephew had actually turned and was looking at him.

"I like her. And I like how you are when she's around you."

"Oh. ...Uh, thanks."

Gordon slapped his nephew's shoulder. Turning away, he said, "Tell the folks hi. And extend my regrets to Vanessa."

Simon watched his uncle walk away and disappear down a side aisle. Then he turned back to the refrigerated case. He set a container of macaroni salad in his basket, debated, then returned it to the shelf. He reached for it one more time, then let his arm fall to his side. He sighed.

At five minutes until six, Simon was standing in front of the barbecue grill in his grandparents' back yard, blinking back the tears as waves of smoke stung his eyes. Squinting, he prodded at the sizzling chicken breasts with a long handled fork. The responsive hiss as juices dripped into the coals was encouraging. It gave him the feeling he must be doing this correctly.

So engrossed was he in the process, that he wasn't aware of his grand-mother's approach until the tap on his shoulder.

"Oh, hey," he said, turning. "How do they look so far?"

"Good, good," Honey said, though she barely gave the meat a perfunctory glance. She wore an odd expression. "Let me do this for a moment. You have a guest."

"A guest," Simon repeated dully. He transferred the fork to her waiting hand. "Vanessa, you mean?"

"Robert," she corrected. "Robert MacKenzie is here to see you."

And then, over his grandmother's shoulder, through the air distorted by waves of heat rising from the grill, he saw him, standing midway across the back lawn: Robert MacKenzie, hands dangling at his sides, chatting with Simon's grandfather.

"What... What's he doing here?" Simon murmured.

"I'm sure I don't know, dear," Honey said. She jabbed at the chicken breasts, flipping each over expertly. "You should probably go and find out."

Simon wiped his hands on the sides of his pants and took a few tentative steps across the grass.

"Hey, Robert," he said, giving Axel a sidelong glance.

"Hi, Simon."

The subsequent few seconds of silence that followed seemed like an eternity. Robert was smiling pleasantly at him. It was Axel who provided the missing piece of the puzzle.

"He's here for the barbecue," he said. Simon's startled gaze traveled from his grandfather to Robert and back once more. Axel raised his eyebrows ever so slightly.

You decide how you want to play this, is what those brows seemed to be saying.

"You... You are?" Simon faltered.

"I thought it was at six. Is that right?"

"Yeah. ...Yeah, that's right." Simon was vaguely aware of a car door slamming, and a moment later, Vanessa appeared from around the corner of the house.

"I smelled the barbecue," she announced. "So I just followed the smoke. My mom just dropped me off."

"That's fine," Axel told her, wrapping his arm around her shoulder in a quick greeting. He smiled at the others. "The party's just getting started."

"Yeah." Simon moved forward, squeezing her upper arms and giving her a kiss. Then he stepped back, slipping his hands into his back pockets, and exhaled deeply. "I guess everybody's here, then. What would you all like to drink?"

"I'm sorry," Simon said a few minutes later when he and Vanessa were alone in the kitchen getting lemonade from the refrigerator. He craned his neck to glance through the screen door, making sure Robert was still standing by the picnic table talking to Axel. "I don't know what he's doing here. I don't know how he even knew about tonight."

"Oh." Vanessa shifted uncomfortably. "Oh, gosh." As Simon studied her curiously, she took a step back, leaning against the counter. "I guess maybe I'm to blame."

She blinked several times, trying to reconstruct her conversation with Robert the night before, the one she'd fallen asleep trying without success to recall.

"We were waiting for you after the concert; we were sitting on the courthouse steps, talking. Well, mostly it was me, talking, I guess. I mentioned the cook-out and how I was looking forward to getting to know your grandparents better, and I asked Robert if he was friendly with them, and he said sort of, but that after you'd moved away, he hardly ever had a chance to see them. I... I..."

"Yeah?" Simon prompted.

"...I don't *think* I invited him. Not exactly, anyway. I think I said something about how they probably would like to see him, too, and he should stop by sometime. Or something like that. I never *dreamt...* I'm so sorry, Simon, if I..."

He laughed ruefully and pulled her away from the counter, holding her against his chest.

"It's okay. It's fine. It's Robert. I should have explained after we ran into him at the marina yesterday. What you *say* and what he *hears* are sometimes kind of different things. Anyway," he waved one hand, "I told him way back in early June that we'd get together sometime over the summer. So now, we have."

The sky turned purplish-blue while they ate. Though it was still light to the west, stars were beginning to glow overhead. There was more than enough food to accommodate an extra guest; Simon had eventually caved and purchased macaroni salad *and* pie, and more, besides. Nobody was going to leave the table hungry.

Elbows folded on the edge of the picnic table, he poked idly at the remains of his dinner and listened to the light and unself-conscious way Vanessa conversed with his grandparents. She laughed easily and made them laugh, as well. It occurred to him suddenly that he felt more adult here than he did at home. Axel and Honey seemed to accept him on his own terms and there was nothing condescending in the way they treated his girlfriend. He felt a sudden rush of love for everyone around the table. Well, maybe not Robert, but in his current mood, he could look upon this interloper with bemusement, as well.

Not surprisingly, Robert had contributed little to the conversation, though he seemed to study everyone with an unabashed sort of interest, looking searchingly into every face, Simon's included, when anyone was speaking. There was a kind of hunger in that look, an eagerness to understand, to comprehend even the little nuances of the interactions taking place around him. Abruptly, Simon found himself wondering what sort of relationship Robert had with his own sets of grandparents. Did he *have* grandparents, even? Simon had never thought to inquire. Not that such a thing came up in typical conversations, but he was a little embarrassed that, in all the years he had known Robert, he knew so little about him.

"Okay," Vanessa announced when everyone stood up from the table. "I'm going to help with clean-up, since I didn't fix any of the dinner. Robert and I can carry everything into the kitchen, and I'll rinse the dishes and put everything away."

"You'll do nothing of the kind," Honey informed her. "I can do it a lot faster and easier, and be done in ten minutes. You kids move over to the lawn chairs, or come inside, if you like. Anybody want to play cards, or something? Axel?"

Simon's grandfather averred that he did not have an interest in games of any kind, that he only wanted to go inside and watch a little television. Yet, fifteen minutes later, when Honey shut off the water and dried her hands, she could hear the distinct sounds of some physical exertion drifting in through the kitchen window. She stepped out onto the back porch to see the four of them smacking a volleyball back and forth over a hastily strung-up net. Axel and Vanessa were on one side and Robert and Simon on the other.

"Join us!" Vanessa shouted, catching sight of her. "You can be on our side!"

"No, she can't!" Simon interjected, leaping to spike the ball solidly into the ground by his girlfriend's feet. "She's a ringer. You stay where you are, Grandma!"

"No worries there," Honey laughed. She settled herself on the chaise lounge and watched the game play out.

The sides had been chosen wisely. Vanessa was an enthusiastic and spry competitor. For all his protestations, Axel was athletic and quick on his feet, if not quite as fast as he'd once been. Robert was clearly the weakest link, standing stiff as a rod in his dress pants and polo shirt. Even in the dusk, Honey could see how his entire body tensed if the ball even threatened to sail his direction, though he would gamely lunge for it, usually with unproductive results.

Simon, on the other hand, could—and almost did—have played the other team singlehandedly. He darted, twisted, and leapt high into the air, seemingly without any effort, returning nearly impossible shots and rescuing some of Robert's wayward ricochets. By the time the game—and a second one—was done, the front of his shirt, his shorts, and his bare legs were smeared green from suicidal dives into the grass to return several volleys.

"That," he gasped, getting to his feet, "Was amazing. Way to go, Robert!" He slapped the other boy across the back. "We showed them!"

Axel picked up the ball from where it had rolled and bounced it off his grandson's head. "I held back on purpose," he informed him, "So as not to shame you in front of your girlfriend. And now, if you'll all excuse me, I'm going inside for a beer. And you kids," he flicked a threatening finger their direction and produced a mock scowl, "Get off my lawn!"

The others collapsed into patio chairs as Axel went indoors, letting the screen door slam behind him.

"I'm dumping you for your grandfather," Vanessa informed Simon while wiping her shining face.

Honey laughed, getting up from her chair. As she opened the door, she turned back. "Just remember," she told Vanessa, "I have a strict no-return policy, in case you're serious about that."

And then it was just the three teenagers, panting, and splayed limply across the lawn furniture, gazing up into the darkness. Simon surveyed the front of his shirt.

"I didn't think we'd be doing this," he said. "I probably should have worn something else."

And then they were quiet for several minutes, listening to the gathering evening taking shape around them. Crickets were chirping. Wind chimes rustled overhead. The sound of a television program reached them suddenly, drifting through the open window. Each seemed occupied with his own thoughts.

"I would like a beer, too," Vanessa said suddenly. She kept her voice low. Turning her head toward Simon, she added, "Actually, I brought some. It's in a paper bag. I hid it under a bush in the front yard when I first got here. Before I came around the house."

"Where the heck did you get it?" Simon asked, amazed.

"Krissy knows some guy. A friend's brother, who's twenty-one. He's done it for some other kids, buying them a six-pack if they'll pay for a six-pack for him, too."

"How did you get it here? Didn't you ride over here with your mom?"

"I just said it's in a bag, silly," Vanessa said. "Hidden under a six-pack of Coke. She only knew about the Coke." She considered this for a second. "It's probably gotten a little warm by now, I suppose. But I'd still like to have one. Wouldn't you?"

"Well, sure. But I don't think we'd better be hoisting any brew around my grandparents."

"How about…" Vanessa paused. She was trying to think of a way to suggest they could return to the dirt road on the bluff they'd visited last night, but without divulging all the details of that trip in front of Robert.

But he saved her the trouble.

"I know a place," he said.

They looked at him in surprise.

Chapter Nine

Simon guided his car down the quiet street, glancing from side to side with growing interest.

"I know this road," he said. He started to say more, but then, from the back seat, Robert's arm snaked in front of his nose, gesturing.

"There! Turn in there! That driveway!"

Simon did as instructed, pulling up the slight incline and guiding the car to a stop. He shut off the engine, and the three of them gazed out through the passenger side windows at the dark, quiet house to their right. For a moment, nobody moved.

"Whose place is this?" Vanessa said at last. She spoke in a near-whisper, though nobody outside the car could have heard her anyway.

"I'm…not sure this is a good idea," Simon added, but Robert had already opened the door and was climbing out of the back seat.

"Follow me around back," he instructed.

Simon and Vanessa exchanged a dubious glance, but obeyed.

Robert had unhooked the gate and was holding it open for them. After they had filed through, he latched it once more.

"We can sit on the patio, and nobody will see us," he explained.

Vanessa set the paper bag containing the beer on a small, wrought-iron table. She glanced around the porch and yard.

"The people who live here aren't going to come home and find us sitting out here drinking, are they?"

He shook his head. "No. She won't be coming back. Her name was Mrs. Scoggins, and she died last spring."

Robert had taken a seat in one of the chairs and was leaning forward, peering down into the sack. He seemed oblivious to the fact that this added bit of information hadn't made his companions feel any more comfortable. Lifting a bottle into view, he twisted off the cap and took a gulp.

"Wow," he said, sputtering a little bit. He ran his tongue over his lips. "Wow." He glanced up, frowning slightly. "Go ahead; sit down!"

Silently, the others obeyed. Simon handed Vanessa a beer and opened one for himself. It was just as she'd warned: A little too warm to be refreshing. Still, it was beer.

"I've been here before," he said. "Well, not here, exactly. Over there." With his bottle, he gestured to the house on the other side of a row of honeysuckle bushes. "My uncle used to live there."

"I guess I knew that," Robert told him. "Except I forgot. So, did you know Mrs. Scoggins?"

Simon took another gulp of lukewarm beer and thought about this. He had vague memories of an older woman he sometimes saw across the way when he was visiting Gordon. He couldn't recall that they'd ever exchanged a single word, though. She was usually working in her yard, or occasionally just sitting on her porch when he saw her, and there was generally something in her posture and demeanor that suggested disapproval.

"Not really," he said. "How did you know her?"

"We were friends." Robert stared into the darkened backyard for so long that Simon and Vanessa looked at each other across his back. He took another pull from his bottle and sighed heavily. "I miss her."

Just then, Simon remembered something from the conversation he'd had with Robert a month ago, the first time he'd seen him since arriving for the summer.

"Is this place yours, now? Did she leave you this house?"

The other boy shook his head. "She donated it to the city. I don't think anybody knows what to do with it. It's just been sitting here since then. I come over and water and mow the yard."

"That's nice of you," Vanessa said.

"She'd be pissed if somebody didn't. Anyway, I like being here." After another pause, he added, "Everything else is mine, though."

Simon nodded. Robert's words from a few weeks ago came back to him. *"I'm rich. I didn't mean to be. But I am."*

"Do you think they'll sell it?" he asked.

"Probably." Robert picked at the label on his bottle with a fingernail. "What do they want with a house, anyway." He shifted in his chair. "Let's talk about something else."

Vanessa, leaning forward in her chair, had been about to ask him something. At this, she rested her elbows on her knees and looked into the darkness across the back yard. She thought of another question, instead.

"So, you two have been friends since you were kids? Tell me about some of the stuff you used to do."

If there had been more light, she could have seen clearly the blank expressions that crossed their faces. The boys looked at each other, waiting to hear what the other would say.

"I don't know," Simon said finally. "Just the regular old crap kids do, I guess. Hung out sometimes. Ate lunch together at school. Things like that. Robert?" he appealed to his friend for more examples. Simon's memories of the other boy were fairly specific, but also limited. He didn't like to think about this now, but as his other schoolmates had done, he'd generally avoided Robert when possible.

"I think we went over to each other's houses sometimes," he concluded lamely. "Once or twice."

Robert nodded. "Yeah. Stuff like that. Talked. Walked home together."

Vanessa was nodding also. Simon wondered what she was thinking. Did that list seem as pathetic to her as it did to him? It occurred to him that what he and Robert had shared was something too distant and formal to be called friendship.

As one, the three of them lifted their beers and drank.

"Do you think," Vanessa said finally, trying a different subject, "That you'll ever come back and live in Stucker's Reach again? If your parents hadn't moved you away from here, would you have left on your own?"

Simon, pulling a second bottle out of the bag, considered this for a moment.

"I always figured I'd go to college," he said. "Even when I was little, because my family always talked about it." He twisted off the cap and watched foam ooze up and over the neck of the bottle and down his hand. "I don't know that I ever though much about what would happen after that."

"How about now?"

He shook his head slowly. "I'd come back for visits. It'll always be my home *town,* but it's not home anymore."

Vanessa shifted her gaze. "And you, Robert?"

Robert was in the process of opening his own second beer. He set the cap on the table, wiped his fingers on his pants and then, as if he'd been waiting years for someone to ask him just this question, said in an even and deliberate tone, "Pretty soon, I'm going to get in a car and drive away from here, to college, and then to someplace after that, and not come back. I won't look back or think back, or even remember what it was like, or anybody who was here."

He seemed resolutely lost in this idea for several more seconds, studying the ground in front of his chair. Then, as if pulling himself free from that image, he sighed and lifted his chin.

"Not you," he said without turning his head. "I'll remember you, Simon."

Simon, looking down at his beer, grinned.

"It's all right, Robert. You don't have to say that, just because I'm sitting here."

"I know," his sort-of-friend answered.

They nursed their second beers mostly in companionable silence. No sounds of passing cars or anything else permeated the darkness. The world seemed theirs alone. Vanessa might have reached across the gap and twined her fingers with Simon's, except that Robert was sitting in the chair between them. She could have gotten up and moved, but the night had a fragile quality that seemed too easily shattered. She stayed where she was.

Vanessa thought about her own plans for college and beyond, comparing these to Robert's. She tried to imagine stepping into a new life, taking nothing of the previous one with her, but was unable to proceed very far with the concept. She turned her head slightly, looking at Robert without precisely looking, intrigued by the attitude of this unrepentant outcast.

From his chair, Simon was studying the house next door. The windows were dark, and he wondered whether the place was occupied anymore. Probably it was, and whoever lived there was either in bed or just away for the Independence Day holiday. A strange sort of gloom had settled over him in just the last few minutes, and he was trying to determine its source.

He recalled the brief encounter with his uncle in the grocery store this morning; the feelings were tied up with that, somehow. But why? A silly discussion about potato salad… Had there been more than that?

Not really. Not to speak of. Except Gordon remembered that Simon had taken the day off, in anticipation of spending it with Vanessa. And when Simon had shrugged this fact aside, Gordon had dropped the subject, as well.

He sighed. The others looked at him.

"What's the matter?" Vanessa demanded.

"Nothing. Just thinking. …About stuff. About… changes."

"What kind of changes?"

He picked at the bits of grass smeared into the front of his shorts.

"Well, Robert plans to leave and never come back here. I'm pretty sure this will be the last year I spend the summer staying with my grandparents and living in Stucker's Reach. We're growing up, I guess. Moving on. I'm trying to decide how I feel about that."

That was part of what he was feeling, but not all of it.

It was a fine art, acknowledging someone's disappointment, and then also having the good grace to let it go without further discussion when it was clear the other person didn't want to talk about it. That's what Gordon had done today in the grocery store, and Simon didn't realize until just now how good it had made him feel, to know someone understood his perspective.

He felt a sudden rush of gratitude. Somehow, with all of the people in his life he loved so much, his mother and his sister and brother, and step-father, and his grandparents, and Vanessa, he sometimes almost forgot about Gordon. Well, didn't forget him, really, but forgot that there was someone else who'd been there from the very start, looking out for him in ways that nobody else took into consideration.

And perhaps because of this unfortunate tendency to relegate his uncle to the background, it now occurred to him that Gordon was another of the things that had changed over the course of the four long winters since Simon had moved away.

Until just now, he'd held onto the image of Gordon from a time when Simon was nine or ten, or possibly even thirteen, the year his family had left for Denver. *That* Gordon was tall and lithe, not muscular, exactly, but quick and agile. They'd snowboarded together, hiked, and played ball.

Nowadays, they stood almost eye to eye; that was a change in Simon, of course. But recalling Gordon this morning in the store, he couldn't quite imagine playing a game of one-on-one with him on the basketball court any longer. Or facing him on the other side of a volleyball net, for that matter.

His uncle had grown doughy and pink-faced. He walked with a kind of weighty trudge, shoulders hunched, the gait of a man settled resolutely into middle age.

It hadn't happened overnight, of course. The changes had to have been creeping over him for months, years even: Simon did some quick mental arithmetic; Gordon must be thirty-seven now. Simon's mother was forty-four, his stepdad a year or so older than that. Had they changed as drastically? It didn't seem so, but of course, Simon saw them almost every day, making it difficult to make an accurate comparison.

Still, no. His mom was a little thicker around the waist than she used to be; she frequently bemoaned the fact that she had been unable to lose the baby weight from when she was pregnant with Joshua. But she wasn't fat. And Kirk... Kirk was stocky, but solid, still firm. Neither he nor Livia had that puffy-faced look Simon had noticed on Gordon this morning. He seemed...old. Older than Simon's grandparents, even.

His uncle had changed in other ways, too. He was more reserved. The corners of his mouth didn't turn up as readily as they had once. The cheerful disposition was still there, but something in his eyes—or behind his eyes—was different. Or maybe not so much different as *missing*.

Yeah, that's what it was, Simon realized abruptly. Though he didn't know what it might be, he understood that Gordon had let go of some part of himself and worse, had now made his peace with its absence. Simon felt a sudden, panicky need to reach out and retrieve it, whatever it might be, in order to bring back the uncle he remembered from years past. Was this what becoming an adult meant? Compromising your plans and dreams, and growing colorless and hollow-eyed in the process?

"I'll never settle!" he said fiercely, startling his companions. His heart, he realized, was pounding hard against the wall of his chest.

"What are you talking about?" Vanessa demanded.

"I...won't just...settle," Simon said again. "Whatever happens in my life, I want to be happy. And if I'm not... Well... No! I... I will be, that's all."

Though he couldn't clearly see her face in the darkness, he knew his girlfriend was staring at him.

"Okay," she said slowly. "Glad to hear it."

"Uh-oh," Robert said. He set his bottle on the table next to his chair and lurched to his feet. "Uh-oh," he said once more, staggering to the edge of the patio, where he crouched and vomited into the flowerbed.

"Oh, jeez," he said. "Oh, man!" And then he threw up again.

After that, he settled back onto his haunches, breathing heavily. He wiped his nose and mouth.

"You okay, Buddy?" Simon was leaning forward in his chair.

Robert nodded. "Yeah," he gasped. "Yeah. You can have the rest of my beer, if you want."

He remained crouched on the concrete with his hands on his thighs, taking in gasps of cool, night air.

"I'm fine," he assured them. "You guys go on talking."

Vanessa moved over to sit in Robert's chair. She picked up his half-full bottle.

"We better make sure he gets home okay," she murmured to Simon.

Chapter Ten

Eulamarie Scoggins had long since resigned herself to dying alone, and so it was disconcerting to her when it didn't happen that way.

In hospice facilities those final weeks, she received more visitors than she quite knew what to do with: Old colleagues, former students, a few neighbors, they all trickled in, uninvited. The near-dead, Eulamarie had discovered, were systematically stripped of their rights, beginning with the right to privacy and followed by, in no particular order, the ability to get up and go to the bathroom unassisted, deciding what and when to eat, when and how long to sleep, and concluding with the most ignominious loss of all: The right to be taken seriously.

People barged into her room whenever they damn well felt like it. She'd informed the staff she didn't want visitors. Nobody except for the boy, that is. And, in response, she'd been told such things as, "Oh, you don't mean that," and "Seeing people will do you good," and "Well, all right, if that's how you want it," all delivered in patronizing tones. Why was it that the very young, the very old, and the very dying were dismissed as if their wishes meant nothing at all?

So, no matter what her protestations, well-meaning busybodies and twerps from all the stages of her life kept coming by to spend a few minutes, bringing flowers and smiles and innocuous chatter that did nothing so much as remind her that she wasn't going to get well, wasn't ever going to get out of here.

"Well, thank you," she said to each guest after a few moments of conversation. "You've done your duty, so goodbye, and please don't come back anymore."

"Oh, she doesn't really mean that," a flustered nurse's assistant said to one visitor.

"Of course she does," the guest, Gordon Perkins, retorted cheerfully. He settled back in the chair next to the bed, crossing one leg over the other. "I lived next door to her for years, and before that, she was my fifth-grade teacher. Mrs. Scoggins never says anything she doesn't mean."

Eulamarie waited until the young attendant had fled the room. Then she turned her glare to Gordon and, through labored breath, said, "You're pretty pleased with yourself about that, aren't you?"

"You're the terror of the whole town," he reported. "Everyone who's been to see you comes back with tales of how awful you were, how rudely you treated them. So I had to come see for myself."

"Oh, stop it."

"I knew you'd be pleased to hear it," he said.

Well, she *was* pleased, though she didn't like having it pointed out.

"Some come to see if I look as bad as the others have said. Those others only came because they wanted to earn a merit badge, or something. I was their good deed of the day. And I do not appreciate being anybody's good deed!" she finished up, wheezing. Those were more words than was comfortable to string together anymore. She waved away the glass of water he was holding out to her.

"I will tell everyone you were so hateful that you made me cry," Gordon promised solemnly, setting the glass back on the stand next to the bed.

From her pillow, she scrutinized him as she regained her breath.

"How are you?" she asked at last.

"Fine, I'm fine. Busy. You know how that is."

"Busy," she repeated, as if weighing the word. Her beady little eyes were still fixed on his.

He shifted in his seat. "There's work. And Ruthie. And Corey, of course. You wouldn't think it would be that hard to coordinate three people's schedules, especially when one of them is a twelve year-old. But hers is probably the worst of any of us, and we hardly ever seem to—"

"—Oh, stop it."

He did. He stopped. For a moment there was nothing but the muffled sounds of activity in the hallway outside their room. Under the sheets, Eulamarie shifted her legs.

"I don't want to hear all that, Gordon. I don't care, can't you see?"

"I... I'm sorry, Eulamarie. I..."

"You have lots of hours left to fill with foolish talk; I only have a few, and I don't want them wasted like this."

More silence. He was hurt, no doubt. Maybe he really would go back and tell people she'd made him cry. She waited for him to get up and put on his coat. But he remained in his chair, hand gripping the crease in his trousers.

"I wish I could die in my house, in my own bed," she said finally. "I wish I could die in Stucker's Reach, not in this ridiculous room in a ridiculous place, twenty miles from home."

"I know."

"I would take that water now."

He waited, hands extended slightly, as she drank. Perhaps he thought she was so far gone she couldn't manage to hold a simple plastic glass. Perhaps he thought he would be able to catch it if it slipped from her fingers. Perhaps he just was trying to demonstrate that he cared. Whatever. She finished sipping and handed it back to him.

"It's the only thing I regret," she continued. "That's quite an accomplishment, I think. In my whole long life, the only thing I regret is that they won't let me die at home."

She closed her eyes. Gordon was half-afraid that when she opened them, she was going to ask him to take her back with him, to sneak her out of the facility somehow, in order to expire in her own house.

"There's a boy, Gordon," Eulamarie said, her eyes still closed. "Maybe you remember him from when you still lived next door. He would come to see me. He still does, in fact. He comes to visit me here."

"No," he said, after some hesitation. "I don't."

"I used to worry about him." She opened her eyes and gazed at the ceiling. "If you knew him, if you met him, well, it wouldn't take you long to understand why."

"Oh?"

"But now, I don't. I can't say exactly when I stopped worrying, but it was awhile ago. He's going to be just fine. He will travel an unusual road, and he will get hurt. But he's been hurt before, and now I see that he deals with it better than many of us do."

She paused, gathering strength to continue.

"I find it peculiar that after all these years, he is the person I am closest to. We're nothing at all alike, not in any way. Except that I suspect, he, too, will have no regrets when he reaches the end of his life."

Eulamarie tilted her head, and for one unsettling second, it appeared to Gordon as if she was smiling at him.

"I'm glad we were neighbors," she said.

"Me, too," he told her.

As he was pulling on his coat and preparing to go, she said:

"Goodbye, and please don't come back anymore."

Gordon had visited Eulamarie Scoggins in late February. She died in mid-March. Because he was not like his old fifth-grade teacher, there were many times in the subsequent months that he regretted not going back to see her again, no matter what she had instructed.

He also wondered, more than once, why she had told him about her other visitor, the boy who would travel an unusual path, and who would ultimately be fine.

Chapter Eleven

"Don't you think it's time you decided what things you want to take to Honors Camp, Robert?" Mrs. MacKenzie asked her son. "I just did a load of laundry, and I put all your clean things on the bed. It would be a good time to pack your bag. You leave next week, after all."

"All right," he said in that agreeable, yet distant way of his.

His sister's response would have been to heave an exasperated sigh and then ignore the suggestion on general principle. Robert wouldn't complete the task, either, not without repeated reminders. Not beligerantly, but because his attention was so often focused on distant, unique horizons, even when it appeared he was present and participating in a conversation. Brenda MacKenzie had known her son to stare raptly at a television program or into the pages of a book for an hour or more without gleaning anything from either.

"What are you doing, anyway?" she asked. He'd just come up from the basement.

"Nothing, just looking for a cold drink," he said, holding up a soda can.

"Aren't there any in the kitchen?"

"Well, yeah. But I thought maybe there'd be a different kind in the downstairs refrigerator. There wasn't, though." He settled himself on the couch and set the drink on the coffee table without opening it. Resting his folded arms across his knees, he gazed at something on the far side of the room, brow slightly furrowed.

Brenda MacKenzie, arms loaded with folded towels, had been on her way to the linen closet. Instead, she remained where she was.

"Everything okay?"

Robert nodded slowly. "You went to college, right?"

"I did." She settled herself on the arm of the couch, balancing a stack of towels in her lap. "How else do you think I became qualified to do all this?"

He glanced at her sharply, indicating this might be one of those rare occasions when he actually sensed subtext. After a moment, he looked away again.

"Did it change you?" he asked. "Do you think it made things different? I'm not talking about if it made you smarter. I know it makes people smarter. I mean, what *other* things did it do for you?"

Brenda contemplated a response. This was the first time in recent memory her son had sought any genuine information from her. It was flattering and intimidating, and a far cry from *What are we having for dinner?*, or *Have you seen my homework?*

"It opened up my world," she said slowly. "Everybody says that, I suppose. But what I mean is, it lessened my sense of…of self. Of self-importance. Every day for the first couple of months, you're finding ways to adjust— to people, to living arrangements, to ways of receiving information. It's overwhelming, and then it's exhilarating, when you finally figure out how to manage it. And you know what else? Nobody cares. Nobody in that whole new environment gives a damn how well or how poorly you do.

"I think how you react to that revelation determines how you handle everything that comes after," she concluded. "Not just in the next four years, but the whole rest of your life."

Robert received this information in silence. Brenda watched him for a moment, and said, "I didn't mean to unnerve you. College can be scary, but I think that's an important part of the learning curve."

"I'm not scared," he said calmly, as if the notion was too insubstantial to warrant contemplation. "I just wonder if it makes you change your mind about what you want to do with your life."

"Well… for some people, certainly."

"Did it you?"

"I…"

"That's where you met Dad, right? College? Do you ever think he stopped you from being what you were on your way to becoming?"

He watched with interest as she considered the question.

"...I wouldn't say that," she said finally. *Really. Where did he come up with these sorts of things?* "He didn't *stop* me from anything. After we met and fell in love, I just decided on a different course of action.

"And never regretted it," she added, interpreting his continued silence as dubiousness.

Robert nodded finally.

"That's good," he affirmed. "I hope that's how you feel after Heather and I are both grown and gone. I hope we were worth it."

Brenda MacKenzie resisted the immediate impulse to respond with, *"Well, of course you're both worth it."* She'd never thought otherwise, but knowing her son, he would see that reply as more obligatory than sincere. He would undoubtedly feel she ought to take a wait-and-see-attitude, just to be on the safe side.

Now he was fishing his wallet out of his back pants.

"Here," he said, thrusting a twenty-dollar bill at her.

She looked down at it without taking it. "What's this for?"

"I'm taking some drinks from the refrigerator for later. I'm meeting up with Simon and his girlfriend Vanessa."

Brenda waved away the money. "You don't have to do that, Robert. Good heavens, just take them. That's what they're there for."

He would not be dissuaded. "I won't take the drinks if you won't take the money."

She did, resisting the impulse to roll her eyes. With Robert, it was generally easier to just acquiesce. She slipped it into her pocket with a vague notion of finding some way to give it back to him later. Maybe hide it in his bag, or something.

"How is Simon, anyway?" she asked, standing. "Here it is, July, and I don't think I've seen him once yet this summer."

"He's fine. We played volleyball in his grandparents' back yard last night. After the cookout."

"And he has a girlfriend with him this year?"

Robert nodded. He opened his soft drink can and took a deep gulp. "Vanessa," he repeated. "She's just up for the week from Denver. She's nice," he concluded offhandedly.

"So, what are you guys all going to do?"

"Don't know yet."

"When are you getting together?"

A shrug. "Don't know that, either."

Brenda sighed. If she were having this conversation with Heather, she would press further, suspecting evasiveness in these responses. But this was Robert, unflappable Robert, who regularly took a haphazard approach to life, confident that whatever plans he made would fall into place.

She stood, tucking the twenty-dollar bill into her pocket and picking up the stack of towels.

"Well, have fun. Tell Simon I said hello, and ask him for me how his mother is doing. I miss having her around, even after all this time."

"Uh-huh," Robert promised vaguely. Peering at the top of his soda can, he offered a soft, squishy belch.

"Where are the kids tonight?" Jim MacKenzie asked his wife as they faced each other across a dinner table set for two.

"Both out with friends," Brenda reported, nudging the bottle of salad dressing his direction. "Heather's across the street at The Powells', and Robert's off somewhere with Simon Perkins and some others." She pretended not to notice her husband's elevated eyebrows.

"Oh," he said. "Simon. Well, good."

They ate their salads in reflective silence for a moment, debating whether to make further comment or merely savor the concept of their son off someplace, engaged in an ordinary social activity for once.

"I guess they've been playing volleyball and things like that this week," Brenda added, affecting a casual tone.

Jim poked at tomato wedges with his fork.

"I always thought he was a decent kid, that Simon. A good influence on Robert. It was kind of too bad—for Robert, I mean—when the family moved away. And you said there were others?"

"Others?" Brenda looked momentarily puzzled. "Oh! Oh, yes. I guess Simon has a girlfriend up for the holiday week. Somebody named Vanessa."

"Really?" There was an unexpected lilt in her husband's voice. "Well!"

"Does that bother you?"

He shook his head.

"I'm thrilled, actually. Robert, hanging around a girl his own age, for a change. No disrespect to Mrs. Scoggins, but you know what I mean."

She did.

As she was clearing the plates, Brenda remembered something from her conversation with Robert that afternoon. She settled back into her chair, pouring a touch more wine into each of their glasses.

"Do you ever wonder, just for curiosity's sake, where we'd be now, if we hadn't met back in college?" she asked. "Or even if we had, but we hadn't decided to get married?"

She expected her husband, who rarely dealt in what-ifs, to dismiss the notion with a derisive snort, but he didn't.

"Oh, sure," he said. "It's crossed my mind once or twice. I think everybody contemplates that kind of thing."

"So..?" she pressed. "What did you decide?"

"We'd be married to other people, I imagine. Or you'd've done something with that English degree. Maybe both."

"Yeah," Brenda said slowly. "That's what I thought, too." After another second, she added, "And we'd have had completely different kids."

"Oh, I don't know about that." Jim held his wine glass aloft, studying its contents through the evening sunlight that filtered through the dining room window. "You and I might not have had them, but it's impossible for me to imagine there wouldn't be a Robert and Heather out there somewhere. The world doesn't hand you personalities like theirs if they aren't needed. And as far as I'm concerned, I'm pretty curious to see what that reason is going to turn out to be. So it's just as well things happened the way they did."

He studied her over the top of his wine glass for a second, then winked and took a gulp.

Every now and then, Brenda could see how Robert came by his unusual way of looking at things.

Simon allowed the handful of dirty dishes he was carrying to slide into the bussing tub with a noisy clatter.

"Hey, easy!" Merilee, one of the waitresses he was working with, cautioned.

"Sorry," he muttered without looking back. He stalked out into the dining room and returned with still more plates. These he settled into the tub with less noisy fanfare. Merilee watched him curiously.

"So, what's the deal? You pissed about something?"

He wiped his hands on a towel.

"I was supposed to be off two hours ago," he told her. "I worked the lunch shift, but Angie called in sick, so I'm still here." He pronounced the word *sick* with a degree of skepticism.

"Well, I'm sorry, but don't take it out on the dishes. Or on everybody else's ears."

"Sorry," he informed her again, but this time he managed a small grin.

"Not that it's any consolation," she said. "But I like having you as my busser way more than I do Angie. You're faster and smarter. I don't have to ask for every little thing."

He leaned against the counter of the wait station and folded his arms across his chest, looking at her.

"No," he said. "It's no consolation." But he nevertheless continued to smile. "Any other week but this one, I wouldn't really care. But, you know."

"Ah, yes. The girlfriend," she acknowledged. She squeezed his shoulder as she moved past him, back out into the restaurant. "Sorry, Sport."

When he'd called Vanessa earlier that afternoon to give her the bad news, she'd said, "Oh. Well, okay, then. Call or text me as soon as you know when you'll be done."

They hadn't made any specific plans for tonight, except for spending it together. But it was Friday, after all. It seemed like most of the week had already trickled right through their fingers. Vanessa would be headed back to Denver on Monday morning, and that would be it; after Sunday, they wouldn't be together again until the end of August, when there would be just a couple of overlapping frantic days as they both packed and prepared to leave for college.

And, well, frankly, it seemed to him that she could have acted just a little bit more disappointed when he'd told her he had to work late.

Another waitress bustled past Simon on her way to the kitchen. "I need two iced teas and a coffee at Table Four," she announced, interrupting his thoughts. "Oh, and you'd better check the syrup canisters under the soda fountain. I think the Coca-Cola may need changing."

He watched her go, then reached for two glasses and the ice scoop.

"Wish *I'd* thought to call in sick," he muttered.

The boy who had settled himself on the dock alongside Vanessa watched as she dropped her phone back into her bag.

"Was that your boyfriend you were talking to?" he demanded coyly.

She glanced at him before scooting half a foot further down the planks. "No. Not that it's any of your business, but it was a friend from back home."

Undiscouraged, he slid himself along, as well, his bare leg brushing against hers.

"What's her name?" he persisted.

Head tilted forward, Vanessa smirked down at the dark surface of the water. There was no denying that the boy on her right, a friend of Krissy's, was cute. He was also fifteen and more enamored of his charms than she was.

Along with the rest of Krissy's crowd, he'd helped Vanessa master a few exhilarating moments spinning across the lake on water skis today. Much more of the time, she'd been flailing in the water or sinking like a stone, but even that had been a sort of fun, too. But now, in the waning moments of the afternoon, without a physical activity on which to focus her thoughts and energy, she couldn't help but notice that he was considerably less agile in his flirting than he was on skis.

Not that she wasn't flattered by the attention, or unamused by his obvious attempts to impress. But he was a high school sophomore, and here on dry land, he was also hopelessly out of his element. Five years ago, Vanessa could have been his babysitter. She resisted the impulse to remind him of this, however.

"Why do you care who I was talking to? Why do you care what her name is?" she asked. "Are you planning on calling her?"

"I don't know; is she as cute as you?"

Oh, brother. Had she once found lines like that to be clever? Unfortunately, she seemed to remember that she did.

"So, Krissy says your boyfriend was from around here, before he moved," he persisted.

"That's right."

"What's his name?"

Vanessa glanced at her companion, who affected a nonchalant pose, squinting into the distance. He'd climbed up onto the dock just minutes ago, and water was still trickling from his scalp, running down his shining arms and back. She had a feeling she was walking into a trap by answering this, but couldn't think of a reason not to.

"Simon Perkins," she told him.

He snuffled and ran a hand through his soggy hair.

"Never heard of him."

"I'm not surprised," she said lightly. "He's a lot older than you are."

"He's not *that* much older!" the boy retorted before he thought better of it. He glanced at Vanessa under the pretext of rubbing his nose. "Krissy says he's a senior. That's how I know."

"*Was* a senior. He starts college next month. Like me."

"So, are you two serious?" His tone was offhanded, yet faintly mocking at the same time.

"Why? What've you got?" she retorted.

"I'm just asking. Jeez! I'm not trying to move in on another guy's girl."

No, not much, she thought. Without turning, she could tell they were under the scrutiny of Krissy and the others, sitting on beach towels in the grass behind them. She could hear their giggles now and then. They might even have put him up to this. Aloud, she said, "You're probably already seeing somebody, anyway."

"Yeah," he said hesitantly. "Sort of, anyway. There's a couple of girls."

Vanessa nodded and tucked a strand of her own damp hair behind one ear.

"Thanks for the water ski lesson. You made it look easier than it is, though. I bet you're good at a lot of sports."

He shrugged, plucking at something on his leg. "Soccer. I play forward on junior varsity right now, but I'll probably be varsity next year. And I wrestled last winter, but I don't know if I'll go out this year, or not. I might do something else."

She nodded as he continued to talk, holding her smile in check.

And that, she could have told him, *Is the proper way to flirt.*

There was one unanswered call on his cell phone, Simon noticed, as he was changing clothes in the employee locker room. He'd felt the phone vibrate earlier, but the number that showed on the screen was unfamiliar to him, so he'd let it go to voicemail. He replayed the message as he walked to his car.

"Hey, Simon. It's Robert. Robert MacKenzie," the voice underscored after a slight hesitation, as if it had no confidence Simon would otherwise know which Robert this was. "I got your number from your grandmother."

Each sentence concluded with a pause, as though expecting a response. "Anyway, I wondered if maybe you and Vanessa wanted to do something again while she's here. Before she goes back. And before I leave, which is next week. Like, you know... volleyball, or just hanging out, or something. Anyway. Okay."

Simon leaned against the side of his car, fingering his keys, phone to his ear. Robert, either in person or while leaving a message, somehow managed to raise a host of emotions in his listener. Simon's ranged from surprise to mild irritation, amusement, impatience, relief, guilt, and even a bit of melancholy thrown in.

Robert had managed to attach himself to Simon at what was a most inconvenient time. Although, to be honest, Simon wasn't sure there was such a thing as a convenient one if Robert was involved. At least it wasn't a union that could last much longer, if the guy was headed off to that genius-camp, or wherever it was he was going.

Simon settled behind the steering wheel and grinned to himself. *Volleyball.* He pictured Robert from last night, and standing alongside him in the back yard, facing Vanessa and his grandfather. His posture was stiff, arms pressed tightly against his sides, moving only from the elbows outward in flailing motions, completely ineffective for returning a serve or even making more than accidental contact with the ball.

Robert, Simon was pretty sure, had no interest in playing volleyball again. Yet, as Simon started the engine and put the car in gear, he understood that he'd be willing to give it another clumsy try, if it meant hanging out some more with Simon and Vanessa. This was both an endearing and burdensome revelation.

SIMON

He sighed, then shifted back into neutral, pulled out his phone and hit *redial.*

"Hey, Robert?" he said after a moment. "Simon. So, I just listened to your message, and I... Yeah. ...Well, I had to work late, so I'm just now... No, actually, I was thinking... No, but how about tomorrow night? ...Uh-huh. Let's say seven-thirty or eight. We can figure it out then. Call me in the afternoon. ...Yeah. Talk to you later."

He slipped his phone back into his pocket and stared through the windshield without really looking at anything. He was just hoping Vanessa would be okay with this plan.

Chapter Twelve

The music from the steel guitars and bass fiddle burst through the open windows and doors at either end of The Community Hall with such vigor it seemed a physical thing, possessing weight and substance. It was impossible to be anywhere in town or even on the far side of the lake, and not be aware that something lively was taking place.

Vehicles were sandwiched tightly into every parking spot along the street, with still more crowded into questionable areas not designated for the purpose. Though the grocery store seven blocks away had been closed since eight, even that parking lot was filled to capacity.

"What's going on?" Vanessa asked, glancing from side to side as Simon guided the car down the street, slowing now and then to allow pedestrians to cross at haphazard intervals, some waving their thanks, some oblivious to stalling traffic.

"Just another one of the events during Fourth of July Week," he said. "A square dance, or something."

She clutched his leg. "Oh! Let's go in! I want to see!"

"Are you kidding?" he stared at her. "It's country-western music!"

"I don't care. Can't we at least take a look?"

He heaved a put-upon sigh. "We're never going to find a parking spot. Not anywhere close."

"Oh, thank you, thank you! Just for a minute, just so I can see what it's like. Oh, look!" she pointed. "Right there! Oh, perfect timing!"

As if to defuse his one feeble excuse, a car was backing out of a parking spot just half a block ahead. Resigned to his fate, Simon guided the car to the curb.

"I think they charge something like ten bucks a person," he said mournfully.

The doomsaying prediction barely registered with Vanessa. She hopped out of the passenger side before he'd even shut off the engine.

"If they do, then we'll just look in through the door," she said. "Come on!"

"Well, hell's bells!" The large woman wedged behind a table in the open doorway bleated when she caught sight of them. She rose from her folding chair with remarkable dexterity, displacing the card table a few inches in the process, and stepped around it to envelope Simon in an all-encompassing hug. "My God, Simon Perkins, look at you! It's been a year or three, but I'd know you anywhere!"

Whether the name was ironic or not, none could say, but his grandmother's friend Teensy Phillips stood at nearly six feet tall with shoulders as broad as a linebacker's and, judging from the intensity of the hug, just about the same amount of strength. She was stout without seeming plump, somehow. Her bright blue eyes surveyed Simon at arm's length once she'd released him from her embrace. He was perhaps half an inch taller than she, yet he felt dwarfed in her presence.

"Hello, Ms. Phillips It's nice to see you."

"Oh, it's Teensy, for Pity's Sakes. What brings you here? Didn't figure you for this kind of a dance. And who's this pretty thing? Your girl-friend?" One arm continued to dangle on Simon's shoulder while the other now rested on her hip as she surveyed Vanessa. "Now, don't be shy; get on over here and say hello!" she commanded, as Vanessa took a half-step back. It wasn't just that Teensy herself presented an overwhelming figure; a half-dozen or so other people in western attire were watching, as well. Their expressions indicated they were enjoying this interaction—and the teenagers' discomfiture—as well.

"Yeah, this is Vanessa," Simon contributed. "We heard the music, and she wanted to stop and see what was going on." He flashed her a quick *You see what you got us into?* sort of look.

"Well, of course she did!" Teensy asserted. For a second or so, it appeared she might envelope Vanessa in the sort of all-encompassing hug she'd given Simon, but she apparently thought better of it, and settled for grasping one of the girl's hands in both of hers and squeezing it heartily. "It's pretty infectious, and what it lacks in tone, it makes up for in volume. Do you two-step?"

"Uh, no, I don't think so," Vanessa said, retrieving her crumpled hand as discretely as she could manage.

"I don't, I can say that for sure," Simon added. "Just ask Vanessa. I don't dance at all."

Teensy was craning her neck and gazing across the crowded interior. She didn't seem to be listening to them.

"Where'd Seth go, anyway?" she demanded of one of the men leaning against the wall. "Isn't it about time he manned the door for awhile?"

"I think he's breaking up a fight out back," another fellow contributed.

"Well, then, one of you can watch things for awhile, especially if all you're doing is hanging out here, anyhow," she decided. She snatched back Vanessa's hand, and before Simon was quite aware of what was happening, she'd nudged him forward. "It's time these two kids learned some new dance moves. I'll pay their admissions."

"No, that's all right, Teensy," Simon said, but somehow the decision was out of his hands. One minute, they had been standing in the open doorway with the cool night air at their backs, and the next, they were in the dim, hazy confines of a large room surrounded by an overflow of people, coupled and spinning in expert circles, jostling them on all sides and then spinning away again without a look back. The air was heavy and rank with a variety of smells, the strongest of which were beer and sweat.

"I really don't want to—" Simon attempted to shout over the noise, but Teensy reached over to pluck the shoulder of a man standing with his back to them, talking to someone else.

"—Hey!" she commanded. "Put down your beer and dance with this girl!"

With that, she handed off Vanessa and turned back to Simon.

"Anybody can learn to two-step," she told him confidently. "For now, I'm going to lead. But pay attention, and next dance, you're going to do what I'm doing. All right, one hand here, and one hand here. Good. Here we go."

And suddenly, somehow, they were another of the spinning couples moving more or less in time to the strokes of a bow across fiddle strings.

Simon might have refused to participate, except that his last glimpse of Vanessa was of her with her arms similarly draped on the lanky balding fellow Teensy had selected for her. She was laughing and shot Simon a quick can-you-believe-this-is-happening look before she and her partner were swallowed into the crowd.

He didn't see her again for several more minutes, by which time he had managed to stumble through one song with Teensy guiding, and another in which he took the lead with just a small amount of success.

"Oh, wait!" his partner said when the music had ended and he attempted to leave the floor. "They're starting a line dance, now. You've got to stay for this. They'll call out the steps, which makes it really easy."

It wasn't, of course. Not at first, anyway. The commands came too quickly, and he was forever turning left when everybody else turned right, but he was surrounded by bodies on every side, and ultimately it was easier to just flounder on than to try to make his way to safety. The back of his shirt was damp and droplets of perspiration trickled off his nose by the time the dance was over, but he had more or less mastered the routine by then. He was actually slightly disappointed when the music stopped.

"Nobody really line dances anymore," Teensy informed him as they crossed the floor. "Except in little backwater places like these. So you probably won't be able to put those moves to use anywhere else."

She was, Simon noticed, neither sweaty nor out of breath. Despite her size and weight, she undertook every dance with grace and dexterity, even when saddled with a clumsy partner.

"I'm not sure I can even do those moves again here tonight," he retorted.

"Of course you can. I'm an excellent teacher. Hey, you guys!" Teensy greeted Vanessa and the skinny guy in jeans and a western shirt waiting for them by the bar.

"That was so much fun!" Vanessa enthused. "Wasn't it?" she demanded of Simon. "And I'm dying of thirst. Can we get a Coke, or something?"

"Yeah, I guess," he said, digging in his pocket for money, but the other man had already turned and was gesturing to the bartender.

"Yo, Sam!" he directed. "Two Cokes and two beers here." Turning back, he thrust his hand at Simon. "Hello, by the way."

"Hi," Simon shook the hand. "Are you, uh, Seth?"

"No," the other man said, dragging his shirt sleeve across his brow. Unlike Teensy, he had sweated some. "I guess you don't remember me. It's been awhile. My name's Miles. I work with your grandmother."

"Oh. Oh, yeah, sure," Simon said, feeling a little foolish. If it hadn't already been red from exertion, his face would have flushed with embarrassment. "My mom used to work for you, too. Uh, here, let me pay for those Cokes."

Miles waved away the money Simon was holding out to him.

"Well, thanks," Simon said. He accepted one cup and passed the other to Vanessa. "I didn't recognize you at first. I guess I just didn't expect to see you here tonight."

"He's my date," Teensy interjected. She took a deep gulp from the frothy cup of beer Miles had handed to her and then patted away her foam moustache. "We're each other's beards this evening."

"How is your mother, anyway, Simon?" Miles asked after arching one eyebrow at Teensy. "She has another baby now, doesn't she?"

"Well, sort of. If you mean my brother Josh, that is. But he's four now, so not so much a baby, except when he thinks it'll get him something."

The others laughed. Teensy nudged Miles in the ribs. "Nothing reminds you of how ancient you are faster than when other people's kids turn out to be older than you remember."

"Yeah, unfortunately, I don't need many reminders," he said with mock ruefulness, patting his thinning hair. "Anyway, tell your mom I said hi. And, if she ever gets up this way, to give me a call or stop by and see me."

Simon nodded. "She keeps saying she'd like to visit Stucker's Reach one of these days and see a bunch of her old friends again. She's just not sure when. With, you know, the kids, and all."

The musicians filed past them a moment later and mounted the stage, picking up their instruments. Vanessa set her cup on the counter behind her and stepped close to Simon.

"Did you want to leave now?" To the others, she said, "Thanks for the drinks and the dance lesson. And for letting us come in. It was a lot of fun."

"You aren't going yet," Teensy informed her. She lifted Simon's Coke from his hand. "Not until you have at least one dance together."

With a gentle push, she sent them stumbling out into the clusters of other couples regrouping for the next number. They faced each other, and after a moment's hesitation, took a deep breath and a first step, hoping to summon back what they'd just learned. They moved tentatively at first, gripping each other as if they were strangers, keenly aware they were under the scrutiny of their instructors. But as they were swallowed into the crowd and could enjoy a bit of anonymity, they relaxed, and the steps came more easily.

"This is a lot harder than volleyball," Simon confided. "Oops! Sorry," he added, as he stepped on Vanessa's foot.

Near the bar, Teensy and Miles stood side by side, sipping their beers and watching the swirling crowd.

"I remember teaching you some of those dances a few years ago," she reminded him. "Lord, at first, it was like trying to lug a six-by-four plank around the floor. I didn't think I'd ever get you to loosen up."

"Yet, look at me now." He squeezed her shoulder.

"Huh." She finished her beer, crushed the empty cup and pitched it into a trash can. "Well, you're a little better than Simon, I'll give you that."

He smoothed the collar of his plaid shirt, then held out his hands to Teensy's. "Come on. Let's show them how it's done."

"I'm supposed to be watching the door," she said. But she allowed him to pull her out onto the dance floor, and a minute later she was laughing heartily as he spun her expertly, clearing a space around them.

An hour later, Simon and Vanessa lay on their backs in the grass in the town square, gazing up at the dark sky. They were only just now regaining their breaths.

"That was a blast," she said, squeezing his fingers. "Aren't you glad we did it?"

"Yeah, I guess. Now I can always say I country-danced once," he answered.

His indifferent tone didn't fool her.

"You liked it!" she accused him. "I know you did."

"I didn't hate it; let's settle for that." He shifted his position slightly, sliding closer to her. "It's funny."

"What is?"

"Well... until I realized who he was—Miles, I mean, my grandma's boss—I was a little bit jealous."

Vanessa turned her head to study his profile, gazing upward. "Jealous? Of the old guy?"

"Well, when I looked over, you seemed to be having a good time. You were laughing."

"I *was* having a good time. I was dancing."

"I know. It was just, you know, a momentary thing. I guess I was worried you were going to learn the dance faster than me, and I wouldn't be able to keep up. You'd only want to dance with guys who were as good as you were becoming."

She bumped her shoulder against his. "That's so dumb."

They were silent for several minutes, listening to the nearby music and the snippets of conversation from other people strolling past. Simon rolled towards Vanessa and rested his other hand on her stomach, fingers stroking the fabric of her shirt.

"You want to go somewhere?"

"Not tonight," she said after another moment. "Let's just lie here for a little while."

"Oh. Okay."

"We were out pretty late last night," she reminded him. "I don't think we should push it."

He took back his hand.

"I can't believe it's Friday already. Practically Saturday. Seems like the whole week's gone."

"Don't do that," she ordered. "We still have all day tomorrow and all day Sunday."

That reminded him.

"Oh, by the way: Robert called me this afternoon while I was at work. He wants to hang out with us for awhile tomorrow."

"Sure," Vanessa said before he could add anything more. "That's fine."

He turned his head to look at her. She lifted her head briefly to disentangle strands of hair caught beneath her back, then settled back into the grass again. Her face was aglow in the glare of the streetlamp on the corner. Her lips were full, her eyelashes impossibly long and eloquently curved, and at that moment, Simon felt astounded that such a girl was interested in him. And he went from being apprehensive to something akin to disappointed that she seemed perfectly okay with Robert joining them tomorrow.

"Do you think he's gay?" she asked, abruptly derailing his thoughts.

"Who, Robert?" He studied her a second longer, then turned his head skyward once more. "I don't know. I never thought about it."

"No, not Robert. That guy at the dance. Miles, I mean."

"Oh."

"The *beard* comment, I mean. When Ms. Phillips—Teensy—said they were each other's beards tonight. So, I was just wondering…" She allowed the statement to go unfinished.

"I think so," he said finally. He tried to remember if he'd ever heard his grandmother or mom mention anything to that effect about Miles. "I'm not sure how I know that, though."

He was still contemplating this when Vanessa said:

"Not Robert. I'm pretty sure Robert's not gay."

And, for some reason he couldn't quite put his finger on, this was the remark that stayed with Simon long after he'd driven Vanessa back to her place and then let himself quietly into his grandparents' darkened house.

Without turning on a light, he sat on the edge of his bed, pulling off his sneakers and socks, then tugging his shirt over his head. He wadded it up and tossed it into a crumpled ball on the floor, then flopped back onto the covers.

Simon was trying to put the evening and his own conflicted feelings into some order. The overriding emotions were of disappointment and frustration.

Not only had Vanessa rejected the idea of making love tonight, she'd waved away his comment about how quickly this week was slipping through their fingers. At the beginning of the summer, she'd been the one lamenting the fact that he would be spending the next three months away from her. She was also the one who'd negotiated a way to spend a week here in Stucker's Reach, just so they could be together. Now, looking back, there'd been something vaguely unsatisfying about most of the past five days. Lying there in the darkness, one hand sliding absently up and down his chest, he tried to identify the source of this feeling.

She'd been staying at a fancy summer home on the posh side of the lake, a far cry from the more humble place his grandparents maintained. Her hosts had treated her to a day at a luxurious spa. She had been able to play the role of tourist to the hilt while Simon was spending his nights refilling water glasses and clearing countless dirty dishes from under the noses of diners who, if they noticed him at all, only wanted more butter and rolls. And today, while he worked an unscheduled extra shift, she'd whizzed across the lake in a high-powered speedboat, or been towed behind it, having a blast learning to water ski with more of Krissy's privileged friends.

So an evening subsequently spent with him, albeit with some country western dance tips thrown in, must have seemed pretty lame by comparison. He sighed.

His hand had found its way down the front of his shorts. He allowed his fingers to continue their massaging for another minute while he considered this. After a minute, he got up from the bed and moved as quietly as he could manage to the doorway. He stood for several seconds, listening for any sign of activity in the house. Only ambient noises from the kitchen clock and from a dog barking somewhere in the neighborhood reached his ears. He carefully closed his door tightly and then turned, sliding his shorts to his ankles and kicking them aside.

There hadn't been much need for self-gratification ever since he and Vanessa had begun having sex. And as a result, he now viewed masturbation as something bordering on the pathetic. But, after all, he had been anticipating a sexual encounter this evening, and merely because she wasn't in the mood didn't automatically derail his own urges.

Simon stretched out atop his bed once more, taking a moment to bunch the pillows behind his head. He settled back and closed his eyes. He plunged his hand into his underwear and began stroking himself in earnest. His hips thrust upward and off the bed in time to his ministrations as he increased his efforts.

With his free hand, he tugged his underwear down as far as his knees. He exhaled in deeper breaths, and behind his eyelids, he summoned an image of Vanessa, beautiful Vanessa with the full lips and incredible eyelashes.

He was making a further mental inventory of her attributes when, unbidden, her earlier comment landed back in his brain.

"Not Robert. I'm pretty sure Robert's not gay."

Simon's hips paused in mid-rise and then settled back onto the mattress.

He allowed both hands to fall at his sides, and he stared at the ceiling. Despite frantic efforts, he hadn't been able to get very hard, and now his half-erection faded entirely. He lay unmoving, except for the continued heaving of his chest.

Not for a second did he think that Vanessa had first-hand proof of what she'd said about Robert's sexual orientation. Nor was it even that remark, exactly, that had so thoroughly banished his arousal. No, it was the image of Robert, affable, goofy Robert, now standing next to Vanessa in Simon's fantasy. There he was, hovering over the bed, gazing down with that impassive expression he so often wore, watching while Simon played with himself.

"Son of a bitch," Simon muttered, yanking up his underwear. With difficulty, he tugged down the bedcovers and crawled underneath them, pulling them up to his face and rolling onto his side. He closed his eyes, trying without much success, to will away the image of Robert, entirely unjudgmental Robert, still watching him. Vanessa, it seemed, had left the picture entirely.

Chapter Thirteen

"So, what I don't get," Krissy began, "Is why you want to be a teacher, anyhow."

She held up a shirt in order to study it from both sides. She fingered the price tag, then returned it to the rack, shuffling several hangers in search of something else.

"I mean, you just got out of high school, now you'll go to college for four years or more, and then you'll want to go right back into another classroom? Don't you think that's just a little too much school?"

Vanessa, bent over a display case looking at rings and other jewelry, didn't answer right away.

"I don't know," she said absently. "It's just something I've wanted to do, ever since I was little." To the clerk standing behind the counter, she said, "Could I see that bracelet, the silver one on the left?" As she waited, she added, "I used to play school with my dolls and stuffed animals all lined up in chairs, and I stood in front of the room. Then later, I'd make the younger kids in my neighborhood play it with me, and I'd give lessons, and things."

"Oh, everybody does that!" Krissy sniffed.

Vanessa fastened the bracelet around her wrist and fingered the coin-shaped ornaments that adorned it.

"The inlaid stones are turquoise," the clerk explained. "The silver's hand-pounded."

"Pounded?"

The woman nodded. "You know: Shaped. It's Native American. Navajo, I think."

"It's really nice. I'll have to think about it, though." Vanessa handed it back across the glass.

"My sister's daughter is a teacher," the clerk said. "Third grade."

"Oh, really?" Vanessa's gaze was traveling down the rows of pendants and necklaces.

"She was teaching kindergarten when she first started out, but she didn't care for that too much. She says children really only start to get interesting by about the time they're in second or third grades. Up until then, she says it just feels like babysitting, mostly."

"You don't make any money teaching," Krissy contributed from over her shoulder as she continued to look at merchandise. "Or not much, anyhow. That's what Mr. Grant, my English teacher said last year. He said, 'I don't get paid enough to take all this grief.'"

"Your *teacher* said that?" The clerk looked aghast. "That doesn't seem very professional."

Krissy shrugged. "Some of us—some of the class, I mean—were being sort of obnoxious. We were discussing this book *Animal Farm,* which is about, well, animals. Except these ones talk, so somebody started using a cartoon voice, like, you know, cartoon animals have on TV and in the movies, and so then more of us did it. People were trying to see who could come up with the funniest voice, and we were laughing and, well, you know. ...It was pretty funny," she concluded somewhat defensively, realizing that both Vanessa and the clerk were staring at her. "Except Mr. Grant didn't think so.

"So, anyway," she added a moment later, coming over to stand next to Vanessa at the counter, "I think that just because you had fun teaching the alphabet and stuff to your teddy bears and Barbies, that doesn't necessarily mean it's going to be like that in real life. I suppose you already know that, though."

She set two shirts on the counter. "I want these," she told the clerk. "But first, I need to know what your return policy is."

"I'm really pretty tired of being around Krissy," Vanessa confided to her mother a few moments later. They were strolling down Main Street several feet behind Krissy and her mother, gazing into the windows of various tourist and gift shops. "I know that sounds awful, but I think I just had to go ahead and say it."

"Well, she's two years younger than you are," her mother observed. "This is a time in your life where two years can make a big difference.

And I know you're really up here because you want to spend as much time as you can with Simon. I do think it's nice you could repay our hosts' hospitality by being as patient with Krissy as you have been. I'm sure it hasn't all been easy."

"It hasn't been bad." Vanessa was somewhat surprised to hear herself contradicting not just her mother's sympathetic response, but her own earlier comment. "In some ways, I guess it's been kind of an interesting education. I must have been just like her, not too long ago, and that makes me feel weird."

Worse, she was thinking, in some ways, she was still exactly the same, and conversing with Krissy was like looking into one of those cosmetic mirrors that magnifies every pore, every blemish.

She stopped and faced her mother who, surprised, gazed back at her.

"Did I always want to be a teacher?"

"I… Well, I don't know, Sweetie. Wouldn't you know better than I do?"

Vanessa persisted. "Don't you remember all the times I would pretend to hold school for my dolls and things, and for the neighborhood kids?"

Her mother's brow furrowed as she thought about this.

"Well," she began tentatively. "I guess I remember that, once or twice. If you say so."

"I don't want it to be because *I* said so!" She clutched her mother's arm. "I want it to be because it *was* so. I mean, when I told you I was going to college to be a teacher, you and Daddy didn't seem surprised. You seemed okay with it!"

Krissy and her mother were waiting at the corner.

"Go ahead to the restaurant," Vanessa's mother called to them. "We'll be there in just a minute or two."

Once the others had begun to cross the street, she turned back to Vanessa, placing her hands on either shoulder and pushed her down onto a bench next to an open doorway. She sat next to her.

"Of course we were okay with it, Vanny. Though, if you're asking me to be completely honest, I wouldn't say we believed that's necessarily what will happen." She waved away her daughter's protest. "You'll turn eighteen this fall. Not many people know what they want to do with their lives at that age. Even some who do, well, they go off to college, and wind up picking something else. Do you think we're going to hold you to the idea of becoming a teacher, just because you've mentioned it a time or two?"

"No," Vanessa conceded reluctantly.

"Well, then, relax. This is your time to explore options. Think about being a teacher, or a veterinarian, or a doctor, or even a ballerina, for that matter. Dabble for awhile. You've got all kinds of core classes you have to get out of the way before you commit to a career."

"I flunked out of ballet when I was seven," Vanessa reminded her mother. "Remember? Madame Pineret told me I lacked passion." She couldn't help smiling at the memory.

"Okay, scratch that one off the list, then. But you understand what I'm saying?" As her daughter nodded, she asked, "Where is all this coming from, anyway?"

"I don't know," Vanessa told her honestly. She thought about it for a minute. "I guess maybe I'm worried there won't be anything I find to be passionate about."

Her mother thought back to the many evenings of the past year since Vanessa had begun dating Simon: The amount of time they'd spent together, the evenings her daughter had crept home far later than promised, and recently, how fervent she'd been to make this trip to the mountains to see him. There had been frank discussions with Vanessa, beginning around the time she turned twelve, and still more when serious boyfriends began to appear on the horizon. Her mother sighed. This moment, seated on a bench outside a gift shop on a sunny afternoon, while dozens of people strolled past, did not seem to be the time to embark on another. So she said merely:

"Passion is an overused word, Sweetheart. And it's a kind of single-minded emotion that can overrule common sense, if you aren't careful. For right now, why not settle for something *less* than passion?"

She half-expected her daughter to balk at this carefully-worded warning. For years now, the resentful credo from Vanessa had been that her parents didn't trust her, were too interfering, didn't think she had any of her own good judgment. But this time, she merely cocked her head, studying her mother, and smiled.

"Message received, Mom. No college pregnancies." She nudged her mother with her shoulder. "We probably better head to the restaurant before they come looking for us."

They both stood.

"I wasn't suggesting *that,*" her mother said, following Vanessa to the corner.

But they both knew that she was.

Chapter Fourteen

If he wasn't nervous, exactly, Robert certainly felt uncertain in his new and unfamiliar role as host. He wandered from kitchen to living room and back again, brushing his hands against the sides of his pants and inspecting the same few items over and over again. He bent to look into the refrigerator, then closed the door and retraced his steps to the front of the house, lifting the curtains and checking the street to see if a car had pulled into the driveway.

Sighing, he turned back into the room, his gaze falling on the bowl of potato chips he'd placed in the center of the coffee table. His twitching fingers reached towards one, but he willed them back to his side.

For a time, he sat in the overstuffed chair facing the front door, but this made him still more restless, so he resumed his prowling, moving through the rooms, both those familiar and the ones he'd never ventured into until more recently, just since Mrs. Scoggins' death.

Books remained on their shelves, pictures on the walls, towels still folded on the shelves in the linen closet. In the bedroom the bed was tidily made, pillows plumped and smooth beneath the spread, even after all these months. Were it not for a slight film of dust coating the top of the bureau and the nightstands, one could almost believe somebody would be coming home any time now.

That used to bring some consolation; now it just angered Robert. It offered false hope, delayed the inevitable. Things were not going to stay the same, not even here. *"Get on with it!"* he muttered again. Though tonight, for the first time in a long while, he was glad no one had. Tonight, he could entertain guests here.

The first time Robert had let himself in through the front door using a key, it had been at Mrs. Scoggins' request. She'd asked him to go and get a few things and bring them to her at the hospice. A book, a pair of slippers, a brush.

He'd felt like an intruder, convinced that at any moment a police car would come rocketing up, red light flashing, and he would have to explain to the officers as they cuffed him and dragged him across the yard why he was here.

But nothing happened. His tentative footfalls disturbed nothing more than dusty silence. Nobody came to ask what he was doing. Still, he was furtive, keeping his eyes averted as he sought out the items on her list, as if even glancing at anything else would be an invasion of her privacy. As soon as he found what he'd been sent to retrieve, he'd left quickly, closing the door and rattling the knob to be sure it had locked behind him.

But after that, he'd returned often, first to retrieve more things Eulamarie wanted, and later, just to sit. Mrs. Scoggins was gone by then. No longer timid, he came in hopes of summoning back something, a feeling or a memory, a scrap of shared conversation with his departed friend.

This gave him consolation for awhile, but then less so as spring gave way to summer. It was as if her presence had left the house gradually, the same way it had departed her weakening body those last few weeks of life. And now, standing here this early July evening, awaiting Simon and Vanessa, Robert realized that his only remaining connection to Eulamarie Scoggins was a faint pull within his chest. This house, these things, they were of no use to her any longer, nor she to them.

He started to say something aloud, but then a noise from the back yard interrupted his thoughts. He descended the stairs two at a time, and rushed into the kitchen, throwing open the back door.

"Oh, hey!" he declared. "I kept waiting for you at the front door."

There was a slight edge to Simon's laugh. "How would we know that? You brought us around the back the only other time we were here."

They faced each other on opposite sides of the threshold for another few seconds.

"Are we coming in, or are you coming out?" Vanessa grinned.

"Oh. Uh..." Robert stepped back, giving them space. "In," he concluded.

His guests stepped into the kitchen, glancing around with curiosity.

"Does anybody know you have a key to this place?" Simon asked.

Robert shrugged. "Probably not. Nobody's ever asked, anyway." He opened the refrigerator. "You want a beer?"

Vanessa looked at Simon, drawing in her breath as if she was about to say something, but then she faced Robert.

"Do... Do you come over here a lot?"

Leaning over the refrigerator door, Robert considered the question. But before he could answer, Simon interjected:

"I'm not sure we should be drinking somebody else's beer. Even if she is...you know...gone, now."

"It's not hers," Robert assured him. He set three bottles on the counter and closed the door. "I brought it from home. Let's go sit in the living room. There's potato chips, too."

He led the way, taking no notice of his guests' incredulous expressions. Numbly, they followed him into the front room.

"Sit there," he instructed, pointing to the couch. He set the beers on coasters and then settled himself in the chair facing the coffee table.

"You swiped beer from your folks?" Vanessa asked. She looked from Robert to the bottle and then back at Robert again.

"No!" he told her indignantly. "I bought it from 'em." For a moment, he couldn't figure out why they both still looked so surprised.

"They didn't know," he clarified. "Not exactly. There's this refrigerator we have downstairs that's mostly for when they have parties, or company comes over. It's full of wine and beer and sodas. I told my mom I was going to take some drinks for us. She thought I meant the sodas."

"Holy shit," Simon declared softly. With a slight shake of his head, he reached for a bottle. "You're something else, Robert," he grinned.

Robert exhaled, not realizing until that second how much he wanted his friend to be okay with what he'd done. He hoisted his own beer and took a small sip. He was determined to demonstrate tonight that he could actually hold his liquor.

For fifteen minutes or so, they ate chips and drank, and talked a little bit about the house and how the friendship with Mrs. Scoggins had come about. But then conversation began to lag, and they found themselves looking around the room, studying the same objects again and again in search of something more to discuss. It was dawning on Robert that he really hadn't planned beyond the introduction of beverages and snacks.

"We could maybe play cards, or something," he suggested. "There's probably a deck around here someplace."

Simon, his arm resting across the back of the couch behind Vanessa's shoulders, looked at his girlfriend and then shook his head.

"I guess not, but thanks."

Robert felt a twinge of despair. He'd been hoping to recapture that feeling from the other night, when they'd come here after the barbecue. But he could sense it; any moment now, his guests would be setting down their bottles and making some excuse to leave, taking with them that new and intoxicating sense of camaraderie he'd only just begun to sample.

"Sorry," he said, expelling the word at the end of a drawn-out sigh. "I guess I don't really know how to do this."

The others exchanged a glance. "Do what?" Vanessa asked him.

"You know," Robert shrugged. "Have a party."

After a second, Simon dropped his chin to his chest, studying his lap. He made an odd snickering noise. Vanessa's brow furrowed. She sucked her lips inward. Then, releasing them, she said:

"This isn't a party, Robert."

"No, but I..."

"It's just a couple of friends over, that's what this is. So, relax."

Robert looked at Simon, who had lifted his head and was nodding in agreement.

Still he was uncertain.

"There's lots more beer," he said. "Lots. But this is it for the potato chips."

"*Relax,* Robert," Simon insisted. "We'll be fine."

And then Robert did relax; considerably. Now on his third bottle and experiencing his first-ever buzz, he regarded the others with a laconic, faintly glassy stare.

"So," he said. "I guess you guys are going to get married someday."

Simon and Vanessa, trailing behind him on the beer consumption, looked first startled and then amused.

"Well...won't you?" he persisted.

"I don't know, Robert," Simon said. "We haven't even started college yet."

"But, you can be engaged."

"We've got our whole lives ahead of us." Vanessa pointed out. "It's too soon to be thinking about things like that."

Robert was not ready to be dissuaded.

"You're going to different schools, though. What if one of you meets somebody else? What then?"

Vanessa shifted against the cushions. Simon's fingers stopped stroking the back of her neck.

"Well, then," she said slowly, "We just have to believe that what we have—" she resisted the impulse to look at Simon, "—is strong enough, or meant to be."

Robert rested his elbows on his knees, holding his beer bottle in both hands.

"My folks met at college. I wonder if they'd been in love with other people before they got there. I never thought to ask."

"What about you?" Vanessa asked, leaning forward and folding her arms in front of her. "Is there anyone you've been serious about, Robert?"

Simon, taking a pull from his beer, thought he knew the answer to that question already. He was surprised when his friend, studying the floor, said, "Yeah. I guess. Once, maybe."

"Do you think he'll be okay?" Vanessa asked Simon sometime later as they sat on the shore of one of the lake's inlets, a finger of water reaching back into the wooded hills. They had walked from the house, following a path that descended the bluff in a series of switchbacks, carrying a six-pack of beer concealed beneath a blanket. The blanket now covered their legs as they reclined in the sand gazing across the water and at the stars overhead.

"He'll be fine."

There was something so dismissive in Simon's response that she gave him a sidelong glance. In the reflected glow of the moonlight on the water's surface, his expression was neutral, but she could see he was working his lower jaw back and forth in a twitching motion.

"How about you, then? Are you okay?" she asked.

She did not receive an answer, and did not press further. She raised herself on her elbow to take another drink from her bottle and to sweep her hair behind her shoulders.

A silhouetted figure rose up from the reeds near the water's edge, outlined against the bobbing whitecaps. It stood, weaving slightly, and facing the lake. At last it turned their direction and, for some incomprehensible reason, raised one hand to shield its eyes. As if this could somehow help Robert locate his friends, sitting in darkness twenty-five feet up the beach.

"What's he doing, do you suppose?" murmured Vanessa.

It seemed as if Simon still wasn't going to answer her, but at last he said, "Who knows? He's buzzing."

"Hey! Hey, you guys!" Robert called, far more loudly than necessary. His voice seemed to shoot out in all directions, over their heads and to either side, rebounding off the trees and striking the ground around them like a shower of stones.

"Robert! Hush!" Vanessa called, looking worriedly over her shoulder. "Somebody might hear!"

He loped up the incline and arrived breathless, dropping to the ground on his knees in front of them.

"What were you doing down there?"

"Just looking around. Checking the water. It's not too cold, you know? We should go in."

"Don't think so, Bud," Simon snorted.

"No, really! I don't mean swimming, just wading. Hey!" he declared. "Are there any more beers?"

"I think you've had enough, Robert," Vanessa cautioned. She looked at Simon. "For right now, anyway."

"Yeah, just relax, all right?" Simon pulled his knees to his chest and wrapped his arms around them.

"Okay," Robert said agreeably. He didn't seem inclined to remind them that the beers were his, after all. Instead, he allowed himself to fall backwards, landing with a thump in the sand. "Wow," he added, gazing up at the stars. "The world just… it just flies, doesn't it? Through the night."

"Oh, Robert," Vanessa laughed softly. "What are we going to do with you?"

"Nothing," he said dreamily. "I wish this had happened sooner, though. *This,* I mean," he added, patting the ground and then folded his hands across his chest.

"I bet this is the last time we ever see each other," he added a moment later.

Simon and Vanessa looked at one another, then at the figure in the sand.

"Oh, you'll see each other," she assured Robert. "The two of you, sometime. And maybe me, too. Probably someplace where we'll never expect it. You never know about these things."

"*I* know," Robert said confidently. He expelled a deep philosophical sigh, as if resigned to the truth. He pounded the sand again and sat up. "I'm going to go wade."

He was on his feet and headed towards the water again before the others had time to react. Vanessa clutched Simon's arm.

"We can't let him."

"He'd probably be all right," Simon told her, but he was already thrusting aside the blanket. "Robert!" he called. "Hold up!"

It appeared for a second Robert was obeying, but in fact, he'd paused only long enough to pull off his shoes.

"Crap," Simon muttered, breaking into a sprint in pursuit of the other boy. Robert was peeling off a sock, hopping on the other foot to keep his balance. He dropped it on the ground and was working on the second one when Simon corralled him by clutching his upper arm.

"No, you're not going in the lake. You just think it's warm because you've got a bunch of beer in you."

"I know how to swim." Robert was doing his best to take back his arm even as he continued to reach for his other ankle and the sock dangling from his toes.

"That has nothing to do with it. It's dark, you could slip on a rock, or something—"

SIMON

They both fell, then, Robert having lost his balance, and pulling Simon over with him. A fiery pain flared on the side of Simon's knee as he made contact with the ground.

"Simon..?" Vanessa's voice, alarmed, drifted towards them.

"Robert..," Simon grunted, but the other boy was crawling away from him, determined as a baby turtle to get to the water. "Fine!" he muttered. "Go, then." He pulled himself to a sitting position and pressed a hand to his knee.

Vanessa came thundering up. "What happened?"

"The little asshole landed on top of me."

"Are you okay?" she asked. Before he could answer, they heard the sound of splashing. "Robert!" she yelled. "Listen to me, please!" And then she was gone, her footsteps pounding away across the sand.

Simon squeezed his eyes shut and hunched against his legs, willing away the pain. "Vanny, don't get in the water!" he commanded, eyes still closed. The last thing he needed was to try and haul both of them to shore. Grunting, he got to his feet and lurched down the slope. He could see only one shadowy outline crouching over an embankment.

"I don't see him, Simon!" she hissed as he reached her side. "Robert!" she called. "Answer me! Answer me right now!"

Now it was her voice filling the inlet like a clarion, shattering the night into jagged pieces. He reached for her hand and gripped her fingers.

"Quiet," he commanded.

"I..."

"*Hush!*" he insisted. And then they were both still, listening for the sounds of splashing. There was only the measured lapping of undisturbed water slapping the shore by their feet. Simon felt his throat tighten with fear, but he forced down the panic.

"Robert?" he called softly. "This isn't funny."

"We need to get back, Robert." The tremble in her voice indicated Vanessa was on the verge of tears.

Simon's mind raced. Even at the height of summer, the glacier-fed lake's temperature was frigid. Swimming—wading, even—was allowed only at the town's roped-off, officially designated beach at the marina. And for good reason. In addition to the cold, there were insidious, abrupt drop-offs below the surface. One minute, you might be wading in knee-deep water, and the very next you could step off a submerged shelf and find yourself plummeting to untold depths. In daylight, and perfectly sober, you'd be in trouble. Here and now...

"Robert!" he screamed, forgetting his own caution to Vanessa a moment ago. "Get your fucking ass back here this minute!"

There were houses concealed in the trees on the hillside above, and this would very likely wake some startled sleepers, but he no longer cared. He was about to call again, when at last they heard someone slogging through the water somewhere down the shoreline.

Simon's hand squeezed Vanessa's in a vise-like grip, but she did not protest. They stood, gazing to their left, waiting, until Robert emerged from the darkness, wading less than three feet from shore.

"Jeez, you guys." In the darkness they could see the exposed teeth in his maddening grin. "Stop your caterwauling. I'm just taking a walk. Jeez."

Vanessa went limp with relief, nearly dropping to her knees as the tension left her body. For a moment, Simon gripped her hand even more tightly, and then he released it.

"I've been around this lake my whole life, for Pete's Sake. I know what I'm doing—" Robert announced, just before he stumbled against something beneath the surface. Arms flailing, he staggered a few steps and then fell face forward into the water.

He was submerged only a second or so before he reappeared, gasping and laughing. "Whoa!" he declared, "Didn't see *that* coming!" He attempted to stand, but lost his footing and slipped once more beneath the black surface. "Holy crap!" he sputtered this time, still laughing.

He was nearly in a standing position before he fell yet again, backwards, and this time his head and shoulders remained above the surface.

Simon left Vanessa's side and walked into the lake, shoes and all. Cupping his hands beneath Robert's armpits, he hauled him to his feet and dragged him up onto the shore.

"Wow," Robert declared, coughing and snorting water out of his nose. "Easier to get in than it is to get ou—"

But Simon, once he had righted Robert on his feet, spun the other boy around and slammed his fist into his jaw. Robert went staggering several feet and landed on his back in a thicket of bushes.

"You fucking little prick," Simon hissed, advancing on him. "Just what the hell is the matter with you?"

The other boy, caught off guard, blinked several times and pressed his hand to his face. Before Robert could manage anything more, Simon had leaned over the thicket and grabbed his shirt front, lifting him to his feet. He held his face just inches from his own, glowering at him.

"What are you trying to pull here, anyway? What do you want, you weirdo? What is it you want from me?"

"Hey, Simon..." Robert managed, the word muffled through the hand he held against his cheek. "Simon," he said again. And then he laughed weakly.

It was the laugh that made Simon lose all sense of reason. Teeth clenched, he lifted the other teen a few inches off the ground and launched him into the air. Robert struck the ground with a grunt, flat on his back, five feet away. His arms and legs flailed as he gasped for air.

"Simon!" Vanessa screamed. Simon, on his knees, was now straddling Robert, one hand raised, ready to deliver another blow. Vanessa threw herself at him, knocking him aside. Both went tumbling through the grass and sand.

"Leave him alone!" she shrieked. "What are you doing?" On hands and knees, she crept to him and as he sat up, she planted both hands in the center of his chest and shoved him to the ground again.

"I... I..." he said.

Ten feet away, Robert was making gagging, wretching noises. Finally, after much struggle, he was able to gulp a fresh breath into his lungs. He rolled away, his back to the others.

They watched him for a few seconds and when at last they looked at each other again, Simon's face dissolved into an expression of disbelief. Vanessa stared at him for a second and then got to her feet. She made her way to Robert.

"Are you all right?" she gasped.

He pulled away as she reached for his arm.

Then Simon was with them, also.

"We have to get out of here!" he said. "Listen!"

They froze. The wail of a siren was drawing closer.

"Somebody called the cops on us!"

"Robert, come on!"

But he shook his head, refusing to move. The others stood to one side, gazing helplessly at him and at each other.

"Grab the beer and the blanket," Simon instructed Vanessa finally. "I'll get him."

She sprinted up the sand, hair flying behind her, to gather the evidence.

"Come on," Simon panted hoarsely. "We're going."

Robert did not struggle as Simon pulled him up, throwing one of the boy's arms around his shoulder as he slipped his own arm around Robert's waist. Slipping and losing traction in the sand, they stumbled towards Vanessa who was waiting for them, beer in one hand, blanket in the other. Simon was aware of the throbbing in his knee, but adrenalin kept him moving, dragging the near-dead weight of his friend with him.

"Come *on!*" Vanessa pleaded. In addition to the siren, they could now hear the crunch of tires on graveled road somewhere above them.

There was the slam of one car door and then another, and the amplified sound of a voice murmuring indecipherable words through a radio. The siren had stopped. Seconds later, a yellowish light swept the shore above the inlet. But by then, the three teens had vanished into the trees.

Vanessa led the way up the path. Branches occasionally slapped her in the face, but she did not stop, merely blinked back tears of pain and kept climbing through the darkness. Simon pulled Robert alongside him, managing to stay no more than ten feet behind her.

"I hope the deputies don't know about this path," he panted. "Or don't think to check it."

After ten minutes, when the immediate fear of discovery had left him, he stopped.

"Hold up," he told Vanessa. "I have to catch my breath."

Cautiously, she retraced her last ten steps, joining them to lean against the side of a lichen-encrusted boulder. They tried to still their gasping to hear if anyone was following them. It appeared they were alone on the path.

"When we get to the top," Simon said a moment later, "Be careful. Don't just burst out of the trees, in case there's anybody waiting up there. There probably won't be, but let me check it out first." He looked at Robert. "Can you make it on your own now?"

Robert nodded without lifting his head. But when, a second later, they resumed their climb, he did not follow. Simon glanced back at him.

"Robert?" he said softly. "You coming?"

Still not looking up at them, he waved them on.

Simon looked at Vanessa.

"Robert?" she asked. When he did not respond, she added, "Are you okay?"

A nod.

And so they went on without him.

Where the path emerged from the trees at the far end of a vacant field, no one was waiting. In silence, they walked through the grass to the street and to Simon's car, parked in the driveway at Eulamarie Scoggins' house.

"What do you think we should do with the beer and the blanket?" Vanessa asked.

"Leave it on the porch, I guess."

They drove through town in silence, each glancing around nervously for a patrol car lying in wait. The digital clock on the dashboard read ten forty-five. Funny. *It seemed much later,* Vanessa thought. The town, on a Saturday evening the night before The Fourth of July, was a hive of activity. Probably the sheriff's department had plenty to keep them occupied besides reports of people screaming and disturbing the peace in a little inlet off the lake someplace.

Simon drove them back to the house where Vanessa was staying. He pulled the car through the gate and up the circular driveway, parking some distance away from the lights of the front porch. He shut off the engine. Both sat listening to the faint *tick tick* noise of the cooling motor.

"Well… good night." She opened the passenger door, flooding the car's interior with light.

"Good night." But as she was about to close the door, he said, "Hey! Uh… I'm… I don't know what happened back there. I *don't*. I'll call you later. Is that okay?"

Both her tone and the expression on her face seemed void of any emotion when she said, "I guess. I don't know."

He did not press her further, just nodded as she closed the door and walked across the grass to the front door. She did not look back once she was there, but opened the door and went inside.

His grandparents were in the living room watching television when Simon walked in his own front door.

"Well, hey," Honey greeted him. "You're home earlier than I expected."

"Yeah."

He wanted only to go to his room, but he didn't want to create even the slightest suspicion of just how far afield this evening had gone, so he stepped into the room and settled himself on the arm of the sofa next to his grandmother.

"Did you hurt your leg?" she asked.

Damn. The woman missed nothing.

"No. Not really," he said. "We were taking a walk, and I just stepped wrong, or something."

"Well, there's a heating pad in the linen closet, if you want it," she advised, letting the subject drop with that.

"Okay. What're you watching?" he inquired with feigned interest.

She waved a dismissive hand at the television set. "Oh, I don't know. Something your grandfather's looking at."

Axel faced his wife with a single upturned eyebrow. "*Me?* I thought we were watching something you wanted to see."

"Oh, well, good heavens, no," she retorted. "I just sat down here thirty minutes ago. It was already on. You were looking at it!"

Simon laughed. It felt unexpectedly good to do so, he realized.

"Well, enjoy it, whatever it is," he told them both. "I'm going to grab a shower and go to bed."

Honey nodded, and turned back to the television program. Simon stood and walked into the hallway, trying to hobble as little as possible in front of the others.

His grandparents continued to watch the screen for several minutes. After they heard the water come on in the shower, Axel, eyes still on the TV, said:

"I wonder what happened. His shoes and socks are all wet. Did you notice?"

His wife nodded again. "And there was that chipper note his voice only gets when he's not really feeling chipper. That's what I'm wondering about."

"A quarrel, you think?"

"Wouldn't be surprised. It's their next-to-last night together before she goes back. That's how these things work."

"Young love," Axel said dismissively.

They both continued to watch the program that neither of them was really interested in watching.

The hot water pelting against his leg felt good, and by the time Simon stepped out of the shower and was toweling off, he decided his knee was probably just bruised. It would be discolored tomorrow, and he'd limp for another day or so, but then it would be all right.

But, would anything else? His stomach felt gnarled and queasy. The look on Vanessa's face just after she'd stopped him from hitting Robert a second time was etched at the forefront of his brain. Worse, he'd punched Robert and then lifted him and thrown him as hard as he could, without regard for the outcome. Even now, Simon could feel in his clenched fingers, the sensation of holding the boy a good eight inches off the ground, Robert dangling like a limp puppet in his grip, and how easy it had been to simply launch him into the air, fueled by pure, unreasoning rage. It had taken no effort at all.

"That isn't me," he told himself, facing the mirror over the sink as he wiped away the steam. "I don't do stuff like that." His reflection regarded him dubiously.

He pulled on his sweatpants and a t-shirt and crossed the hall into his bedroom. He dug his cell phone from the pocket of his shorts, feeling almost certain that there would be a message awaiting him. There wasn't. No one had even tried to call.

Simon flopped across the bed on his stomach, fingering his phone. After a moment's contemplation, he speed-dialed a number and held the phone to his ear.

"You've reached Vanessa's voice mail," her recorded voice told him. *"So I guess I must be doing other stuff right now. Just say the word, and I'll call you back, though."*

He hesitated a second or so, wondering if she was holding her phone, looking at the incoming number, contemplating whether or not to answer.

"Uh..." he said, after the beep. "...Uh... It's me. I... Vanny, I..."

And then he disconnected. Too late, he realized he could have waited and deleted the message. He needed to say something, had to tell her *something* before he could go to sleep tonight. But he didn't know what. What words could possibly take away the images she must have in her own brain right now?

He tapped the keypad idly as he contemplated all this. Then, remembering something else, he pulled up his directory, sought out a recently added number, and called it.

It did not surprise him that it went to voice mail without anyone picking up. He listened to the message and when the beep came, he said:

"Robert, it's Simon. I wanted to make sure you got home okay. I'm home, now, at my grandparents' place. I'm going to leave my phone on all night, and you can call me any time, all right? So, when you listen to this... Robert... I don't even know how it all happened, how I did what I did."

His voice had gotten thick, and Simon realized he was on the verge of tears.

"There's no excuse, none at all, and God, I would give anything to take back tonight, what I... I'm so, so sorry, Robert. ...Anyway... call me."

Simon dropped the phone on the coverlet and rolled onto his back, brushing his eyes with the heel of his hand. He waited a moment, trying to regain his composure. After another moment, he groped for his cell and called Vanessa again.

"Me, again. Look... Even if you never want to see me again, can we at least talk one more time first? I don't even know what I want to say, and I'm not sure I want to hear what you might think, or what you might want to say to me, but... I can't leave it like it is right now. So...please."

Simon got up to turn off the light and then crawled under the covers. He rested the hand holding his phone in the center of his chest, thinking it would be a long and restless night. Instead, he fell asleep almost at once. The world and all its recent developments seemed to float on a surface miles overhead, nothing more than a pinprick of light viewed from the bottom of a deep, dark well. When he awoke, he was still clutching the phone and it appeared he hadn't moved at all during the night.

Chapter Fifteen

"There's just something about the morning of The Fourth of July," Axel declared, standing on the patio, one hand on his hip, the other holding a cup of coffee as he gazed into the distance.

"I mean, look," he commanded Simon who had just stepped out through the screen door. "It shouldn't seem any different than any other summer morning: Same sunshine. Same clear blue sky. But there's just something in the air, a sense of expectation. Feel it?"

Simon settled himself into one of the lawn chairs, holding his glass of grape juice in both hands. He studied his grandfather warily. Such reminiscing—any kind of chatter, in fact—was out of character for the man.

"When I was a kid, my brothers and me, we'd have been up since the crack of dawn today. Earlier than at Christmas, even. It'd be hours until anything got going—the canoe races, the parade, the fish fry—but somehow, you just didn't want to miss a minute of the day."

"Where's Grandma?" Simon asked.

"She said something last night about helping out at the museum this morning. The place is all decked out in bunting, and they're selling old-time, hand-squeezed lemonade. Wearing those authentic, collar-to-ankle dresses with the petticoats and stuff. Which means she'll be back around noon, hands sticky and sore, sour-smelling and grouchy as hell."

"Then why does she do it?"

"She says it makes her feel good." He turned, fixing Simon with a solemn gaze for a half-second before they both laughed. "How's the leg today?" he asked.

Simon glanced down at his knee for the first time since rolling out of bed. It was slightly more pinkish than the rest of his skin.

"Fine," he said. "I barely even feel it."

Axel nodded. "So, you have all kinds of plans for the day?"

"I'm working ten-thirty to six. After that, I dunno."

"Well, you'll be done in plenty of time for the fireworks. The concert and barbecue, too, if that interests you."

His grandson offered a noncommittal nod. Axel studied Simon's downturned head.

"I don't think you'd've been as gung-ho as my brothers and me were, way back when," he observed. "Of course, we were a little young for girls at that point in our lives. Not sure you would have wanted to hang out with us at all, now that I think about it."

Simon drained the last of his grape juice, then wiped his purple lips with the back of his hand. "What will you and Grandma be doing today, once she gets back?"

"Well, I haven't checked, but I imagine we'll find our way over to the cookout later in the afternoon and then claim a spot on the beach to watch the fireworks. You and Vanessa'd be welcome to join us, if you can't find anything better to do."

"I might," Simon said after another moment. "I just might." He got to his feet. "Check with you later, Doo-Dah."

Axel watched in silence as the younger man opened the screen door and slipped back inside. Then he turned to face the back yard once more. He took a sip from his mug.

"Youth," he declared once more, this time to a hummingbird buzzing around the feeder a few feet from his head.

As he dressed for work, Simon tried both telephone numbers again, and got no answer from either. Thrusting his cell into his pocket, he snatched up his car keys and left his room.

"I'm on my way to work, Doo-Dah!" he hollered on his way out the front door.

Crossing the parking lot from his car to The Lodge, he made one last attempt, and was unprepared when Vanessa answered.

"Oh. Uh, hi," he said. "I'd just about given up."

"My cell was dead," she told him. "I just finished re-charging it. Where are you?"

"Just about to start my shift at work. You okay?"

"I'm fine. You?"

"Oh, you know," he responded vaguely. He was climbing the steps and in another moment had entered and was crossing through the lobby. "Feeling like a douche, mostly."

"Oh, well," was her noncommittal response. "So, what's the plan for tonight?"

"Oh. Um, well, you want to see the fireworks?"

"Of course!"

"Great. Well, how about I call you as soon as I'm leaving work? That'll be about six. I can come get you, or meet you, if you're already out doing things."

"Okay."

"Oh, and Vanny? Um... Would you do something for me?"

"What?"

"See if you can't reach Robert. I've got his number here, hold on a sec. He's not picking up, and I don't know if it's just because it's me, or if it's something else. Do you mind?"

"No, I'll do it. Hold on, though; let me grab something to write with. Do you want me to call you back if I talk to him?"

"No. Not unless... I mean, if he's fine, then, no. But if... Well, no, I'm sure he's okay. I just..."

"I get it," she said.

By the middle of his shift, Simon's knee had begun to ache, first just a little, but then with growing intensity. All the bussing, all the carrying of water pitchers and coffee pots, the standing and the walking and the crouching to retrieve dropped napkins and silverware, everything was conspiring to wear down his resistance.

"Sweetie, what's the matter with you?" Merilee asked. She'd watched him make his way across the restaurant floor, one leg trailing the other.

"I banged up my knee last night; I'll be fine." His breath, he realized as he spoke, was coming in ragged little bursts, as if somehow, because of the pain, he couldn't draw enough air into his lungs.

Merilee regarded him skeptically. "Go sit down in the break room," she instructed. "Put your leg up for ten minutes. The other kids can cover for you."

"It's all right," he assured her. "I've got barely an hour to go."

"Go sit down," she said again, more firmly this time. And so he did. Alone in the back, leg resting across the seat of a plastic chair, he attempted to roll up his pants leg, but he couldn't fold it back enough to expose his knee. Just as well, he decided. He could tell from some tentative poking and prodding that it had swollen. It was probably better he didn't have a visual, at least not until he had finished his shift and could do something about it. Damn. He'd given up enough shifts this week already, to accommodate Vanessa's visit; he didn't want to lose more now, because he couldn't walk.

Neither sitting nor elevating his leg for ten minutes seemed to have made a difference. The pain was the same; manageable, but insistent. He scrounged four aspirins from the first-aid kit, swallowing them with a handful of water and returned to the restaurant, assuring Merilee that he felt a little better and trying as best he could for the final hour of work, to conceal his limp.

"It's your leg, isn't it?" Vanessa asked, once she had opened the door and slid into the passenger seat alongside Simon ninety minutes later. She hadn't seen him walk; it was the blanched pallor of his face that gave him away.

"It was fine until I walked on it all afternoon." He put the car in gear and pulled away from the curb. "It really just needs a couple of days of me not doing anything. I've got it wrapped now, and that helps a little."

"So I guess we don't go dancing," she said. "What do you want to do?"

"I just want to sit somewhere, and have something cold to drink, and take it easy. And talk," he added. "I guess we should talk."

"I never got hold of Robert," Vanessa told him later, as they sat waiting in the drive-through lane at the hamburger stand. They'd placed their order for Cokes, but there were three cars between them and the delivery window. "I tried three times. I left a message once, and just hung up the other times. He never called back."

"Me, too." Simon idly slid one forefinger back and forth across the top of the steering wheel. "On my way into work this morning, I swung by that house. His car was gone from the driveway, so I guess that's a good sign. I guess he made it home all right."

He turned abruptly to Vanessa.

"I can't even believe that was me last night, Vanny. I, I hate myself for what I did."

"It's okay, Simon."

"No, it's not. It's not okay. I've been in fights before; well, once, back in sixth grade, when a kid started something with me. But that was different. He swung first. I can't believe that the first time ever I punch somebody in the face, it's Robert. *Robert!*" he repeated for emphasis.

"You'd had a few beers," she reminded him.

He shook his head.

"That's not it. That's not the reason. I... I..." he trailed off helplessly.

"What, then?"

So many thoughts and images were crowding his brain. But how to put them into words without sounding petty, or like a jerk?

"Robert... He... We're not friends, Vanny. Not really. We weren't even back when I lived here, years ago. He probably thought we were, because I tried to be nice to him, but we never were."

The cars ahead of them began to move. He took his foot from the brake and they rolled forward one space.

"He's always been the kind of kid people try to avoid. Not because he was a jerk, or anything, but because...well, you see how he is. Just...you know...so freaking *different.* And if you hung around with him, you worried people would think you were different, too." Simon shot her a quick glance, his eyes troubled, and then he looked away again. "I *hate* that I feel that way, but I do. I hate that I wind up spending time with him because I know nobody else will. All these years later, none of that has changed. He hasn't changed, and it makes me realize I haven't, either."

Now, at last, they were at the window, receiving their drinks. Vanessa held the cups as Simon accepted the change, thrusting it into his shirt pocket.

"And, you see, I let it build up all this week. Every time we turned around, there he was: At the marina, at the concert, at my grandparents' house, even. I wanted to spend time with just you, but there was Robert, always standing around, waiting."

"I know," she said softly.

Simon glanced both directions and then gunned the engine, sending the car out of the parking lot and into the road. Vanessa clutched both Cokes tightly, trying to keep either from spilling.

"Just there, just waiting," Simon continued, "Hoping we'll ask him to do something with us, and inviting us over to some old lady's house where he's got beer and potato chips, but not a fucking clue. And I don't have the balls to just tell him No, to at least say No once. And so, what happens? The week goes along, and I get more and more resentful. For some stupid reason, I think eventually he's going to get it, going to see that we don't want him there *all the time,* but this is *Robert* we're talking about, and I should know better."

He shook his head as she attempted to hand him his drink. They drove in silence for a minute.

"You think you're one kind of a person, and then, in a flash, you see that you're really not," he continued finally. "I knew I was irritated last night, Vanny, pissed that, for no reason I could think of, I'd given away our next-to-last night together, and for what? To hang with some guy I don't even consider a friend? Because I thought I was doing him a favor? And so there we are, sitting in the dirt by the lake, watching him make an ass of himself, and I suddenly realized that he didn't care what we'd given up. I guess he thought we really didn't have anything better to do than be down there with him."

"You wanted him to be grateful," Vanessa suggested.

"But why should he be? And why should I expect that from him? Is that the only reason I'm a nice guy—or try to be—just so people will recognize that about me?"

"You *are* a nice guy."

He expelled a long, slow breath. "I saw the expression on your face, when you stopped me from hitting him again. You didn't think I was a nice guy right then, did you?"

"Where are we going?" she asked suddenly. Simon had turned off the main road and they were driving through the curved, hilly streets of a subdivision with handsome ranch-style homes and well-manicured lawns on either side. A moment later, he guided the car to the curb.

"This is where Robert and his family live," he explained, shutting off the engine and unfastening his seatbelt. "You don't have to come with me, but I just want to check up on him."

But she did accompany him up the walk and to the front porch where they rang the doorbell and stood waiting.

"Maybe they've all gone to the marina for the barbecue and the fireworks," Simon said when several seconds had passed. "I didn't think about that." But then, the door swung open and a slender teenage girl with dishwater blonde hair regarded them warily.

"Oh, hey, are you Heather?" he asked. "I'm Simon Perkins. I don't know if you remember me, or not. I went to school with your brother."

"Yeah?" she said. From her noncommittal tone, they couldn't tell whether she did remember or whether she was merely acknowledging that she understood what he was saying.

"Is he here?"

"Robert!" she hollered, turning her chin slightly to aim her voice over her shoulder, but never taking her eyes from the visitors. "Robert!" she bellowed again, a little louder this time. When no answer came within a few seconds, she said, "Guess not."

"Do you know where he might have gone?"

She shook her head.

They seemed to be at an impasse. Heather remained on the threshold, one hand propped on the door with an expression that indicated their business might be concluded. Vanessa took the initiative.

"Well, have you seen him today?" she asked.

As the younger girl appeared to be thinking this over, they heard another voice from somewhere behind her.

"Heather? Who is it?"

"Some people who know Robert—" was all Heather managed to say before Mrs. MacKenzie had appeared in the doorway, looking with astonishment over the top of her daughter's head.

"—Simon Perkins!" she declared, beaming. "Good Lord, it has been way too long!" She nudged Heather aside and pushed the screen door open wide. "Come in, come in, this minute!" As Vanessa and Heather stood on opposite sides watching, Brenda MacKenzie enveloped him in an all-encompassing hug.

"I was hoping I'd get to see you! I told Robert he should bring you around, but you know how he is." Releasing him, she held him at arm's length, still smiling. Then she transferred her gaze to Vanessa. "And this must be the girlfriend. He mentioned your name, but I'm sorry; I can't seem to remember..?"

Vanessa introduced herself and promptly found herself drawn into a hug, as well.

"Come sit down!" Mrs. MacKenzie urged. "Jim?" she hollered towards the back of the house. "Jim, come in here a minute!"

They left Heather standing by the open front door and followed her mother into the living room.

"Well, we really can't stay long," Simon said, but he was interrupted when Brenda shouted once more.

"Jim? It's Simon Perkins, and Vanessa, his girlfriend. Come say hi!" To her guests, she added, "He's out on the patio, on the phone. We'll get him in here a minute." She patted the back of the sofa. "My Lord, Simon, you've shot up. I guess I shouldn't be surprised; Robert has, too. But I have this memory of you being so much smaller. How's your mom?"

"Well, I'm... She's good," Simon said, trying to select one part of Brenda's chatter to answer. When she patted the back of the couch once more, he and Vanessa settled themselves on the edge of the sofa cushions. "She talks about you every once in awhile; how she misses you and her other friends. Um... where is..."

But now Mr. MacKenzie was there, too, holding a mobile phone in one hand and a glass of tea in the other.

"Well, look at this!" he declared. Sliding the phone into his pocket, he thrust his hand at Simon, who stood once more to shake it. "How are you? No, don't get up," he ordered Vanessa, who was starting to rise, as well. "Sit yourselves back down. You want something to drink? Brenda, did you ask them if they want something to drink?"

Simon glanced at Vanessa and then said, "No, thank you. We just came by for a minute to—"

"A glass of iced tea," Brenda decided. "You can stay long enough for half a glass of tea, can't you? You're probably on your way to the lake and the fireworks, but indulge us. It's been so long. You're working at the Lodge again this summer, right?"

"Yes, yes I am." Simon had to raise his voice as Mrs. MacKenzie had left the room to fetch refreshments.

"What did you do to your leg?" Jim MacKenzie asked. Settling in a chair opposite them, he gestured to the elastic bandage wrapped around Simon's knee.

"Oh. Uh..." Simon felt his face flush. "I just... I banged it against something. It's nothing."

"Water-skiing? Or volleyball? Robert says you guys have been playing volleyball."

"No, nothing like that. I just... I think I bumped into something at work, is all."

"Do you take sugar? Lemon?" Brenda's disembodied voice drifted through the doorway.

"Yes, please," Vanessa answered for both of them.

"College?" Mr. MacKenzie interjected. "I suppose you both start college in the fall, like Robert?"

"Uh, yeah. I'll be going—"

"—Here we are!" Brenda announced, re-entering with a tray, glasses, and several other items. She placed it on the coffee table in front of her guests. "You can add your own sugar. I tossed some cookies on a plate, too. So: What did I miss?"

Simon gave Vanessa a helpless sidelong glance as she reached for a glass of tea.

"I guess Robert isn't here tonight," he said. "That's what Heather said, anyway."

The MacKenzies exchanged a glance. Brenda shrugged.

"I'm not sure where he is, actually." She smiled. "I suppose we thought he was somewhere with the two of you. That's where he seems to be all the time any more. We've barely seen him all week. Funny, I usually find myself tripping over him once or twice a day, but not lately."

Only Vanessa was aware of how Simon's shoulders sagged. She stirred her tea.

"Do you think he might be at the lake?" she asked. "Did... Did he say anything to you before he left?"

Both adults considered this a second, brows furrowed. Shaking his head, Jim spoke first.

"Truth to tell, I don't think I've seen him today at all. I had a tee time at seven this morning, so I was up and gone by six-thirty. Nobody else was awake yet. I only got back middle of the afternoon. Has he been around since?" He looked at his wife.

"I don't think I've seen him since breakfast," she said after some hesitation. "I noticed we were running low on milk, and so I told the kids if they wanted cereal, then I'd have to... No, wait; that was just Heather, now that I think about it." She tapped her chin meditatively with her index finger. "Robert was still in the shower, then. I don't think I've actually spoken to him face to face today, either." She leaned around the corner. "Heather?" she called.

"What?" came a petulant reply from down the hall.

Brenda rolled her eyes at the others in a this-is-what-I-have-to-deal-with sort of way.

"Did Robert tell you where he was going today?"

"He *never* tells me where he's going, and I don't ask."

"Heather, come here!" her father commanded. A second later when she appeared in the doorway, he said, "We're not going to conduct a conversation shouting from one room to the next. Do you have any idea where your brother is?"

"I already said that I don't," she retorted in a put-upon whine. "The last time I saw him, he was putting things in his car. Then he got in and drove away. It was maybe ten o'clock this morning. I don't know if he's been back since then, or not."

"What kind of things?" Simon asked.

"I don't know." Heather's tone softened. She didn't know Simon well enough to be as dismissive with him as she could be with her family. "A bag... Just stuff. Maybe he was going to do yard work at that old lady's place again. Mow the lawn and things."

"Oh. Oh, sure," her mother said, brightening. To Simon and Vanessa, she added, "There was an older woman in town who died last spring. She and Robert had become friendly, and he still goes over to water her yard and cut the grass, even though nobody's asked him to, and he doesn't get paid for it. But that's Robert, for you."

Vanessa and Simon received this news with impassive nods.

"Well, we'll check for him down at the lake, then," Simon said. He stood. "But if he comes back here first, would you tell him I'm looking for him?"

"Of course." The others rose to their feet, as well.

"Thanks for the tea," Vanessa told Brenda.

"So nice to meet you, and to see you again, Simon," Mrs. MacKenzie said. "Please come by anytime, whether Robert's here, or not."

It was when they were at the front door, ready to step onto the front porch that Simon wheeled abruptly.

"I... I have to tell you this," he blurted, facing their hosts.

"Robert and I had a fight last night. It was my fault, completely my fault, and I've been trying to find him today, to apologize. He hasn't returned my calls, and so that's why I came here: To tell him I'm sorry."

"Oh..."

With the exception of Heather, who, for the very first time, appeared interested in what was happening, everyone in the crowded entryway shifted uncomfortably. Jim MacKenzie cleared his throat.

"Oh," Brenda said a second time. She looked at her husband who was still staring at Simon. "I'm sorry to hear this, Simon."

"I'm sorry, too, Mrs. MacKenzie. Ashamed, actually. I want to tell Robert that, face to face, but I'm not sure he'll let me."

"Simon, I'm sure it's not all that bad."

"It's bad enough," Simon responded.

"What happened?" Heather was looking eagerly from face to face.

"That's really none of our business," her mother told her, although her tone had an uncertain quality to it. She glanced at her husband. "Maybe... Maybe we should try calling him. Just to see..?"

He shook his head. "I think this should be between the boys." He looked at Simon. "Unless you disagree?"

Simon wasn't entirely certain. But as he pondered, another thought came to him. He said, "I got jealous. I thought Robert was hitting on Vanessa. I... I completely overreacted."

This produced an astonished silence that lasted several seconds. Heather was the first to speak.

"You're kidding," she said flatly. "You have got to be kidding."

"No. I'm not." He regarded her solemnly and she lowered her eyes.

"Simon, I... I'm sure you must have been mistaken," Mrs. MacKenzie said dazedly. "Robert wouldn't do that. Not to a friend."

"I know that now," he offered contritely. "I was a complete jerk, and now I want to make things right, if he'll let me."

"We'll have Robert call you," Jim MacKenzie promised.

"No, don't do that. Don't make him call me. Like you said, it's really just between him and me. But maybe I'll just check back, if that's all right."

Just before he stepped off the porch, he turned to face the family, still clustered in the gap of the open screen door. He pointed to his bandaged knee.

"Oh, and this? Robert kind of did it. But I had it coming."

Simon was settling himself behind the steering wheel and Vanessa had just closed the passenger door. Fastening her seat belt, she murmured, "They're still standing there watching us."

"I know." He turned the ignition and pulled the car away from the curb.

Vanessa waited until they were some distance down the street before she faced Simon.

"Why did you do that? Why did you tell them all of that? Are you crazy?"

"Well, they needed some of the details, Vanny."

"Not all of them! Not that many! Now they're all going to be mad because you and Robert had a fight!"

For the first time all day, a smile began to form at the corner of Simon's mouth.

"Maybe a little bit, right now. But after they think about it for awhile, they're gonna try to picture it. Their boy Robert got into a fight, and not only that, but he kicked some butt, besides. Do you suppose they ever thought that could happen?"

"It didn't happen!"

"Didn't it?" He patted his wrapped knee.

Vanessa turned away, folding her arms in front of her chest. "I don't believe you, Simon Perkins. You are a boldfaced liar."

"Says you."

"Yeah, says me! What was that crap about how you thought Robert hit on me? That never happened!"

Simon grew solemn once more. "Actually," he said. "That part is exactly true."

"What are you talking about?"

"Think back to last night, sitting in the living room at that house," he instructed. "Do you remember what you asked him?"

"No!" she retorted. But then she tried to recall the conversations from the previous night. "No..," she said again a moment later, "I can't remember any... *Wait!*" she said abruptly, interrupting her own response. "Are you..? You don't mean when I asked him if..."

"...If there was anyone he had ever been serious about."

Vanessa let her hands drop into her lap as she stared at Simon.

"No!"

"Yes."

"No! There is no possible way he was talking about me when—"

"—When he said Yes, that there had been one person, one time."

"Simon, Robert just met me! A week ago, he didn't even know I existed. You can't get serious about a person when you've been around them like, what, three times? And anyway, I certainly didn't say or do anything to make him think..."

"I didn't say you did."

Vanessa shook her head vigorously. "No," she declared once more emphatically. "I don't know who he was talking about when he said that, but it certainly wasn't me."

They drove in silence for more than a minute.

"I mean, do you really think..?" she ventured finally.

"Yes," Simon told her. "I do. I knew as soon as he said it. All those questions about whether you and I were going to get married? He was curious, Vanny. Not that he was ever going to do anything about it, but he'd fallen under your spell."

"My *spell?* I don't have any spell, Simon."

"You're probably the first girl who's been nice to him, who's treated him like he's just another guy, and not some dork. Of *course* he was saying he could be serious about you."

"So, you…you really were jealous of him? For a minute, anyway?"

"For a minute," he conceded. "Because, this week, when you were treating him like he was just another guy, there were times he started acting like just another guy." He chewed his lower lip reflectively. "And so then I started acting like an asshole."

They were driving on Main Street now, moving at a snail's pace as the other drivers inched their way along, everyone seeking a parking space for the evening's events. The town square was a throng of bodies, and people dashed from one side of the street to the other, threading their way through traffic, seemingly confident nobody would run them down.

"Are we going to go check at that lady's house?" Vanessa asked, once they'd negotiated their way to the other side of the business district where the road was less congested. "To see if that's where he is?"

Simon nodded.

"I have to," he said. "This isn't over."

Chapter Sixteen

Simon was lying in bed, feeling an enormous emptiness in the center of his chest. It was July fifth, dazzling sunlight streaming through the parted curtains above his head. Birds chirped with frenzied good cheer, and the intoxicating scent of fresh-cut grass wafted through the window. Today could very nearly be the twin of the morning almost a week ago when he'd awakened to find that Vanessa was in the kitchen with his grandparents, waiting for him.

But now he was at the other end of that week. Vanessa was gone, or would be soon. She and her family were leaving this morning, so that she could be back to Denver in time for her shift at day camp by this afternoon.

Stucker's Reach was going to seem ridiculously empty now. Eight long weeks stretched between now and the end of August, days to be filled with work, with clearing half-finished plates, re-filling water glasses, folding napkins and re-setting tables. It all seemed so pointless, and it wouldn't have, if she hadn't come to visit and provide a contrast he wouldn't have otherwise noticed.

Simon kicked aside the covers and forced himself to his feet, trying to shake off malaise in the process. He'd spent previous summers in this house, sleeping in this room, working the same job, enjoying evenings and days off with his grandparents and other friends. It had been enough then, and it should be enough now.

Returning from the bathroom, he pulled on a jersey and running shorts. It was only as he stooped to tie his shoes that he remembered he probably wouldn't be able to run with the injured knee.

"Damn," he muttered. After a moment's consideration, he went ahead and finished dressing anyway. He moved down the hallway to the kitchen,

SIMON

testing the weight on his leg. It seemed to be okay this morning, but he recalled how quickly it had begun to hurt at work yesterday afternoon.

"Better not push it," he muttered to himself.

The kitchen was empty, the table and counters bare. His grandmother was probably at work this morning, and his grandfather off on some errand, likely. Simon poured himself a glass of juice, drained it, and then let himself out through the back door.

He retrieved a basketball from a shelf in the garage and stood in the driveway, shooting hoops, not moving much, enjoying the sunshine and soft morning sounds of summer. He couldn't have guessed how much time had passed before he heard a small voice behind him say:

"I know how to play."

Holding the ball against his hip, he turned to find a small boy watching him from the sidewalk.

"You do, huh?"

The boy nodded. He unfolded one of the hands twined behind his back and pointed. "What did you do to your knee?"

"I fell on it." Simon gestured in return. "What did you do to your forehead?"

The boy's hand found its way to his temple, the fingers poking at the center of a dull purple scab as if he needed to touch it in order to remember how it had gotten there.

"I fell on it," he said, nearly parroting Simon. "I was on the swing, and Jennifer pushed me, and I fell off the swing, and that's when I got it. When I fell out of the swing."

"Ouch," Simon said sympathetically. "Was it an accident?" From the description, it was difficult to tell if what he meant was Jennifer—whoever she was—had been pushing him back and forth in the swing, or if she had deliberately shoved him out of it. He found himself thinking about the random acts of mayhem his sister and brother occasionally visited on each other.

But the boy just continued to regard him solemnly.

"I fell in the dirt," he added finally, as if this was all the clarification needed. He was perhaps five or so, right between Joshua and Madeleine in age and size. Simon felt a momentary pang, thinking of them. He crouched on his good knee and held the basketball in front of him.

"Do you want to shoot a couple of baskets?" he asked.

After a second or so of hesitation, the boy stepped forward and took the ball from Simon. It was huge in his small hands, and his face disappeared behind the ball completely as he held it up, preparing to shoot. Simon stood and took a step back.

"You got it?" he asked. For a moment, it appeared the weight of the ball might actually topple the kid. But then he thrust it into the air with surprising strength. It went nowhere near the basket, but it did achieve a respectable height.

"That's pretty good," Simon told him, catching it on rebound. "You've got a lot of power behind you, but you might want to hold the ball a little bit lower, so that you can aim it better. You want to try again?"

He placed the ball back in the boy's hands. "And maybe you want to stand a little closer to the basket," he suggested.

The kid obligingly took a couple of steps forward before launching the ball one more time. He staggered back under the effort, and Simon pressed a hand into the small of his back to keep him from falling backwards into the driveway. This shot was no more successful than the last.

"It's too high!" the boy complained, pointing to the basket.

"Yeah." Simon considered this for a second. Then he placed the ball in the kid's hands one more time. "Can you hold onto that real tight?" he asked.

He put his hands on either side of the boy's waist and lifted him overhead.

"All right, wait until we get closer," he instructed. "Now!" he declared, once he'd carried him up the driveway and they were standing just inches from the rim.

The kid lifted his arms and released the ball. It swooshed neatly through the basket, and he laughed with delight.

"I did it!" he declared.

"Yeah, you did."

"I want to do it again!" the boy said as Simon lowered him to the concrete.

"Here's what you need to do: Do you have a smaller ball at home? You could practice with that. That's what I did when I was younger. I used a littler ball at first, and when I got good with that, I switched to one like this." Simon dribbled the basketball a couple of times, then tucked it under his arm.

"You know what?" he mused. "We might have one in the garage you could have, if you want. You want me to check?"

He lifted the garage door and walked inside. The boy stood outside in the driveway watching as Simon moved around the interior, inspecting shelves and looking into boxes.

"Do you have little kids?" he inquired after a moment.

Simon, lifting the folds of a cardboard box to check within, laughed.

"No. I have a little brother, though. His name's Joshua. If he was here, the two of you could hang out."

"Is he coming?"

"No, probably not any time soon."

The boy collapsed cross-legged in the grass next to the driveway. He had no use for empty promises about playmates who weren't going to show up.

"Ah!" Simon produced a somewhat grimy soccer ball from behind a row of empty flowerpots. He bounced it experimentally on the floor of the garage. It didn't have quite the spring of a basketball, but it wasn't too bad. "Here's something that could work."

As he stepped out of the garage, he heard a female voice. "What are you doing way over here?"

An adolescent girl in jeans, a pink t-shirt and flip-flops was clomping up the street. She stopped at the base of the driveway, placing her hands on her hips and looking at the boy.

"Talking to him." The kid poked a finger Simon's direction. The girl turned, catching sight of him for the first time. She took a half-step back.

"Well, you're not supposed to go further than the corner, you know that," she said. She was talking to the boy, but her eyes were fixed on Simon. "Mom'll be mad if she finds out."

"Hi," Simon greeted her. Noticing her wary expression he stayed in the open garage doorway, keeping a respectable distance between them. "I was trying to find a ball he could take home to practice with." As evidence, he held up the soccer ball.

"He isn't supposed to talk to strangers," the girl said. "He knows that."

"Oh. Oh, sure. We… Uh, he saw me shooting baskets, and…" Simon paused. It occurred to him there was really nowhere for this sentence to go that wasn't going to get one—or both—of them in trouble.

"This is my grandparents' house," he said, instead. "Do you know them? Mr. and Mrs. Perkins? They've lived here forever." Now he was grasping for authenticity. "Are… Are you Jennifer?"

She looked startled. "No." To the boy, she instructed, "Get up."

"Oh. I thought…" Simon gestured to the kid. "He mentioned a Jennifer, and so I thought maybe…" Yet another sentence died unfinished on his lips. What was he going to say? *"He said somebody named Jennifer pushed him and made him get that scab on his forehead, and I thought maybe it was you?"*

The boy had pulled himself to his feet and was walking across the driveway towards the girl. Simon held up the soccer ball.

"Hey… Do you want to take this? It's yours, if you want it."

Both of the children surveyed it dubiously. It was, Simon had to concede, now that he saw it in the sunlight, pretty crappy-looking. He lowered it once more, even before the boy shook his head. Who could blame him? Now they were headed down the street, the kid walking a step ahead of the girl, who had one hand on his shoulder.

"Well…uh… keep practicing!" Simon called after them. They did not look back. Feeling unfairly judged, he lobbed the ball towards the rear of the garage, landing it in the trash can, and then stooped to pick up his basketball where he'd left it alongside the concrete. It was strange to realize that somebody thought he was old enough to have children of his own, and that somebody else apparently thought he might be trying to lure little kids into his garage by offering them used toys.

He had just climbed the steps to the front porch when a car stopped at the curb. He turned to watch as Brenda MacKenzie shut off the engine and climbed out from behind the wheel. Shading her eyes, she looked at Simon over the roof of the car.

"I was hoping to catch you, Simon," she said. She closed the door. "Do you have a few minutes?"

"Oh, sure. Come on up."

They sat in the porch swing gazing across the front yard. Simon balanced the basketball between his knees, fingers resting atop it.

"Robert left for his honor's camp," she began, after a few seconds of silence. "Did your grandmother give you my message last night?"

Simon nodded. "Yes. Thank you. I didn't see him last night at the fireworks or anywhere else, so I was glad when I found out you'd called."

"He left yesterday morning," Mrs. MacKenzie said, after a few seconds of silence. "Apparently when Heather saw him putting things in his car, he was preparing to go right then. He called us about seven last evening."

"Oh." Simon watched her out of the corner of his eye.

"From somewhere in the middle of Kansas. We were fit to be tied." She was running her hands up and down her pants legs. "You think your teenaged son is downtown playing miniature golf, or having a Coke with friends, and then you find out he's four hundred miles across the country, and heading even further east. It calls your parental supervising abilities into question, let me tell you."

"Oh. ...My grandmother didn't tell me any of that. I..."

"There was no point in giving her all the details, or you, either, Simon. What could you have done, except worry, and we already had that covered. Besides, Robert insisted he was fine." She sighed. "It probably comes as no surprise that we've had our...*concerns*...about him over the years. He's not your average kid; never has been."

There was a slight pause. Simon wasn't certain whether she was expecting agreement, but he opted to maintain tactful silence.

"He was supposed to fly to St. Louis. Driving—especially by himself— was never part of the plan. We already had his plane ticket purchased. Of course, Robert was perfectly unflappable about the whole thing on the phone. *'We can always turn the ticket in for another trip,'* he said. As if there was nothing more to the whole thing than that."

"So, what happens now?"

She lifted her hands and then let them fall back into her lap. "Robert's dad and I discussed one or both of us flying out there. So we could...I don't know...shake him until his teeth rattle, to express our displeasure. In fact, we'd have to fly into St. Louis, at this point, anyhow. I'm not sure it's worth spending four hundred bucks or more for the privilege of lecturing him face to face. That might still happen, but in the cold light of day, we're more inclined to let him go ahead and finish his drive and then punish him later."

"Maybe one of you could fly out there when the honor camp thing is over, and drive back with him," Simon suggested.

Brenda MacKenzie nodded. "That's one of the possibilities. In the meantime, he's under strict orders to call us as soon as he arrives, and every day after that. I think we're hoping that will teach him some sort of a lesson."

She looked down at her fingers curled in her lap. "One of the problems with confronting Robert is that he can always offer some fairly reasonable explanation for whatever it is he's done. He doesn't get defensive. He doesn't shout or become emotional. He lets *us* do those things, which definitely weakens our side of the argument."

Simon set his basketball on the floor next to the swing.

"Well, I'm sorry for whatever part I played in all this," he told her. "And for the worry I caused you."

She rested her hands on her knees. "That's why I wanted to come by and tell you this in person. From all appearances, Robert put a lot of thought and planning into this little scheme. He got his car serviced last week so it would be ready for a long trip. He packed half the clothes he owns, judging from the way his room looks right now. He even found a way to get himself a debit card, so money isn't going to be a problem." Brenda shook her head and rolled her eyes, contemplating the depth of her son's alarming ingenuity. Then she shifted in her seat to look directly at Simon.

"He was planning this before you and he got into that fight the other evening; I don't want you beating yourself up, thinking you're somehow to blame for this. You hear me?"

She stood, causing the swing to jostle back and forth slightly, and turned to gaze down at Simon, who was leaning forward, head lowered. She touched his shoulder lightly.

"You and Robert will make up," she said. "I'm sure of that. Friends fight, Simon. It's just what happens sometimes. You've always been so good to him. In case you think I hadn't noticed."

Simon nodded without looking up.

"I'll keep checking in with you, if that's all right," he said. "And let me know what you hear from him."

"I will," she promised. As she descended the porch steps, she turned back to Simon one more time.

"I mean it," she said. "You and Robert will be friends again."

He lifted his head and managed a halfhearted smile as he returned her wave.

Simon spent the rest of the morning pushing the hand mower back and forth across his grandparents' front lawn. As he worked, he tried to recall something Robert had said one night early last week, when they'd all been sitting on the back porch of the old lady's house. What was it, again?

"Pretty soon," he'd said, *"I'm going to get in a car and drive away from here, to college, and then to someplace after that, and never come back. I won't look back, or think back, or even remember what it was like."*

Simon paused the mower midway across the grass to lift the front of his jersey and wipe the streaming sweat from his face.

"He'd had a couple of beers by then, though," he reminded himself. Still, he couldn't stop thinking about this as he guided the mower carefully around the edges of the flowerbeds and lilac bushes, and then turned his attention to the back yard.

It had sounded so resolute.

Chapter Seventeen

The distant, flat horizon shimmered, distorted by a heat-generated optical illusion.

Robert had seen this effect in movies before, but had never experienced it first hand until now. He stood alongside the gas pump, half-listening to the thrumming sound of gasoline rushing through the hose into his tank while experiencing a curious sort of lethargy in his extremities.

St. Louis was less than thirty miles away; his journey nearly at an end. It had been exhilarating up until now, starting with the quiet, well-managed departure yesterday morning, conducted right under his family's nose. Really, the trick was simply in acting natural, not furtive, and then nobody even bothered to ask what he was doing, or what he was loading into his car. And there'd been the first day's drive, descending from the mountains into the eastern Colorado plains. Denver loomed at the base of the foothills, and Robert whizzed along the interstate that bisected the city, buoyed by a heady sense of purpose. *Simon and his family live around here somewhere, and Vanessa and her family, too,* was his fleeting thought as a thousand nameless buildings of all sizes and shapes drifted by on either side. Gradually, these thinned out, finally falling away altogether, conceding to open rolling farmland.

For awhile, there was the thrill of traveling a route he'd never experienced before, though gradually that was overtaken by the tedium of a landscape that seemed unchanged for hundreds of miles. He stopped now and again, sometimes at rest stops to use the bathroom, or to get something to drink, and once just because an exit promised an interesting-sounding museum.

There, Robert had driven down a two-lane highway bordered by tall stalks of corn on either side that seemed to lead only to scattered farmhouses and a decrepit, deserted building that had once been a tavern of some sort.

A humongous tractor was pulled off to one side of the parking lot, and a sunburned man in overalls and baseball cap leaned against one enormous tire, texting on a cell phone. He lifted his face, squinting at the car as Robert drove past him. On impulse, Robert made a u-turn and pulled alongside the tractor, rolling down his window to ask if the fellow knew anything about a museum. The man had scowled at him for several seconds before shaking his head and then turning his attention back to the phone. So Robert had given up and returned to the interstate, disappointed and no longer placing faith in any of the signs posted along his route.

Around five, he'd found a motel off one of the larger exits, situated back from the interstate in a grove of tall green trees and near some restaurants and curio shops. He'd approached the clerk in the front desk lobby with trepidation, but she seemed indifferent to his youth, barely glancing up while processing his debit card. She gave him a cursory glance while inspecting his driver's license, but seemed satisfied with everything on both the license and his face. This had been another exhilarating moment, another threshold crossed. He had checked into a motel all by himself for the first time.

Robert had eaten dinner in one of the nearby coffee shops, sat by the motel swimming pool for half an hour, and then returned to his room where he'd fallen asleep while watching television. In the morning he awakened early, but remained in bed flipping randomly through the channels while trying to forestall beginning his day.

Far away from home, the full weight of his decision was now beginning to press in on him. His carefully orchestrated plan had covered the journey, but nothing beyond its conclusion. St. Louis—his destination—was just over the horizon, but he felt a curious reluctance to reach it. Every move until now had been conducted with bold assurance. It seemed ridiculous for his resolve to falter now, and, lying face down on the bed, Robert tried to ignore the trepidation he was feeling, pretending to be engaged in the snippets of television programs.

Finally, though, he aimed the remote one last time, silencing the TV, and pulled himself off of the bed. He showered, brushed his teeth, and with a final lingering glance around the room, stepped out onto the balcony with his bag and closed the door behind him.

The waitress wiping the counter in the truck stop diner viewed with some interest the shiny-faced boy who shuffled up to one of the stools and paused uncertainly.

"Breakfast or lunch?" she inquired and received a startled look in response. "It's almost eleven," she clarified. "You've got about ten more minutes, if you're wanting eggs or pancakes. After that, you gotta order from this side." She slapped a laminated menu on the counter, flipping it over to demonstrate that one side depicted the breakfast selections, the other side lunch.

"Oh," Robert said. He straddled the stool and sat down.

"Coffee?" she asked, the steaming pot in her hand poised over his cup. The startled expression made a reappearance, which she took as a refusal. Instead, she settled a glass of ice water by his hand.

"Um, waffle, I guess. And a glass of milk." He handed back the menu which she accepted, turning away with what might have been a shake of her head.

He ate slowly, methodically, studying his surroundings with unabashed interest. If aware that he himself was the object of curious glances from the other diners, mostly mechanics, farm hands and the drivers of the large rigs parked outside, he gave no indication.

"Anything else?" the waitress asked when his waffle had been reduced to a few crumbs floating in a pool of syrup.

"No, thank you," he said. But when she brought his ticket, he asked, "Have you ever been to St. Louis?"

"Now and then." The facetiousness of her tone seemed escape his notice. "Why?"

"I'm going there today. I've never been. I'm not sure what to expect."

"Well, I guess you could expect just about anything," she mused. "Depending on what you're going there for."

"It's an honors camp." The boy was looking through his wallet, counting out bills.

"Honors camp... What's that?"

"It's for kids going into college. I guess, anyway. It's two weeks of classes and tours of places. We get one college credit in advance if we complete it."

"Well. You must be pretty smart, then."

Robert shrugged. "It starts tomorrow. Check-in is at noon in Maryville. So I don't know what to do until then. What do you do when you go to St. Louis?"

A man seated a few stools to Robert's left snorted as he settled his coffee mug on the counter. Both Robert and the waitress glanced his direction, but he did not look up.

"I usually do some shopping; visit friends. Take in a movie, sometime. Do you know anybody there?" When he shook his head, she said, "I think you should go right to the campus, then. Do you know how to get there?"

Robert patted the phone in his shirt pocket. "I pulled up directions. I can find it okay. But I don't think I can get into a dorm room until tomorrow."

"Well, try," she urged. "Explain that you're a day early. I'll bet they can figure something out. If not, get a motel room close to the campus, and then stick close. Even in the summertime, there's probably plenty of activities right there at the college in the evenings."

Robert looked uncertain, but he nodded. He settled some money atop the bill and slid it towards her. "There's seven dollars and fifty cents," he said. "With a twenty percent tip, the total would be seven forty-four, so just give me six cents change."

The waitress dutifully brought him a nickel and a penny and then watched through the window as Robert crossed the parking lot and got into his car. She picked up his sticky plate and set it in the bus tub before carrying the coffee pot along the counter, refilling cups as she went.

The man who had snickered earlier nodded his thanks.

"I'm thinking of going to St. Louis next week, Barb," he mimicked. "What do you think I should do while I'm there?"

"Oh, hush." She poured herself a cup and then returned the pot to its burner. She took a gulp and surveyed the thick green landscape and blue sky on the other side of the parking lot.

"What're you worried about?" the man asked, watching her curiously. "He's got to be seventeen or eighteen. Old enough to take care of himself."

Barb set her cup aside with a grimace. She'd had too much coffee this morning already. Her tongue felt sour and acrid.

"I suppose," she sighed. "But it's amazing how stupid those smart kids can be."

Seizing a damp cloth, she proceeded to wipe the counter in wide, vigorous circles.

Chapter Eighteen

His grandparents, separately observing Simon the few days following the July Fourth weekend, had arrived at similar conclusions.

"Do you suppose he and Vanessa had a real falling-out, not just a quarrel?" Honey asked. "He seems awfully quiet lately, even for Simon."

Axel shifted his newspaper to reach for his coffee cup. "Passion at that age, hormones; everything seems more dramatic than it actually is. Kids invite that sort of intensity, if you ask me. Crave it, almost." He settled his cup back on the table and folded the paper across his lap.

"She's a sweet girl," Honey pointed out.

"I wasn't saying anything against her; Simon's a good kid, too."

His wife was quiet for a moment, pondering whether they were arguing or in agreement.

"She's his first serious girlfriend."

"They'll fix whatever's wrong," he predicted. "For awhile. And then they'll go their separate ways. There will be others. For each of them."

"You're such a cynic."

"I'm a father," he reminded her. "I've been through this a time or two."

Their thoughts drifted back to Simon's dad.

"I don't know." Honey shook her head slowly. "Larry was so different at that age. He dated, but he was never really serious about a girl until later. He... He seemed to float above all the drama. Girls came and went so fast I stopped trying to remember their names. There never seemed to be much anguish. But Simon..." She let her hand drop into her lap.

"He takes things differently," Axel conceded. "But that doesn't mean we should. We'll watch, and make ourselves available if he wants to talk. Otherwise, we stay out of it."

Her husband spoke with such assuredness that Honey found herself wondering where he'd come by that confidence. How did he know these things? Would he be this knowledgeable if they'd had girls and granddaughters, instead?

They both gazed across the backyard as if Simon was present, occupied with some activity and barely out of earshot. He was, in fact, already at work, and they were looking at nothing more than the empty lawn and trees and lilac bushes with dark, heavy leaves bobbing in the sun.

"It has occurred to you, hasn't it," Axel began, "That this may be the last summer he spends with us? Now may be the last real time we have with him."

This was a startlingly self-revelatory thing for her husband to say, bordering on the maudlin. Honey's impulse was to offer up a contrasting opinion: Oh, surely not. There would still be those summers between the college years. Simon would still need employment, and why not here another time or two?

But something stopped her. There *had* been a different feel to his stay this time, from the day he'd arrived, though she couldn't pinpoint where the feeling originated.

Simon's return in the summers always brought startling changes, of course. Each time, Honey felt as if she was meeting a new version of her grandson: Taller, leaner, a deeper voice, a gauzy suggestion of facial hair. There was an initial kind of shyness around the boy she'd known from the first day of his life, as they readjusted to each other during those first tentative hours. But within a day, he would be *Simon* again and she was *Grandma,* stoically accepting that still more aspects of the little boy she'd known so well were gone.

But Axel was right. If Simon were to come back next summer to stay with them and work, it would be with a year of college under his belt, a year spent on his own, learning and growing in all sorts of ways. A chasm would have opened between them in that time. How would he not be restless in tiny Stucker's Reach by then, saddled with a pair of doddering, out of touch grandparents?

"Then it's been a good time," she said, reaching across to Axel's chair, resting her hand on his. "I want more, but if this is all we get, well, I'll take it."

Simon had been uncharacteristically sloppy at work all week. He'd delivered things to the wrong tables, forgot to restock silverware, and had to be reminded repeatedly to complete other tasks.

"What is *up* with you?" Merilee demanded in exasperation. "On Monday, I figured you were just hung over from Fourth of July. Then I decided you were missing your girlfriend. Now, I'm wondering what drug you're on. Either knock it off, or share some with me, so that I can float around in a daze, too." With a clatter, she dropped the dinner dishes he was supposed to have cleared into a bus tub. "Now, take all this into the dishwasher. We're nearly out of bread plates."

Simon lifted the heavy tub and carried it to the back of the kitchen without comment. On his way back, he collected a stack of clean bread plates and brought them to the serving station. Merilee watched all of this, frowning slightly. Since he hadn't offered an explanation, she didn't press further.

"Decaf to the booth in the corner," she instructed. "Remember: *Decaf!*"

"Simon!" his mother declared with delight, and then regretted it. The kids, barely settled at the table in front of their dinners, vacated their chairs instantly and clustered around her legs, jumping towards the receiver she held to her ear.

"Simon! Simon!"

"I want to talk to him!"

"No, me!"

"Where are you, Simon? When are you coming home?"

Livia moaned. "My bad. You'd probably better talk to each of them for a minute, or we're not going to get any peace."

"Sure, Mom. Put the monsters on."

She handed the phone to Madeleine. "One minute!" she advised sternly and then turned and swept Joshua up in her arms to forestall the jostling for the receiver that was sure to follow. He waved his arms frantically over her shoulder as she carried him into the living room.

"No, me! I wanted to be first!"

"It'll only be a few seconds," Livia promised her youngest, knowing this was scant consolation for a four year-old.

"And there were these big purple ones, Simon!" Maddie was describing the fireworks they'd seen. "And gold, and this one red one that kept falling and falling, and I bet you could have caught some of it, if you'd been here!"

"She's telling all the stuff!" her brother howled. "I won't have nuthin' to tell him!"

"Of course you will. You can tell him how you've learned to do the backstroke, and that you've helped Dad paint the house."

Madeleine, somehow managing to talk and eavesdrop at the same time, immediately switched topics.

"Oh, and wait 'til you see the house, Simon! We've been painting it, and—"

"—That's enough," Liv commanded, coming back into the kitchen. "Tell your brother goodbye now. Your minute's up."

Several seconds of mayhem ensued during which Josh cried and struggled out of his mother's arms, and his sister attempted to elude capture by ducking under the table with the receiver while delivering snippets of any additional things that occurred to her.

"You!" Livia snapped, once she had retrieved the telephone receiver, "Will go and sit on the couch in the living room, young lady, and be perfectly still while Josh has his turn."

"But I—"

"—This instant! One peep while Joshy is on the phone, and there will be no ice cream all week!"

Livia handed the receiver to Josh, who held it to his tear-stained face and quavered, "…Simon?"

An instant later, the sunshine had broken through, trauma forgotten, and he was chattering excitedly about painting the house, about a bulldozer he'd seen moving dirt at the end of the street, and a variety of other topics. He was determined to get his money's worth of his moment on the phone.

He wasn't even deterred by the sudden blare of noise from the next room. Livia marched across the hall to silence the TV that Madeleine had turned on to full volume.

"I didn't make a peep," she informed her mother nonchalantly. "I just wanted to watch television."

Livia turned off the TV and carried the remote back with her into the kitchen. She allotted Joshua an extra minute's conversation and then took back the phone.

"I'll pay for those extra minutes," she told Simon.

"Nah," he said. "It was worth it."

"I can't remember," she mused. "Were you that big a handful when you were their age, or was it only because you didn't have siblings to fight with and make me crazy?"

He laughed, but ventured no answer.

"So, what's up?" she asked.

"I wanted to run an idea by you. It's going to sound kind of crazy, but just let me get it all out before you say anything…"

Chapter Nineteen

"What are you doing here?" Robert asked. His tone was dull and flat. His hands dangled at his sides, fingertips brushing against each other.

Simon had just come through the airport's security gate. He stepped to one side, away from the flow of people emptying out of the concourse.

"I'm here to ride home with you," he said.

Robert peered over Simon's shoulder, craning his neck to look through the sea of travelers moving past him into the main terminal.

"Did you come with my dad?"

Simon shook his head.

"I came instead of him."

Robert, brow furrowed, studied the other boy and then shook his head. "I don't believe you." He looked again past the *Do not enter* signs and down the corridor.

Simon adjusted the strap of his carry-on bag, sliding it up his shoulder. "Well, call your folks, then."

Robert scrutinized Simon's face for a few seconds with an expression that wasn't quite a scowl, but close. Abruptly he turned and strode briskly across the tiled floor towards a set of escalators. Simon broke into a trot to follow. At the top of the moving stairs, he placed a hand on Robert's shoulder.

Robert shrugged it off with a shake. The two of them rode to the lower level in silence, Simon perched one step behind.

"Why didn't they tell me?" Robert inquired of the empty air in front of him. "It doesn't make sense." Though, despite his astonishment, it was starting to. This was the sort of exercise his parents would devise to teach him a lesson. From earlier phone conversations, he knew Simon had told them some of what had happened at the lake that night. Robert had downplayed the whole thing as insignificant, and volunteered no details of his own. Perhaps that had been his mistake. That was probably why Simon was now standing less than a foot behind him.

He stepped off of the escalator on the lower floor and walked some distance without looking back, though he knew Simon was keeping pace. It had been his intention to pull out his phone and call home, but that impulse had faded. It was probably what they were expecting, and he didn't want to hear the smug, amused tone that would accompany the confirmation that *yes*, they had sent Simon to retrieve him.

Now Robert faltered just slightly. He didn't know for sure where he was, in relation to the parking lot where he'd left his car. He'd chosen the escalator route as a handy escape, not because it was the way he'd come or because he knew where it led. He stopped and faced Simon.

"You're not riding home with me," he announced.

"I'm not, huh?"

Simon's expression and tone seemed innocuous enough, yet faintly challenging.

"You're supposed to be bussing tables back in Stucker's Reach. You don't have any business here," Robert informed him.

The other boy shrugged.

"Well, here I am." He looked around the terminal. "I really need to pee. I wonder where the restrooms are. I should have done it on the plane, I guess, but I didn't think about it then." His gaze returned to Robert. "I'm going to go find one. I guess now would be the time for you to take off. I only have a one-way ticket and nowhere near enough money with me to buy another. If you left now, I'd be totally screwed."

He swung his bag over to his other shoulder and went in search of a bathroom.

Robert remained where he was, shifting his weight from one foot to the other, glancing around for some indication of where in the airport he might be. A tall counter ran nearly the entire length of the wall to his right, housing countless different car rental services. Opposite these were floor-to-ceiling windows and sliding glass doors through which he could see buses, shuttles and bright yellow taxis lined up next to the curb. His car, he remembered suddenly, was on the upper level of a parking structure.

He turned and retraced his steps. At the foot of the escalator, he stopped. Standing just off to the side, he watched the flat silver grids slide into view and fold themselves into steps. They rose to the floor above like a metallic, reverse waterfall, flowing upward in precise, perpendicular waves. He heaved a sigh while he waited for Simon to return from the bathroom.

Simon offered no more apologies. He'd left enough in Robert's voicemail days ago. At first, the conversation in the car was infrequent, hesitant. Primarily one-sided.

"Did you like Honors Camp?"

"It was okay."

"What all did you do?"

"Just stuff. Classes. Tours."

"Did you go to that arch-thing?"

"The Gateway Arch, you mean?" Robert snorted derisively, but did not otherwise answer the question. He gripped the steering wheel more firmly and kept his eyes on the road.

"I've never been," Simon said. He was watching the St. Louis outskirts whiz past his side window. "I was at the Grand Canyon, once. And we went to Yellowstone. But that was when I was really little, and I don't remember much about it. I don't remember seeing any geysers, for instance, but I probably did."

This disclosure was met with silence. Simon shifted in the passenger seat and settled back against the headrest. The prospects of a dreary, uncomfortable ride home loomed in front of them, but then, he'd expected as much. He folded his arms and abandoned any further attempts at conversation.

Forty-five minutes later, a band of dark blue had developed on the western horizon. Within minutes, it had risen, looming over them, turning ominously black. Raindrops began to spatter the windshield, though it was still sunny and clear directly overhead. Even with the windows rolled up, the air within the car took on a leaden, murky feeling. The wind rushed at them in bursts, and Robert fought to keep the car in its lane. Simon's fingers dug into his thighs and he clenched his jaw.

A tarp covering the bed of the truck in front of them billowed and flapped in the gusty assault. Abruptly, one corner pulled loose, waving frantically and timed so precisely with an abrupt crack of thunder that it seemed as if the noise had come from the canvas itself. Both teens jumped, and Robert tapped the brake. They dropped back a car length or so.

"Jeez," he gasped, breaking his own icy silence, "No warning. I didn't even see any lightning; did you?"

Simon merely shook his head, too startled to respond.

And then the rain was upon them, slapping across the hood and windshield like someone angrily shaking out a bed sheet. It rippled the view and pummeled the car, sounding like hundreds of pebbles hurled from all directions. Suddenly, the truck in front of them was no longer visible, obscured by gray water that seemed to be falling both down and up at the same time. Robert lifted his foot from the gas pedal altogether.

"What should we do, do you think?" His voice was taut with fear. "Should I pull over?"

Simon looked in his side mirror and then twisted in the seat to get a better view through the rear window. He could see headlights of a car following some distance behind, but guessed the driver of that vehicle couldn't see them any more clearly than they could see the truck in front of them, not with the rain and the backsplash.

"Not yet," he advised, facing forward once again. He tried to summon back scraps of information from his driver's education class, something that might be useful to this situation. "Somebody might rear-end us if they don't see the car in time. Maybe we'll come to an overpass or an exit soon. It would be safer to stop there."

Robert nodded. His face and neck had gone very pale. Occasionally the boys caught glimpses of the truck some distance ahead of them, but then the curtain of water would close once more and they were left with the eerie sensation of not moving at all, having no point of reference by which to gauge momentum.

Simon was terrified they might at any minute plow headlong into the back of the truck, should it slow or come to a stop, or that somebody driving blindly behind would do the same to them. Or that Robert might miss a curve in the road and send the car rolling through a field of alfalfa or something. But there seemed to be no logical course of action except to keep going until they could find a safe alternative.

"This can't keep up for long," he murmured, almost offering it as a prayer. The back of his shirt, he realized, was soaked through with sweat and clung to the back of the seat.

"Okay," Robert said suddenly, leaning so far forward his chin was nearly in contact with the steering wheel. "I think we just passed a sign. Maybe we're getting close to something."

A flat gray shape whizzed past Simon's window.

"Yeah," he said. "I saw one, too. I'll keep looking. You watch out for that truck—it might slow down if we're coming up to an exit."

"There's one," Robert announced and twisted the steering wheel. Simon couldn't see it, though, and placed a hand on the dashboard as the car veered from the highway and began to rise. He was momentarily convinced they were airborne, hurling to their demise, but no. Robert had indeed guided them up an exit ramp, though the airborne sensation was because their tires had lost contact with the pavement, and they were hydroplaning, riding a thin sheath of rushing water between the wheels and asphalt.

"Robert..." Simon uttered weakly as the car fishtailed and seemed to pick up speed, even though Robert was tapping the brake.

The ramp was a long, gently rising one, however, and Robert removed his foot from the pedal. Simon could feel the wheels regaining traction. And whether it was the car leaving the interstate or the rain lessening in intensity, they could now see a greater distance in front of them, enough to discern earth from sky, at least. Further up the ramp, Robert pulled off onto the graveled shoulder and put the engine in park.

"I... need to stop for a minute," he said in a voice weak with relief.

Simon nodded, heart pounding.

"I'll get us someplace out of the rain in a little bit," Robert added.

"Here's fine," Simon assured him.

They sat, saying nothing more, staring through a windshield that was rapidly fogging over due to their deep breaths of relief.

Everything about the drenched, silvery landscape seemed abruptly wonderful to Simon.

Gradually the sensation of blood thudding in his ears receded as his pulse returned to normal. He rubbed his moist palms against the legs of his jeans.

"You handled that really well, Robert. I figured we were toast."

Robert nodded, as if he couldn't quite believe it himself. His fingers still clutched the steering wheel.

"Look," he said. "There's a car pulled off up ahead. Probably waiting out the storm, too."

"Yeah." Simon squinted through the glass. The other vehicle was a hundred feet or so ahead of them and though the rain was slackening some, they couldn't tell if it was occupied.

"I'm gonna need gas pretty soon," Robert said. With that, he turned off the ignition. For a few seconds, there was just the sound of the rain hitting the car. He sighed. "So, did my folks tell you when they expect us back?"

Simon shrugged. "They didn't say for sure. A day or so, I guess. I don't even know how many hours it takes to drive home."

"You can do it in a day, if you leave early enough. But I stayed overnight in a motel on my way out. We should probably do that, too, especially since it's already afternoon." He raised the lid of the compartment between the seats. "You want a candy bar, or something?" He lifted out a Snickers bar.

Simon inspected the contents of the storage compartment. It was well-stocked with snack items. Pawing through them, he selected a package of M&Ms.

"Thanks."

He tore open a corner of the pouch and dumped several into the palm of his hand. The scent of chocolate filled the car's interior as they ate. Their near-brush with mortality had evidently caused Robert to re-evaluate his hostility towards Simon, at least temporarily.

"I don't know what I expected that honors camp to be like, exactly," he said finally. He licked his candy wrapper and then wadded it into a crumpled ball. "But not what it turned out to be. It was like high school, except with a bunch of people I didn't know."

His tone disclosed nothing about whether he thought this was a good thing or a bad thing. He studied the wadded-up wrapper in his hand, turning it over and over.

"Well," Simon began hesitantly, after some consideration, "Was it supposed to give you a taste of what college is going to be like, maybe?"

The other boy's shoulders rose and fell. "I guess," he said at last. "I mean, we were staying on a campus. In dorms, and everything. We had roommates."

"Yeah? How was yours?"

Another shrug. "Fine. I guess. He was almost always off somewhere, hanging out with other people. He didn't like that I had brought my alarm clock," he added. "He said it was summer, and he didn't want to have to wake up to that every morning. We argued about that."

"Oh. Well, who did you hang out with, then?"

This time Robert shook his head, a fairly vague gesture, although Simon guessed its meaning.

"And yeah, we went to The Gateway Arch," Robert conceded. "Naturally. And to a museum, and on this restored riverboat one evening. And there were guest lecturers, and seminars."

"Did you like those?"

"Some. One about computer applications that are supposed to help with homework and writing papers, that one was good. But some of the stuff, well, I don't know. *Time Management and Effective Study Techniques? Marketing Yourself in School and Beyond?*" He transferred his gaze from the candy wrapper to Simon. "What's any of that, anyway? But I went to everything, because, well, isn't that what you're supposed to do? But a lot of the kids didn't, or went for awhile and then stopped. And you know what's weird? Nobody seemed to care. Not the instructors or the people in charge."

The sigh that followed was one of both frustration and bewilderment.

"I just don't get it," he added, quite unnecessarily. "Why would you even bother coming to an honors camp, in that case?"

Offhand, Simon could think of a few reasons, but none, he suspected, that would carry any weight with his companion.

"Well," he asked instead, "Was it fun? The whole experience, I mean."

"I already told you: It was *fine.*".

Simon was debating whether there was anything to be gained by trying to explain that *fine* did not automatically translate into *fun,* but their attention was drawn to something else. A hundred feet ahead, an arm had extended from the driver's side window of the other car, and was beckoning through the rain.

"What do they want, do you think?" Robert asked.

"I guess they want you to pull up closer."

Robert gave Simon a sidelong glance, then turned the key in the ignition. Putting the car in gear, he crept along the shoulder of the ramp until they were just a few feet behind the other vehicle.

The door opened and a young woman in shorts and a t-shirt emerged. She unfolded a sweatshirt and held it over her head in an attempt to shield herself from the rain as she trotted through the mud back to their car. Robert lowered his window a few inches at her approach.

She bent over, peering in at them. The shirt she held over her head hadn't prevented the rain from soaking her. Her bangs were plastered to her forehead and one droplet of water was making its way down the bridge of her nose.

"You guys know anything about cars?" she asked.

"We pulled off because of the rain," she continued without waiting for an answer. "The engine died as I was coming up the ramp, as soon as I took my foot off the gas, but since I was only trying to wait out the storm, I didn't really care. But now, it won't start at all. Just makes a chugging noise when I turn the key."

She looked from one to the other. She was, Simon estimated, a couple of years older than they. The sweatshirt she held bunched over her head displayed the embossed letters of a college logo, though he couldn't make out a name.

"Sounds like a loose cable," Robert said. "Or maybe your fuel filter's clogged."

"Can you fix it, do you think?" she asked eagerly, heartened by his knowledgeable-sounding response.

"Probably not," he said with equal offhandedness. "Not if it's a fuel filter." As her shoulders slumped, he added, "We can try jumping it, if it's just the battery. Though I doubt it is, not if you've been driving for awhile and only pulled over a little bit ago."

"Oh, that would be great, if you'd try," she said. "So...what do we need to do?"

Robert gestured over his shoulder. "Get in back," he said. "I'll need to pull up in front of your car, so that the engines are facing each other."

She needed no additional encouragement. More quickly than Simon could take it all in, the girl had opened the door and dived into the back seat. She wriggled to the center, tossing her dripping sweatshirt to one side and leaned forward, hands resting on the front cushion between Robert and Simon.

"I'm Cherie," she said. "Thanks so much. I thought we were totally screwed. This is one of those no-service exits. There's nothing around for miles. I was so glad when we saw your car pull up onto the ramp a little while ago, because at least then, we weren't out here all alone. Glory was all worried you might be a freak—or a couple of freaks. She didn't want me to get out of the car. But, hell, what else was I going to do?"

She paused to draw breath, and look appraisingly at each of them.

"I guess you still *could* be freaks," she conceded. "Baby-faced ones." Abruptly she produced a small canister and pointed it at each of them in turn, causing both Robert and Simon to flinch and blink. "But I have pepper-spray, so I figure I could spritz you and get a pretty good running head-start, if I have to."

And just as abruptly, the menacing canister was gone, returned to what-ever pocket she'd produced it from, and she was resting her chin on her hands on the back of the seat. "Glory is my cousin," she volunteered. She's probably sitting up there all prepared to dial 911 if she hears me scream. Like anybody could get here in time. So, what school do you guys go to?"

Robert had started the car, and after a careful look over his shoulder, pulled out onto the asphalt. Ahead of the other vehicle, he cut the wheel sharply to the left, steering them to the far side of the ramp, and then shifted into reverse. In another moment, he'd nosed the car so that it was facing the other one.

"We probably need to wait a little while longer," he said. "The rain's letting up, but let's give it a little bit more time. And we're not in college. Yet. We just graduated high school last month. Did you want to go wait in your car?"

"Nah," Cherie said. "Glory's actually starting to get on my nerves. It's nice to get a little bit of a break." She scrutinized the boys some more.

"I kinda figured you might be freshmen. What're your names, and what are you doing out here, anyway?"

"Robert MacKenzie and Simon Perkins," Robert announced formally, pointing to himself and Simon in turn. "I've been at a seminar in St. Louis."

"We're headed back to Colorado. That's where we're from," Simon interjected. He wasn't entirely sure how much of their recent history Robert might be inclined to share with Cherie. A fairly embarrassing amount did not seem out of the question, and he was hoping to forestall that.

"Oh, yeah? Is that where you're going to go to college, too?"

Both boys shook their heads.

"Tucson. University of Arizona," Simon answered.

"Polytechnic," Robert said. "San Luis Obispo."

"Wow. Rocket scientist."

He shook his head. "No, architecture. That's what I'm going to study."

Simon, jiggling the last few M&Ms in the palm of his hand, lifted his chin abruptly. He was about to speak when Robert opened the door.

"Rain's just about stopped. Go pop your car's hood while I get the cables out of my trunk."

Both Robert and Cherie exited the car, leaving Simon to ponder his next move. Robert seemed to have the situation well in hand, but it seemed impolite for Simon to just remain inside. He tossed the last of the candies into his mouth and climbed out the passenger side.

Cherie had unlatched the hood, so he stepped forward to raise it as Robert approached, untangling a set of black and red cables.

"Hold these," he instructed Simon, handing him one end of each color. "And don't let 'em touch each other."

Simon opened his mouth to say, with some irritation, that he knew this already, but changed his mind. It didn't matter, particularly, except that he didn't want Cherie thinking he was inept when it came to automotive repair. Instead he held a cable in each hand while Robert attached the opposite ends to the other car's battery and then wordlessly passed his ends to Robert a moment later. A tiny orange spark crackled as Robert secured the last clamp to a terminal.

"All right. Try starting it now."

Cherie slipped into the driver's seat, leaving the door open. Robert and Simon stood to one side as the engine lurched and struggled to turn over. At first, it appeared it might, its rhythmic chug nearly flaring to life, but whenever Cherie stopped turning the key, the motor settled back into moribund silence.

Robert shot Simon a dubious look, but called out, "Hold off a minute."

He hovered over the motor, adjusting the clamps on the battery terminals. Simon, meanwhile, was aware of another girl standing to one side of him. Raven-haired, solemn-faced, she had apparently exited the car from the passenger side very quietly. She gave Simon a fleeting sidelong glance when he looked at her, but then focused her attention on the project at hand.

"Try it again," Robert instructed.

The results were the same—the engine rumbled promisingly, but was unable to sustain any momentum once Cherie stopped turning the key.

"It's not going to work," Robert reported, and lifted the clamps from the battery. Simon closed both hoods as Robert coiled the cables and returned them to his trunk.

"Well, what do we do now?" the dark-haired girl spoke for the first time. Her tone was both annoyed and accusatory, and when she looked at Simon, it was with the implication that he now shared responsibility for finding a solution.

"Do you have some kind of roadside assistance?" Robert asked, rejoining the group. "Triple A, or something? You could call them, if you do."

Cherie shook her head, looking slightly bewildered.

"No. I guess I better call my dad and ask him what I should do. He'll come get us. Or send someone."

"Where is he? Where would he be coming from?" Simon asked.

"Grand Island." She sighed. "He's going to be so pissed. But he'll come."

Robert glanced at Simon then back at Cherie. "That's in Nebraska, right? How long will it take him to get here?"

"A long time," the other girl interjected. "Like, eight hours or more."

"Well, what else are we going to do, Glory?" Cherie snapped. She flipped a dismissive hand towards her. "This is my cousin Glory," she added somewhat redundantly.

Glory and the boys looked at one another, but no one said anything.

Cherie had climbed out from behind the driver's seat and was holding a cell phone to her ear. To the east, there was a rumble of thunder. Simon glanced up and realized that the storm was retreating at last. Raindrops fell sporadically, but overhead, seams of blue sky had begun to force their way through the blanket of clouds.

"Dammit!" Cherie said. "It's going to voicemail. They must not be home." She waited a second and then spoke into the phone. "It's me. Car broke down. We're like, stranded, somewhere on I-70 about an hour west of St. Louis. Call as soon as you get this. We need someone to come get us!"

Ending the call, she faced her cousin. "What about your folks? Can you call them?"

"They're still in Michigan!" Glory wailed. "They're not going to be any help. Try your mom's cell phone. Or your dad's."

"You know what?" Robert said abruptly. "It's nearly five o'clock now. Even if your dad could leave right away, he's not going to be here until the middle of the night. You guys can't just wait around in the car until then."

Cherie, in the process of making another call, lowered her phone. She and Glory and Simon all stared at Robert.

"Here's what we should do," he continued, frowning at the ground as he laid out his plan. "Simon and I were going to stop for the night in another hour or so, anyway. Just get some of your things—especially the valuable stuff—out of your car and put it in mine. We'll all go on until we find a motel someplace. Your father can meet you there and you can decide what to do then."

He walked back to his car and opened the driver's side door.

"Start getting your stuff out. I need to check something."

For a moment, nobody else moved. They just watched as Robert climbed inside, started the engine and then pulled out onto the ramp. Cutting the wheel sharply, he put the engine in reverse and circled again so that the car was facing forward once more. But rather than pulling back onto the shoulder, he proceeded to back the vehicle all the way down the incline until he was nearly on the interstate again.

"What... What's he doing?" Glory asked.

"I don't know," Simon said. He watched in bewilderment as Robert veered off onto the shoulder once more and then jumped out of the car. He ran another fifty yards or so, along the edge of the interstate, stopping at last to peer up at a road sign. Then he dashed back to his car, climbed inside, and drove back up to where they waited.

"Well, come *on!*" he urged. "Get your stuff!"

"What were you doing?" Simon asked as they tucked suitcases and a few random items into the trunk and backseat of his friend's car.

"Checking which exit number this is," was the response. "So Cherie and her dad will know where to find the car."

"Wow," Simon said, impressed. "I wouldn't have thought of that."

When he closed the trunk and moved up along the right side of the car, he was startled to see that Cherie had taken ownership of the front passenger seat. Since she was talking into her phone, he didn't say anything, but climbed into the back. Glory was already sitting directly behind Robert. A small duffle bag had been positioned on the seat next to her. She did not acknowledge Simon's presence with so much as a sidelong glance, though her continued discontentment was still in evidence.

"Yeah, Mom," Cherie was saying. "We're with these two nice boys who're giving us a lift." She looked at Robert and then twisted in her seat to scrutinize Simon for a second. Still looking at him, she said into her phone, "From Colorado. They seem okay. No, I didn't ask to see some identification. And, anyway..."

Though she lowered her voice and turned her head away to the window, everyone in the car could still hear what she was saying. "...If it came to that, I don't think we'd have much trouble handling it. So don't worry. And when Daddy gets back, tell him what happened. And tell him to start taking his phone with him from now on, for God's Sake!"

She lowered her phone and shook her head.

"He'll call when he gets home," she said. "Whenever *that* will be." She sighed and threaded her fingers through her damp hair, shaking her head from side to side. Simon, sitting directly behind her, received a face full of flying droplets.

For the next few minutes, they rode in silence as Robert steered the car in the direction of the clearing western horizon.

Chapter Twenty

"What's that look for?" Mrs. Reynolds asked her daughter as Vanessa stepped out onto the porch, letting the screen door swing closed behind her. It was late afternoon, perhaps early evening already. It was difficult to tell when the transition actually occurred on sluggish July days like these. The slanting yellow sunlight lingered endlessly, trapping everyone in a sticky amber limbo.

"What look?" Vanessa flopped onto the lawn chair alongside her mother's. When a suitable length of time had passed, enough to suggest that what she was about to bring up now had no correlation to the original question, she said casually:

"I just talked to Simon. He and Robert are at some motel halfway across Missouri. He says they should be back up in Stucker's Reach tomorrow."

Mrs. Reynolds nodded and sipped her iced tea. "Will you get to see them on their way through Denver?"

Vanessa lifted her feet and fanned her toes, allowing her sandals to slide free and drop to the ground. She shook her head.

"Didn't you suggest it?" her mother asked.

Another shake of the head.

Mrs. Reynolds stifled the urge to sigh audibly. This was one of those times when Vanessa wanted whatever was on her mind to be coaxed out slowly.

"Well, it isn't too late. I imagine you'll be talking to him or texting him between now and when they're passing through. Did he say how it was going? Is Robert still angry?" She'd heard just a little of what had happened between the boys the night on the lakeshore.

"He didn't go into it." Vanessa was studying the tops of her feet. During their brief conversation, she'd gotten the impression Simon wasn't at complete liberty to talk. "I guess maybe Robert was right there. All he really said was they'd gotten caught in a big storm that's delayed them a little."

"Are they all right?"

"Yeah."

Mrs. Reynolds nodded and leaned back in her chair. She did not re-open the book sitting in her lap. For another moment, mother and daughter reclined side by side, gazing out across the lawn. Finally, Vanessa lifted one leg and folded it beneath the other on her cushion.

"You know, I love Simon," she announced.

Mrs. Reynolds felt her breath catch in the back of her throat. As she was pondering what—if anything—she should say to this, Vanessa continued.

"I do. I love him." Yet, in the repetition, it sounded as if the person she was most trying to convince was herself. She plucked at a stray thread on one corner of the cushion. "When he was getting ready to leave at the beginning of summer, to go up and work in Stucker's Reach, there were moments I felt I couldn't breathe, almost. I knew I was going to miss him so much. And I didn't understand why he didn't feel the same way, how he could just pack up and go like that."

Her mother turned away slightly to conceal a smile. She remembered the drama of the parting all too well.

"I was so happy when you said we could go up there for The Fourth of July," Vanessa continued. "I was afraid of what would happen if Simon and I didn't see each other for three months."

"That he might meet another girl, you mean?"

Vanessa shook her head.

"Sometimes when he talks about Stucker's Reach, and his grandparents, and the things he used to do when he lived there, I would get this weird feeling that *that* was his real life, and this one, the one with me in it, was just a dream to him, or something."

"Sweetie…"

"I couldn't help it. That's what I thought. So when he first left, I was calling him all the time. I would listen so hard, listen to see if there was anything different in his voice, if he seemed… less interested, or maybe to see if he was turning into somebody else."

"And was he?"

"No. He was still just... Simon. But I couldn't wait to get up there, to see him and be sure, and to make myself a part of Stucker's Reach, so that from then on, whenever he thought of the place, I would be part of it, too."

"You... You were jealous of the *town?*"

"No. ...Well, yeah. I guess. It... It seems dumb, when you actually say it like that."

Mrs. Reynolds bit her lip, resisting the impulse to confess that it didn't seem dumb to her at all, actually. Instead, she asked, "Do you still feel that way? Did being there—even for just a week—make you see what Simon sees?"

Vanessa considered this for a long moment. "I had a good time. It's in a pretty place. But it's just a town. Some stuff is the same as anywhere, some things are different. The people aren't really any different, though."

"So, you aren't worried any more that it's going to change Simon into someone else."

Her daughter shook her head slowly. "No. I'm not. I'm... I'm not exactly sure what I think now."

"Well, Hon, you'll figure it out." Mrs. Reynolds reached across to squeeze Vanessa's wrist. "And, for better or worse, the summer's nearly half over already. Simon will be back home in barely more than another month. You'll have a couple of weeks with him before you both head off to college."

Vanessa, thoughts elsewhere, didn't notice the slight hitch in her mother's voice just before the word *college.*

"I guess," she said. And then she got up and went indoors.

Her mother remained in her chair, once again gazing across the yard, but seeing something else altogether.

She understood, even if Vanny didn't just yet, what her daughter was struggling with. The mystery of Simon—and some of his allure—had been diluted by the week in Stucker's Reach. The town itself wasn't to blame, not entirely. But the mystique it had held when it was a place Simon had talked about, but Vanessa hadn't yet visited, vanished the moment she began to see it for herself. It was, as she'd pointed out, *just a town.* And Simon was, after all, just a boy.

This was the first big hurdle they were facing in their relationship: A recognition of the...*ordinariness*...of it. Or the moments of ordinariness, at least, with the realization that more of these would follow. Mrs. Reynolds suspected, but didn't want to know for a fact, that Simon and her daughter had already slept together. And what an easy threshold that was to cross, after all, compared to most of the others a couple would face if they really wanted to get serious.

"Sex is easy, Sweetheart," she muttered under her breath. "It's the other twenty-three and a half hours of the day that are hard."

Simon leaned against a soft drink vending machine, absently turning his phone over and over in one hand. He'd just finished talking to Vanessa, telling her that he and Robert had stopped for the night. And he had lied to her.

For most of his life, it had never occurred to Simon to lie about anything. It wasn't so much that he was morally opposed to the practice; it simply struck him as inconvenient. Lies required ongoing maintenance, and ultimately seemed a waste of time, since more often than not, the truth would come out anyway.

Nor did he buy into the myth that leaving out some of the facts was less dishonest. A lie was a lie, and it didn't come in degrees or in shades.

But he had quite deliberately chosen not to mention that he and Robert were sharing a motel room with two college girls this evening. He could think of no efficient way to present this information in a phone call across a great distance without significant repercussion. It would be much easier to explain this in person, once he was home again. Although now, standing here in the breezeway of this motel in the middle of nowhere, Simon wasn't entirely sure how he was going to do that, either.

He made his way back to the swimming pool area, where Robert and Glory were sitting in vinyl-slatted chairs, and Cherie was splashing around in the water.

"Come join me, Simon!" she urged. "Since these two party-poopers won't."

"I don't have a suit," he told her.

"So what? Wear your boxers, or something. There's nobody else around. Who cares?"

"Yeah, I don't think so," he said, settling in a chair by the others.

"Fine! Buncha wusses!" she taunted, before disappearing dipping her head and diving below the water's surface.

Securing a motel room had proved to be more problematic this time than before. It was the weekend, and when they'd finally located a full-service exit from the interstate, the first two motels they'd checked had no vacancies.

At the third, the front desk clerk, an older man wearing a blazer embossed with the motel's insignia over his breast pocket, studied Robert for several seconds, then shifted his gaze to Simon and the girls, standing some distance away.

"This is a family establishment," he'd informed them. "I'm not going to rent a couple of rooms to kids who are out to party and trash them."

"We only want one room," Robert said. This, he realized a second later, noting the clerk's raised eyebrow, was not the best response he could have offered. "We just met those girls," he added quickly, thrusting a hand in their direction. "We gave them a lift. Their car is just off the interstate a ways back, and they're just waiting until someone can come fix it."

"It's Saturday night," the older man had pointed out. "You won't find anybody around here who can work on an engine until Monday."

"My dad is on his way," Cherie said, stepping forward and resting both hands on the edge of the counter. "He'll get the car running again. We may not even be here the whole night. Give us a break!"

But she hadn't helped their cause any more than Robert: Her hair was askew and damp from standing in the recent downpour, she was wearing a t-shirt tucked into a pair of short shorts, and also, there was just a faint, but distinctly suspicious smell hovering around her. The clerk shook his head once more.

"Try in town," he'd advised, relenting slightly. He flicked his thumb over his shoulder. "About half a mile down the road that way. "There are a couple of places that don't fill up as fast as we do. They're cheaper, too."

Simon recognized that the man was steering them to some of the less discriminating lodging establishments in the vicinity. He, too, was aware of the scent of marijuana on Cherie's clothes.

They had managed to find a motel—or as the weathered neon sign had advertised, a *motor lodge and trailer court*—not too far down the road.

And the heavy-lidded man who checked them in seemed indifferent to their appearance, their youth, and even the faint pot smell hovering over the girls.

"Ice and soda machines are through the breezeway," he'd informed them, handing Robert back his debit card as well as two room keys. "Pool and hot tub are there, too, down the steps on the back lawn. Don't leave towels out there, 'cause they get moldy. Office is locked at nine, no smoking in the rooms. Any questions?"

The whole spiel was delivered by rote in a halfhearted monotone. At its conclusion, he'd lifted his eyes and looked at them as if, despite asking, he neither expected—nor desired—to give out any more information.

Therefore it seemed likely that Cherie's assertion was probably true. Nobody—least of all the front desk clerk—would care if Simon wore his underwear into the pool. Just so long as he didn't leave a towel behind to mold. Judging from the cars in parking lot, only two or three other rooms were rented so far this evening, anyway.

"So," Simon called to Cherie when she resurfaced a moment later. "If you're from Grand Island, what were you doing in St. Louis?"

"Visiting our grandmother," Cherie said. "Glory and I have come out here every summer since we were little. "Our moms are sisters, and she's their mother."

"Usually we fly," Glory interjected. It was the first substantive comment she had made to any conversation up until now.

"Guess that's what we should have done this time, too, huh?" her cousin said. Both girls laughed. Cherie floated her way to the pool's edge, resting her arms on the concrete near where the others were sitting.

"Grammie is awesome," she explained. "But it's sort of confining when we fly there. It means we're pretty much stuck at her place the whole time. Having our own car this visit was great! We went all kinds of places we couldn't have otherwise: Clubs, a concert, some parties. We met some guys one night."

"They were jerks." This from Glory.

"They were not!" Cherie was silent for a half-second. "Okay," she conceded. "They sort of were. But they took us to this awesome party. *That* was fun."

Out of the corner of his eye, Simon watched Glory shrug indifferently. "We didn't get home until after four the next morning," Cherie laughed.

"What did your Grammie think about that?" Robert inquired.

More laughter.

"We did a kind of bad thing; she'd been waiting up, but when we sneaked in, we saw she'd fallen asleep on the couch." Cherie looked at her cousin, who didn't meet her gaze, but was nevertheless smirking. "So, I whispered to Glory to run into Grammie's bedroom and change the time on her clock. I did the same thing to the one on the TV. Then I shook Grammie awake, and we made her think it was two o'clock, instead of four. She was still upset we were so late getting in, but it would have been way worse if she'd known what time it really was."

"How did you know she'd been asleep three whole hours?" Robert asked. "She might not have fallen asleep until three-thirty or some other time. Or she might have waked up a few times and noticed it was already past two before you got home."

"It was a calculated risk," Cherie acknowledged. "But, hey, it was worth a shot. And it paid off."

Simon watched with interest to see how Robert, methodical and practical in his approach to everything, would respond to the concept of such a playful, haphazard notion. But, disappointingly, Robert simply extended his feet in a stretch and announced, "I'm hungry. Let's find somewhere to eat."

When Cherie had changed, they trudged across the street to a hamburger stand, the only restaurant within walking distance, the motel clerk had advised them.

"Great," Glory muttered as they squeezed into a booth. "What a craphole." Two men sitting in a booth across from theirs looked over at them with interest.

Without looking up from the laminated menu, her cousin asked, "Do you think you could maybe go one day without being a raging bitch?"

If Glory took offense at this, she kept it to herself, merely wrapping her lips around a straw and sucking a deep draught of ice water from her glass. The girls apparently shared a curiously confrontational dynamic that somehow worked for them.

"So, did you tell your dad how to find the motel?" Simon asked. "And do you have any idea what time he'll get here?" He was trying to imagine how irritated and out-of-sorts a father who had just finished an inconvenient and unplanned eight hour drive was likely to be by the time he arrived at their door. He had already decided that if he slept at all tonight, it would be fully clothed, atop the bed.

"I didn't," Cherie informed him nonchalantly. "I told him to call when he got to the truck stop down by the exit, and we'd come meet him." The amused look she gave him over the top of her menu indicated she knew what was going through his mind.

After they'd ordered their food, she propped her elbow on the table, rested her chin in the palm of her hand and smiled lazily at Simon.

"So, do you have a girlfriend? Is that who you were talking to awhile ago?"

"Her name's Vanessa," Robert contributed helpfully, before Simon could say anything.

"Oh, yeah?" Cherie shifted her gaze to the other boy. "How about you? You have one?"

Robert shook his head. He lowered his eyes and tapped the straw in his water glass with his forefinger.

"Now, or ever?" Glory asked. She was sitting alongside him in the booth.

A faint blush was coloring Robert's ears and face. "Not ever, really," he muttered.

"Why not? You're cute," Cherie told him.

Now his skin was fully crimson. "No," he said. "I'm not."

Cherie turned her attention to Simon once again.

"So, you and Vanessa," she began. "Are you, you know… true to her?"

"Yeah," he said. "I'm true."

He was aware of the amused glance that passed between the women.

"He doesn't know what you mean," Glory informed her cousin.

"Order up!" the woman behind the counter called, nudging a plastic tray piled with sandwiches and drinks their direction. Simon slid out of the booth. When he returned with their meals, he said:

"I know what you meant. I should have just said it's none of your business, I guess."

Robert, peeling back the waxy paper from his burger, observed matter-of-factly, "I guess you guys don't have boyfriends, either? I mean, since you called your dad to come get you."

Unwrapping his own sandwich, Simon fought back a smirk. Surely this was just an incidental comment, delivered in Robert's offhanded way, not a calculated retort. It just wasn't in his character to be that pointed.

The girls, for once, seemed to have nothing to say.

Back at the room later, Cherie produced a bunched-up t-shirt from among her things, unrolling it atop one of the beds. She held up a square of aluminum foil encased in a sandwich baggie.

"How about we have a little smoke to unwind?" She looked at each of them in turn. "Who's up for it?"

Simon shrugged. Glory managed another indifferent expression.

"Not here in the room," Robert instructed. "Remember what the guy at the front desk said."

"These aren't Marlboros. You realize that, don't you, Bobby?"

"I know what it is," he told her evenly. "But it's my name on the room registration, is what I'm saying. I'm the one in trouble if we get caught. Smoke outside, understand?"

They moved in single file past the row of motel room doors, ducking around the hanging baskets of geraniums and petunias that swayed back and forth somehow, without benefit of breeze. The air was heavy and dark blue in fading daylight and the parking lot was still as empty as it had been when they'd arrived. Cherie led the way through the breezeway down the short flight of steps to the lawn and pool area.

They sat at the furthermost umbrella table, nearly concealed behind the leaves of a sprawling honeysuckle bush.

Cherie touched one end of a joint to the open flame from a disposable lighter. She inhaled quickly, holding the smoke behind pinched lips while stuffing the lighter back into the pocket of her cut-offs. At last she exhaled and passed the tightly rolled cigarette to Robert.

Simon watched, unaware that he was holding his own breath as the friend he'd known since gawky childhood gripped the joint between thumb and forefinger, lifted it to his lips and took a hit before handing it on to

Glory. He wondered for a minute if Robert was faking, playing along to be one of the gang, but no. A plume of smoke rolled elegantly from his mouth and nostrils as his chest sank with release. Simon was so surprised at this that he was barely aware of taking his own turn at the traveling bomber.

Dusk and then darkness settled over them. They'd finished the joint by then, but continued to sit, gazing up at a sky faded to dappled black.

"Look," Cherie said laggardly. She'd lowered her face and was studying the immediate vicinity. "The pool lights have come on."

"They've been on for awhile now," Glory added after a considerable pause.

"They've always been on." Robert raised his legs in an extended stretch and then tilted his neck against the back of his chair. "You just didn't notice them until it got dark."

Simon, chin resting on his chest, smiled but said nothing. Those comments, he decided, easily defined each of the people who'd made them. He found this amusing.

A clattering noise caused them all to turn, leaning around the honeysuckle branches to watch another guest scooping a bucket of ice out of the machine in the breezeway.

"That's the first other person we've seen," Glory said. "I'm glad there's somebody else here. Maybe we aren't staying at The Bates Motel, after all."

They watched until the guest had filled his bucket, closed the hinged door and disappeared around the far side of the building.

"That reminds me," Cherie said. She was silent for so long that the other three were looking at her expectantly before she continued. "Does anybody have some money for the soda machine? I've got a bottle of rum back in my bag, if somebody'll get us some Cokes."

When she returned from their room with her bag and the bottle, she was barefooted and wearing a bathing suit under her t-shirt. Simon and Robert had pooled their change and there were cans of Coca-Cola sitting on the table.

"Great!" she said approvingly, setting down the rum and a stack of shrink-wrapped plastic glasses she'd grabbed from the bathroom vanity. "I'm getting in the hot tub, by the way. Even if nobody else does."

She unwrapped one of the glasses, filling it nearly halfway with rum and then began to add Coke in sporadic dollops. It was a slow process, since she had to wait for the foam to settle between pours. Glory and Simon watched, far more entranced than they might have been without the benefit of a few tokes. They were so distracted, in fact, that it was another moment or so before they realized Robert had gotten up and moved a few steps across the grass. By the time Cherie had finished filling her drink, Robert had unbuttoned his shirt, kicked off his shoes, removed his socks and pants, and was standing next to the hot tub in nothing but a pair of briefs.

"Well, look at you, Bobby!" Cherie crowed.

"My name is Robert," he informed her. "It's not 'Bobby.'" Then he pulled off his shorts and descended, naked, into the bubbling water.

Chapter Twenty-One

Simon was stretched out on the grass near the pool, hands folded behind his head.

After a few minutes, Glory left the umbrella table and sat cross-legged some distance away from him.

"I'm surprised you didn't get in the hot tub, too," she said.

"Maybe later. What about you?"

She made a sort of dismissive snort and sipped from her rum and Coke.

Simon shifted his position slightly to study Glory's profile. She was gazing at the ground, her skin luminescent in the glow of the pool lights. Facing downward, she displayed a double chin. She wasn't heavy, exactly, but her features were rounded and soft. She tucked a strand of hair behind one ear and sniffed suddenly, making him wonder if she was sad, for some reason.

As if sensing his stare, she turned to him suddenly. "What?" she demanded.

He shook his head. "Nothing."

He was surprised she'd moved to sit so near when her demeanor up until now had suggested she had utterly no use for him. But then again, everything about this day seemed as distorted as the reflection of the rippling water across Glory's face. He couldn't pinpoint for certain when things had diverged so sharply from reality. Maybe when he and Robert had driven into the rainstorm? Or maybe as far back as this morning, when he'd first stepped onto the plane in Denver. That moment certainly seemed to have taken place a very long time ago.

Cherie's laugh rang out over the sound of the churning Jacuzzi waters.

Simon and Glory looked towards the hot tub. Through the rising steam, they could see Cherie gesturing animatedly as she talked, though the distance was too great to make out her words. Her golden hair, carelessly pinned up, had nevertheless gotten wet, and now appeared darker. Even disheveled, she was pretty, and Simon wondered if her cousin was jealous.

Abruptly Glory struggled to her feet. Simon assumed she was leaving, heading back to the room, maybe, but she crossed back to the table and returned with Cherie's bottle of rum.

"Hold out your cup."

"No, that's okay," he demurred.

"Hold out your cup!" she insisted, so he did. She poured some of the clear liquid atop what remained of his previous drink, then more to her own. Capping the bottle, she dropped it in the grass and collapsed heavily on the ground again. She pulled her knees up against her chest, wrapping one arm around them.

"Bet you never expected your day to wind up here."

He laughed. "Nope. You, either."

"Doesn't surprise me too much about the car. Cherie treats it like crap. I told her to get it serviced before we left home, and she said she did, but she was probably lying. It's no wonder we're here tonight." Glory took a healthy gulp from her glass and sighed. "So, you guys were at some sort of college fraternity thing in St. Louis?"

"No." Simon had just taken a sip from his own cup and was blinking back tears. His mouth seemed to be full of rum and nothing else. "Just Robert was there. And it wasn't a fraternity thing. At least, I don't think so," he said hoarsely. "I'm just along for the ride."

"Huh," she offered noncommittally. She glanced over her shoulder towards the others and then back again. "Are you guys related, or just friends?"

"We're...friends. Actually, we went to school together back when we were kids. In this little town where I used to live. Now I... He..."

It all seemed too complicated to explain, at least here, tonight, stretched out on a motel lawn, head buzzing for a variety of reasons, and he stopped trying. But Glory didn't seem to mind. She nodded.

"You're like Cherie and me," she suggested. "You don't seem like two people who would hang around together."

Intrigued, Simon set his cup aside and folded his legs underneath him. "Yeah? What does that mean?"

She flicked a thumb over her shoulder, gesturing towards the others.

"We were best friends when we were little. Then, by about middle school, she got like *that,* and I didn't. She just knew, somehow, how to look and talk and act. Didn't even have to work at it. So then, she didn't really want to associate with me anymore. This trip to visit our grandmother each summer is the only thing we still do together." She laughed softly. "I don't think our parents have ever even noticed that."

Across the grass, things had grown much quieter. The figures in the water were sitting close to one another. So close, in fact, that Simon would have had to look hard—much harder than he felt comfortable doing—to be able to tell precisely what was going on. There was only the sound of bubbling, lapping water. He turned his back to all of that.

"The reason she's over there, and not here, is because you're all noble about your girlfriend," Glory declared loftily. "Otherwise it'd be you she was on top of right now."

He couldn't decide if the bitterness in her tone was directed at Cherie or himself or both.

"I think everybody is pretty much where they want to be," he said, more in defense of Robert than for any other reason.

"Yeah, right. You really want to be sitting here with me."

"Why not?"

"Oh, please." She ripped up a handful of grass and let the blades fall between her fingers. "You can afford to be nice. What's it going to cost, after all? Tomorrow, you're on your way home again."

"Or maybe," Simon said, "I'm just nice."

He was abruptly irked. He didn't mind Glory scorning his motives without justification so much as he disliked her defiant attitude that it was somehow her destiny to accept whatever life—and anybody with whom she came into contact—cared to throw at her.

"You save yourself the trouble," he told her, "Of waiting to find out whether somebody's going to be a jerk. You go ahead and make that assumption so that it's all right to be one to them first."

"You don't even know—" she began, indignant, but then fell silent.

Simon glanced at her curiously, but she was looking past him. Not even a second later, a shadow fell across the both of them.

"Evening," a masculine voice spoke from over his shoulder. "How are you guys?"

Simon swiveled in the grass to see two men standing over them.

"Fine," he said, startled, but trying to sound composed. "You?"

Though both guys were smiling, Simon was on his guard. His heart began thudding against the wall of his chest.

"Looks like you're having a little party," one of them said, choosing to ignore the question. He gestured to the bottle of rum lying in the grass. Crossing around them, he pulled out a chair from one of the tables and sat, elbows propped on his knees. The other man remained where he was. Both appeared to be in their late twenties or early thirties, dressed in jeans and boots. The one standing behind them was wearing a baseball cap.

"Not a party," Simon said. "Just hanging out for a little bit before going to our room." He recognized them now. They had been eating dinner in the booth across from theirs in the diner. In fact, he'd had the sensation that the men had been watching them with more than just a passing interest. And now, here they were once more. Something didn't feel quite right.

"Nice night. Mind if we join you?" The tone was casual, affable, but there was something harder behind it. Simon didn't like the positions they had taken up; with one sitting in front of them and the other standing behind, he couldn't watch them both at the same time. The seated man leaned forward to pick up the plastic glass Simon had set to one side in the grass. He sniffed its contents. "Whoa!" he declared, wrinkling his nose and recoiling slightly. "*That's* a toddy!" he affirmed. The other man laughed.

"There's Coke on the table over there," Glory said. Her face was the picture of calm, but her voice was tight. Her eyes settled fleetingly on Simon, looking indifferent yet conveying her concern before she looked away again. "Help yourself to that and the rum."

"We were just getting ready to go inside," Simon informed them. He tried to glance towards the hot tub without being obvious, wondering if the men had spotted the others. That depended, he supposed, on how long they might have been watching them before making their presence known.

"Are you, now?" This from the man standing behind him.

"We've got an early start," Simon fought to keep his tone casual, friendly. "We're meeting someone." He nodded at Glory. "Her uncle."

The seated guy thrust his chin in the direction of the Jacuzzi. "How about them?" he asked. His eyes were still on Simon, and his sly smile conveyed a sense of mastery. "Are they getting ready to go in, too?"

"I'll go ask," the man in the baseball cap volunteered.

"No!" Glory blurted as he started to move. "They're not... They haven't got anything on..."

"That's all right; I won't peek," he assured her. It was his buddy's turn to snicker. He had taken a couple of steps through the grass when Simon called out:

"Guys? Get out of the hot tub and get some clothes on."

For just a half-second, everyone froze. Then the man in the baseball cap turned back to him. His body blocked the light from the pool, making him just a tall, featureless shape standing in front of Simon.

"Now, why did you do that?" he asked in a wounded tone.

Simon rose on one knee, preparing to stand. "Why do you think?" he retorted.

He sensed a quick motion, but it was only the stab of pain on his cheekbone and the abrupt contact with the ground that belatedly told him he'd just been kicked in the face. Behind his eyelids, he saw a wall of fire. Glory screamed.

Still blinded, Simon felt the hands on his shirt lapels, hauling him off the ground. His arms flailed at his sides.

"I'll get the ones in the water," he heard the more distant voice say.

"Let him go!" Glory was pleading.

"Hands off me, bitch!" the voice directly in front of Simon snarled. That was enough to guide him. He raised one knee with as much force as he could muster, making contact with soft flesh—belly, or perhaps something more tender—and was rewarded with a strangled gasp. In the scant second before the fingers holding his shirtfront released their grasp, he drove his forehead upward, bone making contact with bone. The sensation, on top of his already stinging face was nearly unbearable, but he fell back to the lawn knowing he'd inflicted damage of his own.

Through half-lidded eyes, he had a blurred image of his assailant, no longer wearing his baseball cap, stagger to one side, hand clasped across his nose.

"What the fuck..?" The other man came into view, clutching a terrified, disheveled Cherie by the shoulders. Her arms were folded in front of her bare torso, hair hanging loosely about her shoulders. He shoved her roughly to one side, sending her spiraling into the grass, and lunged for Simon.

Simon rolled to one side and attempted to crawl onto his knees, but then his assailant was atop him, one arm wrapped around his neck, choking him and driving his other fist into his ribcage. Simon gurgled as the air left his lungs. He feebly raised one arm in an attempt to ward off a second blow to his side, knowing he was about to go down for the count.

Now there was added weight atop him, and he sank to the ground. Glory, in an attempt to help, had thrown herself atop the man on Simon's back, yelling and clawing at him. Simon was effectively pinned, unable to move until someone else did first.

And now the other man reappeared, limping, but recovered. Blood trickled from his nose, his face a mask of fury as he glared down at Simon.

"I'm going to kill you," he said between clenched teeth. He lifted one leg in preparation of another well-aimed kick, when a white, glistening form appeared from nowhere, tackling him around the neck and shoulders. The man and a naked Robert tumbled down the sloping grass, disappearing from view into the tall weeds bordering the lawn.

The weight atop Simon lessened then. His opponent had succeeded in throwing Glory to one side, but in so doing, had left himself open for attack from the other side. Cherie, no longer shielding her breasts and her own blanched face displaying wide-eyed rage, brought down a lawn chair she'd been holding over her head, slamming into the man's head and back. Again. And again. And yet again.

It was a lightweight piece of furniture, and though delivered with all her strength, the blows weren't damaging so much as distracting. Still, they served a purpose; the man was so busy shielding his face and trying to deflect the assault that he couldn't maintain his grip on Simon, who slithered from beneath him and crawled to his feet.

For a moment, he fought to keep his balance, woozy from pain and loss of breath. Nausea also gripped him, but he forced the sensation down, looking from side to side. Glory had joined her cousin in the attack on the first man. He was crawling on all fours as the women kicked him and pelted him with lawn furniture. In the other direction, Simon could hear grunts and landing blows from somewhere in the darkness. He made a hasty decision and sprinted down the slope and into the weeds.

The bloody-nosed man was straddling Robert and delivering a series of punches to his face. Robert's arms and legs floundered uselessly to either side as he received blow after blow. Copying his friend's earlier tactic, Simon launched himself into the air, his shoulders and torso slamming into the man and sending them both tumbling across rocks, burrs and more tall weeds.

Spitting dirt and dried grass, Simon climbed to his feet. He could hear the other man gasping in the darkness, but couldn't spot him. Hastily, he made his way back to Robert, grabbing his arm and pulling him to his feet.

"Thanks," they gasped simultaneously. With another glance over his shoulder, Simon pushed his friend back towards the manicured grass below the motel. They had just reached it when Robert, looking back, dug his fingers into Simon's shoulders and panted, "There he is."

A slouching form had risen out of the untended field and was making its way slowly towards the lawn.

"Look," Simon called to it. "It's over, all right? You and your buddy, you just... just go away, okay? Let's just all walk away from this."

"Simon..." Robert cautioned.

Their foe stepped into the light. One eye was partially closed. Blood continued to stream from his nose. His shoulders rose and fell in heaving gasps. He remained at the edge of the grass, and seemed to be considering the suggestion.

"Simon," Robert whispered again, and this time, Simon saw what Robert was looking at. In one grimy hand, their attacker clutched a knife, turning it over and over as he glowered at them in silence. Each time the flat side of the blade caught the light from the pool behind them, it appeared to radiate an icy heat. The boys took a single step backwards.

"Go find the girls," Simon whispered. "Make sure they're okay, and tell them to go lock themselves in the room."

"What about..."

"Go! *Go!*" Simon hissed.

And then his friend was gone, slipping and staggering up the slope.

Only after Robert had vanished did the man begin a slow advance towards Simon.

"It's not over," the man declared in a raspy breath. "Not yet."

Simon took a few more steps backward. Each move he made was countered by his assailant, who matched his pace, keeping the distance between them the same. Simon didn't bother to plead or speak at all. He could tell from the other man's stony expression that he was past any sort of reason.

Abruptly, he heard feet pounding on the hill behind him.

"Robert," he began, turning his head, but keeping his eyes on the other man, "I told you..."

But it wasn't Robert. It was his attacker's companion, evidently escaped from the girls' assault. He clamored down the hillside and stopped a few feet away, panting. He looked from one to the other.

"Let's get out of here!" he told his buddy. "One of those kids has probably already called the cops."

"I don't care," the man with the knife said. "We've got time, first. Get hold of him."

For a moment, the other guy hesitated, and Simon thought perhaps he was in the clear. But then the buddy sighed and said:

"All right. But make it fast."

The two of them closed in on Simon who ducked first left, and then right, eluding capture. He made for the slope and was climbing and slipping in the grass when one of them grabbed the back of his shirt, pulling him backwards. He lost his balance and fell. Face against the ground, he felt one of them kneel on the back of his calves. He was pulled up onto his knees, the rest of his legs still pinned to the earth.

"Hold his arms behind his back."

The man with the knife advanced slowly on them. His face, bloodied and swollen, seemed to hold no emotion, neither anger nor triumph.

"This is your fault," he informed Simon, crouching and breathing heavily in his face. "You hurt me."

It was a ridiculous thing to say, and in his disbelief and fear, Simon actually uttered a gasp of laughter. The others didn't seem to notice. The point of the knife pricked the hollow fleshy spot of his throat below his Adam's apple. He swallowed and felt the knife break the skin.

"I won't kill you," the man said. "But the blood loss might." The knife made its way just below his jaw line, dragging and pulling the skin, but not tearing it. It paused just below his left ear.

"Here would be good. The jugular's right here. You'll spurt like a fire hydrant." There was a sudden flick of the man's hand, driving Simon's head upward. "See?" he gloated, lifting the knife for inspection. A quarter-inch of the tip was shiny and red, and Simon could feel liquid pulsing down his neck.

"Hurry *up!*" the man holding his hands said. His companion ignored him. He studied the blade for another second or so and then leveled it at Simon's face.

"Maybe through the eye next," he said.

From slightly further away, a command pierced the darkness. "Simon! Close your eyes and mouth!"

And then a sticky mist settled over him, over all of them. The acrid smell reminded him of bug spray, but stronger. Unable to close his nostrils, he inhaled some and promptly gagged. He wrenched to one side, and realized that his wrists had been released.

He heard the sustained and agonized screams of the other men. They, unlike Simon, had not closed their eyes. The leg of one of the men kicked Simon's sharply, not in anger or defense, but merely in spasm. Still holding his breath and shielding his eyes with the palms of his hands, Simon rolled to one side. Arms linked through his and pulled him still further away.

"It's okay, you're okay," he heard Glory say. Helped to his feet, he finally risked opening his eyes which, despite Robert's cautioning, were streaming tears. Through his watery visage, he caught glimpses of his attackers, both writhing and rolling back and forth, fingers digging at their eyes. They alternately yelped and heaved great bowel-wrenching gags. And hopping back and forth over their thrashing bodies was Robert, holding a towel over his mouth and nose, and continuing to douse them in Cherie's pepper spray anytime their faces became available. He was otherwise still entirely nude, a gaunt ivory figure performing some pagan ritual beneath the stars.

"I think that's enough," Cherie told him finally.

"Yeah," he agreed, stepping around one of the men, now on his hands and knees vomiting even as he continued to wail. "I just wanted to be sure."

The four of them watched from the top of the rise for another thirty seconds. From all appearances, their opponents would be incapacitated for quite awhile yet.

"What does pepper spray do to a person, exactly?" Glory wondered as they turned and made their way back to the hot tub.

"It says *'may temporarily impair vision and breathing,'*" Robert said, holding up the nearly empty container and squinting at the print along one side. "*'Seek immediate medical treatment following sustained exposure to contents.'*" He shrugged and looked at the others.

"Do we call somebody?" Glory wanted to know. Now they all exchanged glances.

Robert tugged up his briefs, gathered up the rest of his clothes, and they started back to the room.

"Here's what I think," he said. "We probably shouldn't stay here, after all. Let's go get our stuff and we'll find another motel further down the interstate, just to be safe. The last thing out the door, we'll call the front desk and say somebody's lying out by the pool making a lot of noise, and somebody should go check. That is, if somebody else hasn't done it already."

"How about you?" Cherie asked Simon. "Shouldn't you see a doctor? There's blood all down your neck."

"I'll be all right," he said. He pressed his fingers to the wound and then held them up for inspection under the light just outside their door. They were sticky and red, but there wasn't as much as he feared. "He didn't get anything vital."

In the room, the four of them moved quickly, efficiently, saying little as they gathered up their things. Both Simon and Robert hunched over the basin, washing their faces. Robert's temple, Simon noticed, was raked raw in one spot.

"When did that happen?" he asked. "When you rolled down the hill with that guy who was starting to kick me?"

He shook his head. "When the other dude came over to the hot tub. He shoved me down as I was getting out, and I hit my head. I guess he thought he'd knocked me out, since he just left me there."

"He underestimated you," Cherie said admiringly.

Robert made the call to the front desk while the rest of them waited in the car, engine idling. Then he climbed behind the wheel and they left the motel parking lot, steering back towards the interstate. Just as Robert turned onto the entrance ramp, a police car came racing across the overpass from the opposite direction, lights flashing. It zoomed passed them, disappearing in the distance from which they had just traveled.

No one said anything until they had joined the flow of traffic moving westward on I-70. Then, as one, they exhaled in relief.

"I guess we're safe," said Cherie.

"Well, even if they somehow manage to tie us to any of that, we didn't do anything wrong," Glory pointed out.

"But it might be their word against ours. And if they're a couple of local boys, and the police can track us down, who knows what they'll believe."

"My blood is on that guy's knife," Simon reminded them. "That's probably pretty good evidence in our favor."

They rode in silence for a few more minutes. Then Robert said, "Uh-oh."

"What? What is it?" Alarmed, they all looked at him.

He was shaking his head.

"We forgot to bring the towels back from the pool. Now they're probably going to get moldy," he said.

Chapter Twenty-Two

When Simon woke, it was gradually, and from the bottom of a deep, dark well.

The light was a tiny circle overhead, and he floated toward it leisurely, feeling as if he had been drifting in a warm, safe tunnel below the earth's surface for a very long time. There was no sound in the well, and no sound when he opened his eyes and found himself staring into the folds of his pillow.

He knew immediately where he was, but that realization only made him wonder if he hadn't awakened at all, but was trading one dream for another. Yesterday couldn't have happened; it was a day so completely unlike any of the others he had experienced in seventeen and a half years that it surely wasn't one of his. In fact with one exception, it had been populated entirely by people he'd never even met before in his whole life.

Yet, as he lowered the covers and rolled to one side, he saw it was indeed that one familiar person who was occupying the bed across from his.

"Hey," Robert said, bringing sound back into the world. He was lying on his back, arms resting on his chest, gazing at the ceiling.

"Hey," Simon said hoarsely. He watched his friend for a moment, then twisted beneath the sheets to glance over his shoulder. The other side of the bed was empty. As he turned back, a host of pains shot through his body and he settled gingerly back into his pillow. Yes. Yesterday was definitely his, all right.

"Where...?" he started to stay, but Robert cut him off.

"Gone. Cherie's dad called about six, so they left to go meet him downstairs. They said to tell you good-bye. They didn't want to wake you. You were really out of it. Snoring, and everything."

"Sorry." Simon lay still, taking quiet inventory of the things that hurt. There were a lot of them.

"It's okay. I didn't really notice, until it was already starting to get light out. How do you feel?"

"Lousy. You?"

Robert nodded. He pulled himself into a sitting position and tucked an extra pillow behind his back. For the first time, he faced Simon. He broke into a broad grin. "Oh, man."

"What?" As carefully as he could manage, Simon raised up on one elbow.

"You should see yourself! Dude, it's... it's..." He started laughing. "I know it's not funny, but..."

Simon began to chuckle as well. His left eye was swollen half-shut, but even with impeded vision, he wondered if he could possibly look any worse than his friend. The skinned section of Robert's temple was raw and pink. There were greenish-yellowish welts on both cheekbones and a jagged vertical cut slicing through his upper lip. His shoulder and chest were a spider's web of intricate red scratches received, no doubt when he'd tumbled through the weeds and brambles. He remembered now that after they had checked into this new motel room late last evening, the girls had spent some time extricating burrs, thorns and slivers from Robert's back, chest, legs, and the bottoms of his feet.

They both continued to laugh and to wince at the added pain that laughing caused them.

"Your eyes," Robert gasped between snickers, "They're all bloodshot, I guess from the pepper spray, even though you had them closed. You look like you've come off of a three-day bender."

"How can we go home looking like this?" Simon grinned. As gingerly as he could manage, he wiped away tears from his throbbing cheek. "Your folks sent me to bring you back, and *this* is how I'm going to deliver you?"

"Maybe it won't look so bad in a few hours," Robert ventured. They considered this remark in silence, and then began to laugh all over again. Finally, Simon sighed as deeply as he could manage and settled back onto his pillow.

"I never saw you smoke pot before last night," he remarked. "I didn't think you ever did."

Robert was tracing a particularly deep scratch down the center of his chest with one finger.

"I never had," he said absently. "First time anybody ever offered me any."

"Really? You handled it like you knew what you were doing."

"Movies. TV," he shrugged. "I just did what I'd seen."

They were silent then, occupied with their own thoughts. Simon began to contemplate a series of images all collected in the last twenty-four hours. Tallied together, they presented a different impression from one he'd carried for a long time, now:

There was Robert's quiet assurance in diagnosing the girls' car trouble. Backing his car down the ramp to determine the number of the interstate exit where they were leaving the stranded vehicle. Reminding Cherie that his name was not *Bobby*. His ass, pale as a fish's belly, rolling over and over down the hill as he tackled a guy about to deliver Simon a vicious kick to the ribs. Coming to Simon's rescue a second time, still naked, but nevertheless willing to confront two men, one wielding a knife. Calmly deciding a subsequent course of action as the rest of them looked to him for leadership.

"Do you know," Simon said at last, studying his folded hands atop the bed sheet, "That you and I are both planning to major in the same thing? Architecture? I never even knew that until I heard you tell Cherie that in the car yesterday."

Robert nodded. "Yeah. That's pretty cool, I guess."

"Yeah. Of course, you'll probably be a lot better at it than I am."

"I dunno. Maybe." Robert yanked back the covers and set his feet on the ground. Standing, he raised his hands high overhead in a stretch. "I'm going to go stand in a hot shower for a long time," he said. "I hope it will make me feel better."

Simon had averted his eyes. "Geez, Robert," he said. "I saw enough of all that last night. At least put on some underwear, would you?"

His mouth turned up in a grin, Robert reached for a corner of the bedspread, yanking it up and wrapping it around his waist with a flourish. It trailed several feet behind him as he strolled into the bathroom.

His smugness was to be expected, Simon supposed. Last night, before falling into deep slumber, Simon and Glory, lying back to back, a chaste distance separating them in the bed they were sharing, folded pillows over their ears and tried hard not to listen as, across the way, Cherie and Robert completed the act they had begun in the hot tub earlier that evening.

The boys had a late breakfast an hour later in the motel's brightly lit coffee shop. Their mangled appearance drew curious stares from the other diners.

"Car accident," Simon informed their waitress as she poured their coffee, regarding them with a concerned expression. "During that big thunderstorm yesterday afternoon."

"Oh, hon!" she wailed. "That's just awful! I heard there were a bunch of accidents up the road a ways. One with about thirty cars, all crunched together like an accordion. Were you in that?"

"That was us," Robert nodded. He flicked his thumb towards the window facing the parking lot. "Now we're driving a rental."

"You just gotta be so careful, especially this time of year," she mused. "We get those storms almost every afternoon. Not always that bad, of course. I hope you don't have any more trouble!"

They grinned shamefacedly at each other as she hurried away to place their order.

"I don't like doing crap like that," Simon admitted. "And it sort of bothers me that we're getting so good at it."

Robert added a generous amount of sugar to his coffee. "I'm glad there was a legitimate alibi we could use this time, though. Otherwise, it might be pretty easy to tie us to what really happened." He finished stirring and looked up at Simon. "Thank you for pulling that guy off of me when you did. He was pounding my face into mush until you got there."

Simon shook his head. "You did the saving. He never would have been on you in the first place if you hadn't kept him from kicking me while the other guy was sitting on my back."

"Funny." Robert tasted his coffee and set the mug back on the table. "I'd never been in any fights my whole life, and now I've been in two, both in the same month." He grinned. "And both with you."

Simon felt his face color. "Yeah," he said. "At least we were on the same side in this one."

Robert tentatively touched the cut on his lip. Returning his hand to his lap, he looked at Simon. "Can I tell you something?"

"Sure. What?"

"I know we're not really friends. Or that you don't think of me as one."

"Robert... That's not—"

"—I know that when we were kids, your mom made you come over and play with me because she and my mom were friends. You didn't really want to be there."

This time, Simon didn't offer a protest.

"But you never said that," Robert continued. "You could have; you could have said that you were only there because your mom made you, and you hated me because of it. You could have ignored me at school, or made fun of me like some of the other kids did, so that nobody would think you were...you know... a geek like me."

"I would never have done that."

"I know. That's not how you are. You just...you always went along, putting up with me, because you're that kind of a person."

Simon sighed. "Robert..."

"And then, when we were thirteen, you moved away. And so I learned to get along without anybody who would let me eat lunch with him sometimes, or walk home with me, or be my lab partner. I even mostly got used to it. It only bothered me when I remembered what it was like when you still lived in town."

Simon sank back against the cushions of the booth, as though such frankness was a physical thing pushing against his chest.

"But then you showed up at the beginning of this summer," Robert continued. "I'd seen you other summers, but usually only once or twice. And this time, you introduced me to Vanessa, and we all started doing some stuff together. And because it was fun, and because she was nice, I started to forget that I had actually mostly made up the friendship. I let it go too far, I realized that finally, but only after... after..."

"Robert, I shouldn't have done what I did on the beach."

"I wasn't mad when you hit me, Simon. Not then. I figured I was getting what I deserved."

"That's... That's crazy! Why would you deserve it? I was jealous... an asshole."

"*That's* when I got angry at you, Simon. When you started leaving me those messages, apologizing for being jealous."

Simon frowned. "I... I don't understand. Why would that..?"

"I'm your *friend,* Simon. Even if you aren't mine, it doesn't matter. I don't care what most people think, not the ones who were never nice to me to begin with. But *you:* Your opinion meant something to me, because you were the person who didn't pick me last for baseball. You came to my birthday dinners, when it was just my sister and my parents and me. And you thought I'd repay all that by trying to steal your girlfriend?"

"I was wrong, Robert."

"Yeah, you were." As the waitress settled their plates in front of them and stepped away, he spread his napkin across his lap. With a sigh, he picked up a strip of bacon. He turned it over and over between two fingers, scrutinizing it. Then, before taking a bite, he transferred his gaze to Simon. "But now, you flew out to St. Louis to ride home with me. We got our asses kicked together. I smoked my first joint and slept with my first girl while you were right there. I guess it's all evened out, somehow."

Simon, plunging his fork into his hash browns, burst out laughing.

"I don't know how your brain works, Robert. I guess I never really have."

For just a moment, the other boy looked hurt. But then, reconsidering, he grinned back at Simon.

"You sound just like my folks."

In mountain communities like Stucker's Reach, perching just below the Continental Divide, spring is a tentative thing. It might peek out from under drippy blankets of April snow, cautiously putting forth a green shoot here and there, only to retreat hastily when a furious storm sweeps off the mountain peaks, obliterating blue sky in minutes. These Arctic blasts, active as late as May sometimes, curdle the blood and remorselessly freeze the green shoots back to the ground's surface.

But there are some years, like this one, when a series of sun-filled days occurs as early as March, warming the earth and summoning back a few hardy—or foolhardy—robins who bounce from branch to bare branch and towards dusk, even find something in their dismal surroundings to sing about.

It was one of those evenings last spring when Robert MacKenzie got out of his car in Wardlow, a town just eighteen miles down the canyon from Stucker's Reach and crossed the hospital parking lot. He stepped over streams of melting snow flowing over the asphalt and paused for a moment to tilt his head and listen to some of that birdsong. As he did, he felt the late afternoon sun warm his face.

His spirits were further buoyed when he got out of the elevator and the nurse—one of the friendlier ones—smiled at him as he approached her desk.

'Good," she greeted him. "She's been asking if you were coming this evening."

"How's she doing?"

The nurse bobbed her head sideways in a noncommittal way. "Oh, well. It was a rough morning, but she's resting more easily now." Those among the staff who had taken the time to really get to know Robert had learned not to skirt the truth or offer him vaguely promising but ultimately empty platitudes. Though he was unfailingly polite and respectful, a loss of trust still showed in his implacable features. "I just put ice chips in the water pitcher next to her bed. Maybe she'll let you give her some."

But it was Robert himself who allowed himself a ray of hope when he stepped through the open doorway of Eulamarie Scoggins' room. Her head was elevated on her pillow and she faced the door expectantly.

"Hello," he said. Mouth open slightly, she nodded her response. The fingers of her upturned hand, lying alongside her, curled slightly. Further up that same arm, near the crook of her elbow, an intravenous tube, held in place by murky clear medical tape over a piece of gauze, ran from the needle plunged into the withered gray skin to an inverted bag attached to a hook behind her bed.

For some reason, Robert had a sudden impulse to grasp that hand, to squeeze the curling fingers, but he did not. Though he and Mrs. Scoggins had been close friends since he was twelve, theirs had never been a relationship based on even the most casual physical display of affection. Even now, if he were to initiate that sort of gesture, she would think less of him for it.

"Sit," she instructed. "Here."

He dragged the heavy visitor's chair across the linoleum and placed it alongside her bed. Seated, his head was just slightly lower than hers.

"You want some ice chips?" he asked.

"No," she said. "But...help...yourself."

In just the last few weeks, she'd begun to take in gulps of air between almost every word or two, and so had learned an economy of speech she never used to practice when she was well. Now most responses were succinct and terse, but occasionally when she deemed the situation worthy, she'd go for something blithe, even if it left her winded.

"I got accepted to two more schools," he told her. "California PolyTech, and Colordo University."

Eulamarie nodded.

"Poly... PolyTech," she decided.

"Really? In-state's cheaper."

She lifted her hand dismissively. "Too close. ... Any...way, schol... scholar...ship."

"Yeah. Dad's pushing for one of the places back east. Thinks it would look better on job applications."

She had no reaction to this which he understood to mean that back east would be fine with her, too.

"I'll be glad to be done with high school, that's for sure," he sighed. They were quiet for a moment. Robert studied the floral painting on the opposite wall without really seeing it. Eulamarie likewise looked at things beyond the confines of her room.

"House?" she inquired suddenly, bringing them both back to her bedside.

His head bobbed up and down. "I was there this morning. Everything's good. I checked the taps. It hasn't been too cold for awhile, but I wanted to be sure. Nothing's frozen. I took your plants—I bundled 'em up first, like you said—to the lady at the museum. She said she'd take good care of them. She'll find homes for them. Some might stay right there, she said."

Eulamarie blinked several times. Neither of them acknowledged the single tear that appeared in the corner of one eye. It wobbled there, then slid out of sight down the far side of her face.

"Ice," she decided abruptly, and opened her mouth to receive a single chip from the spoon that Robert had tilted towards her tongue.

"Enough?" he asked, and when she nodded, he set the pitcher and spoon back on the table.

"I wonder," he speculated a moment later, "What it would have been like if you had still been teaching when I was in fourth grade. Imagine, if I'd been one of your students."

"No." Eulamarie moved her head from side to side in the most vigorous gesture he'd seen from her in weeks. "No... No... Not..." Her fingers were twitching, as if reaching for something, and for a second it appeared she might actually want to clutch his arm. "...No good," she concluded.

"I know," he sighed. "It was just a thought."

He studied the edge of the mattress, his hands folded across his legs, unaware that her eyes, sharply blue, were regarding him closely. It was one of the only times that he had failed to understand what she was trying to tell him.

The sky was sullen azure when he left the hospital nearly an hour later. The afternoon warmth had been chased from the air by encroaching nightfall. He zipped his jacket as he walked to his car, but the bracing cold was comforting on the back of his neck.

As he was pulling into the street, a small bird swooped abruptly in front of his windshield, darting so close that he could hear the flapping of its wings through the glass. He hit the brake and lurched forward. Chin nearly against the steering wheel, he caught a glimpse of one shiny dark eye regarding him intelligently before the form lifted itself into the gathering dark and was gone.

He sat for a moment, car poised halfway into the intersection, his heart thudding. Finally, when he had regained his breath, he leaned back against the seat and lifted his foot from the brake pedal.

"Shit," he muttered.

It was dark by the time he was home. All during his drive up the canyon, he held the wheel in a grip so hard that his knuckles were dotted bright pink, the blood trapped there below the surface of his skin. In his shirt pocket, his cell phone had buzzed twice, but he'd ignored it.

He parked his car in the driveway and was just coming up onto the porch when his mother opened the front door.

"There you are," she said. Her hands dangled at her sides, fingers working, and he knew she was trying to decide whether to embrace him or not. He could see his sister Heather standing just inside the open doorway, bathed in yellow light and watching with some interest.

"The hospital called," his mother began, and Robert nodded.

"I figured," he said.

Made in the USA
Charleston, SC
17 April 2013